Love Next Door

Love by the Golden Gate, Volume 2

J.C. Fairbanks

Published by J.C. Fairbanks, 2023.

LOVE NEXT DOOR

First edition. June 2, 2023.

Copyright © 2023 J.C. Fairbanks.

ISBN: 979-8223184836

Written by J.C. Fairbanks.

Also by J.C. Fairbanks

Love and Desire
Two Days In Florida
A Kiss in Carolina
Love and Desire in Paradise
Daphne, Woman of Law

Love by the Golden Gate
Love Next Door

Standalone
Eternal Flame

Watch for more at https://www.facebook.com/jcfairbanksromance.

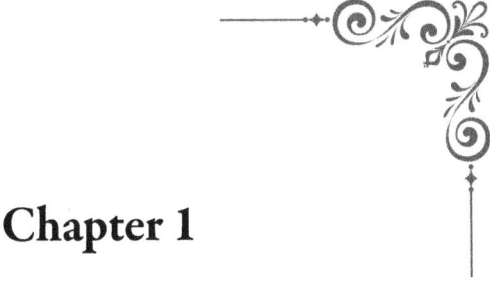

Chapter 1

An intelligent man is like a piece of cake. Book smarts are good. That's the cake part. Alone it's pretty tasty. A woman would go a little out of her way to have some of that in her mouth. But, if you want her to open her heart too, you've got to have the chocolate ganache frosting. A man with emotional intelligence is the frosting. Too sweet on its own, but put the two together and it's a guaranteed orgasm.

Then there's the fluffy, creamy filling. That's all the extras you hope you can find- sexy, successful, a great lay- but the cake works without it. Still, a girl can dream of having her beefcake and eating it, too.

SHAE RAN IN HER FRONT door, dropping her lunch sack on the kitchen table and her laptop in the study. She gathered up the perishables she was taking to the farm and transferred them to the trunk of her car, carefully arranging everything so it would be secure.

She looked back at her house as she stepped into her car. The pink dahlias she'd planted a few months ago popped against the moss green walls. The bright white trim glowed, clean and fresh. She sighed a contented sigh, until her gaze wandered slightly left and the real estate sign caught her eye. She sighed again and got into her car.

The house next door just went on the market. Again. Great. When Shae bought in this neighborhood it was because it was quiet,

1

and stable, and the house next door was occupied by a nice couple and their adorable three-year-old son. They'd promptly sold two months after she closed escrow, and what followed was a string of short-term renters, each one worse than the last.

The neighboring house was now the eyesore of the block. No, of the surrounding ten blocks. Even from the outside you could tell it hadn't been taken care of. The inside must be even worse.

Shae knew there was flood damage, the last tenants having left the kitchen sink plugged and running just before going away over a three-day weekend. Shae had been relaxing on her back patio when the peaceful sound of running water drifted to her. She wondered momentarily when the neighbors had gotten a fountain, then realized that was highly unlikely. Looking over the fence, she spotted a waterfall cascading out the vent on the side of the house. She ran over and pounded on the door. When no one answered, she shut off the water supply to the house from the outside.

All the houses in this neighborhood had the water supply in the same place. It was a planned community at one point, though the days of HOAs and regulations were long gone. Unfortunately, Shae thought. Maybe a Homeowners Association could do something about the jungle of crabgrass taking over the front lawn and crawling into her neatly tended flowerbed.

The neighbors came back, confused about why their house was wet. The 'For Sale' sign went up a few weeks later. Whoever the current landlord was, they must not want to deal with the mess. Shae wondered what kind of person would want to take on that project. The housing market was pretty hot, people fighting for houses all over town. Still, it would probably be one of those bottom-feeding house flippers that would slap some paint over the soaked drywall, stage it with fancy furniture, and sell it for a tidy profit, ignoring the black mold that would likely grow in the walls. Or a complete sucker. Either way she wasn't hopeful she'd get anyone decent next door. Not up to her standards, anyway.

Shae Mitchell had lofty standards. She was proud of everything she'd accomplished in the first thirty years of her life. She hadn't come from much and expected the same level of motivation from others. It was something her Bohemian mother was constantly nagging her to change; one of the many ways she wished Shae would 'relax'.

She pulled out of her driveway and headed out of town to her parents' home. They had finally settled down when Shae was in high school, buying a piece of property out in the country and living out of their van, then a yurt, and eventually building a little cabin. The only bathroom was still outdoors, including the shower, which in Northern California was only comfortable to use about three months out of the year.

Shae drove, her mind drifting into the past, until she hit the gravel of her parents' road. She slowed and turned into their drive. Parking the car, she took a deep breath, steeling herself for the onslaught.

"Shae Marley Indigo Mitchell, you get in here!" her mother said loudly, emerging from the front door. A woven poncho, complete with fringy bits, covered her body down to her knees where a brightly colored skirt took over, continuing the journey to her bare feet. She held her arms wide as Shae climbed out of the car.

"Hi, Mom," Shae said as her mother wrapped her in an embrace. The familiar smell of the amber her mother rubbed on her wrists enveloped her.

"Oh, it's so good to see you," Mom said.

"You too, Mom. Help me with the boxes in the back." Shae motioned to the trunk.

"Oh, now. You didn't go and bring a bunch of stuff again, did you?" Mom asked, annoyed.

"Yes, you know I did. Just the essentials. No plastic, all organic," Shae said, holding her hands up in surrender. Her parents never went shopping for themselves. She was worried they'd waste away eating only whatever came out of the garden or was foraged off the land. It would be blackberry season soon, and Shae had picked up several flats of canning jars.

"Look at all of these!" Mom said, holding the jars up.

"I promise I will help you pick berries and apples and whatever else you want to can for winter. And I brought the other things you wanted for the garden. How many hose connectors do you guys need, anyway? Where's Dad?"

"He's just taking a nap. Should be up soon. And you know I'm not going to waste the old hoses. I need as many connectors as there are pieces of hose," Mom said, carrying a sack of flour inside. Shae followed with the rest of the bulk items as her mother made her way into the kitchen, stowing the large sack in a basket in the corner. Shae set her boxes on the kitchen table.

The cozy kitchen wasn't nearly big enough for a table, but her parents squeezed one in there anyway, forcing four chairs to fit around it. Three would have made more sense and would have fit much better. But Mom insisted on keeping a place for River, though he would never come back to use it.

Shae gripped the back of 'River's chair' and took a deep breath. "Miss you," she whispered to the sky before her mother turned around. Shae curved her lips into a smile for Mom.

"Hey, Shaky-Bakey, what's the haps?" her father said behind her. Shae turned around and Dad grabbed her in a bear hug. He was always smiling. No matter what was going on, Vern had a smile on his face. Even after a nap. Shae could never wake up smiling after a nap. She was always crankier than she'd been before.

"Hi, Dad," she said, hugging him back. Shae was several inches taller than her father and had to bend down to hug him. Even so, she always felt like a child again when he wrapped those warm arms around her.

"Let me get a look at you," Dad said, releasing her. "Nope, no grays yet. Gosh, it's been so long since we've seen you, I thought for sure you'd have a few more wrinkles, considering you're getting up there in years now," he laughed.

"It has not been that long," Shae objected. "And yes, ha-ha, I'm thirty now. I'll probably go through menopause any day."

Vern and Veronica looked at each other. Yes, her parents' names were Vern and Veronica, and it was as disgustingly cute as they were.

"Well, you'd better get busy on that grandchild for us," her mother said. Dad nodded in agreement, his walrus moustache curving into a smile.

Shae had heard this too much lately. Her parents were suddenly dying for a grandchild. They'd been bringing it up more and more often, and she had just fallen into their trap again.

"I'll tell you what," she said. "I'll get busy on the grandchild when you two get married."

"We *are* married!" Mom said.

"Not legally," Shae countered.

"Legally," her mother scoffed. "What's that got to do with anything? Our marriage means much more than that."

"Still," Shae said, teasing them now, "I want my future child to have respectable grandparents."

"Well, then you'd better hope the father has some of those lying around," Dad laughed. "You won't find any of those types around here."

Shae laughed. She knew they would drop the subject now. They didn't like her harassing them about conforming socially any more than she appreciated their hounding her for a grandchild.

Her parents were dead set against anything conventional. They'd been married by a shaman in a forest circle of some sort when Shae was four years old. She still vaguely remembered it. There was tribal dancing, and people wearing strange costumes. But that wasn't the part that stuck out in her mind. Growing up in communes, that was the norm. What Shae remembered from that day was River.

He was only nine years old, but he acted like he owned the place. He was alone, as he always was, and Shae thought he looked sad. She was drawn to him for reasons she still didn't really understand. She wandered over to stand next to him that day, and she remembered feeling happy there.

"Now it's ruined," River said, kicking pebbles in the dust of the forest floor and looking angry.

"What?" Shae asked.

"They're gonna be angry at each other all the time now. That's what marriage does. My parents got married and that's what happened." River kicked another rock and spun around, dust rising around him.

"What's married?" Shae asked.

"It's what they're doing right now. Your parents."

"No, they're not," Shae said, upset at what this boy was saying. "They're having a spiritual joining."

"Same thing," River said, and marched off, leaving little Shae bewildered. She didn't want her parents to be angry all the time.

The next day River jumped out of a tree in front of her as she wandered through the woods. She'd been allowed to run wild since she could walk, even going down to the lake. How she survived she would never know. So many things could have happened to her.

River growled as he jumped in front of her. He had hoped to scare her, but she only giggled. Shae didn't scare easily. River scowled at her.

"Aren't you scared, little baby?" he said grumpily.

"I'm not a baby!" Shae yelled, getting right in his face. River flinched and pulled back, but then he laughed.

"Alright, little firecracker," he grinned. "You swim?"

From that moment on, Shae followed River around like a lost duckling. Wherever he went, she went. River never minded. In fact, he would seek her out when she didn't show up, which wasn't often.

Her parents lived in that commune for five years, far longer than they stayed at any other place. But one day the wind changed and called to them again, and they packed up the van to go. Shae cried for two days when they told her what they were doing. River didn't cry. River didn't say anything at all when she told him. His face just went dark.

The morning they were supposed to leave Shae hid in the forest. It was hours before anyone found her. The entire camp was frantic, especially her mother, who had passed by Shae several times in her searching. Shae watched her, holding her breath each time her mother passed by the tree she'd climbed. In the end River found her and convinced her to come down.

He was fourteen then, all gangly limbs and scraggly beard. But he was everything to nine-year-old Shae. When she did climb down, she clung to him and refused to let go.

"Alright, little firecracker, you've gotta go now," River had said quietly. But he held onto her, too.

"I'll never leave you, River!" she'd cried.

"I can't do this, Vern," her mother said, tears still in her eyes from the fear and relief of the search.

"Me either," her father whispered. "He's like my own son now."

Shae heard him and hope sprung up in her little heart. "Come with us, River!" she'd shouted, smiling up at him. It was so simple to her then. Of course he would come with them. His own parents didn't even like him. He spent more time with Shae and her parents than anyone else.

"Can I?" River had asked, his eyes big and round, his voice small. He was waiting for the inevitable rejection and disappointment he'd become used to in his life. No one had ever genuinely cared for him until Shae.

"I don't see why not," Veronica had said.

"Let's go talk to your folks," Vern said, his trademark smile raising the corners of his thick moustache.

River's parents weren't overly concerned that he wanted to leave with another family. They told him he was a man now and could do as he saw fit. Shae felt like she had saved the day. It was many years before she realized how strange the entire situation really was.

But none of it mattered because she had the best big brother in the entire universe. For the next six years they shared everything. They lived in the van, all four of them, for five of those years, until the yurt went up. It felt like a palace to her. She was so happy.

"Shae baby, would you mind driving us out to the coast tomorrow for that festival I mentioned to you last week?" Mom asked, pulling Shae out of her reveries.

Shae sighed inside. Another vegan fiber and food festival. All her mother needed were more batik tapestries to hang up. Who needed wallpaper?

"Why don't you let me buy you guys a nice car? It can be all electric," Shae tried, hoping her hundredth attempt might convince them.

"Oh, that's silly. No, no. We would never use it," Mom said, smiling and patting Shae's arm.

Maybe you could use it on the weekend when you want to drive down to Bolinas instead of asking me to devote my entire Saturday to granola-fest. That was what Shae wanted to say. "Sure, Mom," was what she actually said.

"Good, good. It'll be so fun! You really should add more color to your wardrobe. There will be some beautiful batiks there," Mom said, gesturing to the taupe slacks and cream blouse Shae had worn to work that day.

Shae smiled inside at her mother's predictability. "You know that's not my style. But it'll be nice to spend the day with you guys."

Dad reached an arm around her and squeezed. "That it will," he said smooching her cheek with his bristly mustache.

"Well, I brought dinner," Shae said, unloading the last of the parcels. "I'm starved and I know you guys will want to get to bed soon."

Mom yawned as if the very mention of bed made her sleepy. Her parents rose and retired with the sun, and they tended to get pretty tired when the days started to get longer as they were now.

They sat around the little table, holding hands to say a few words of gratitude for all the good things in their lives, including each other. As they did every time, they included River in their blessing. Shae missed him more tonight for some reason. She thought she could almost feel his presence. If only she could have her brother back.

Shae passed out the tempeh slices and fresh salad she'd prepared the night before. She chewed on the rubbery wheat-meat, pleased with the braise she'd made. It was actually edible. Her parents dug in and finished off every last bit. Shae was glad to see their appetites.

Her phone buzzed in her pocket, and she fished it out as she stood to clear the dishes. She glanced at the screen and smiled a wicked grin. Grabbing the lychee fruits she'd found at the local market, she placed them on the table for dessert and turned back to the sink to send a quick reply.

"Well, I suppose I should let you old folks get to bed," Shae said, smiling brightly.

"I am beat," Dad said, standing from the table. "That sure was tasty, Shaky-Bakey. Thank you."

"Anytime, Dad." Shae hugged her father and gathered her things. Giving a quick kiss to Mom, she headed for the door.

"About ten a.m. work for you tomorrow?" Mom called as Shae opened the door.

Shae turned and smiled, "Yep!" She slipped out into the dark night, closing the door.

She almost ran to her car, careful not to trip in the dark. Her parents didn't believe in outdoor lighting, either. She was in a hurry to ease the burning that had started low in her belly and was only going to get hotter over the next half hour while she drove home.

"Call Liam," she told the robot that lived in her dashboard. Honestly, technology really was the best thing ever. Well, besides a hot, hard body. None of her toys could compare to the real thing.

"Hey, baby," Liam's smooth voice answered the phone. "You home already?"

"No, just leaving the folks' house," Shae said, her voice already breathy.

"Couldn't wait?" Liam asked, a smile in his voice.

"It's been five days, Liam," she breathed. "You know how I get. I haven't even touched myself. I'm about ready to pop. Talk to me until I get there."

"What are you wearing?" Liam asked, his voice husky.

"A silk blouse and slacks," Shae answered. "And the blue panties." Shae knew Liam was partial to the lacy thong and bra set. She hoped to get a *rise* out of him and wasn't disappointed.

Liam sucked in a breath, his words coming out in a quiet moan. "Oh, Shae baby. You've got me so hard already it hurts."

"Yeah?" Shae said, untucking her blouse. "Tell me what you want to do."

"Unbutton your blouse," Liam said, his voice low and commanding.

"Already there," she said, opening the last button. Her nipples tightened against the cool air as she pushed the fabric aside and the air conditioning bit at her skin through her bra.

Thank the goddess Liam had texted tonight. Shae was almost going out of her mind. He'd been so focused on work the last few months he'd hardly been over. Shae had healthy appetites, which Liam seemed to appreciate at first. Lately she wondered whether he was becoming bored.

Liam's dirty talk turned downright filthy, and Shae knew he was still hot for her. The normally stuffy lawyer almost growled at her through the phone line, "Damn, Shae. Tell me you're ready for me."

"I'm ready. So ready," she whispered as she turned down her street. Rounding the corner, she spied Liam's car in her driveway. As she pulled up next to it, she saw Liam standing on her porch by the front door.

He looked good enough to eat. He was still in his suit, just the way she liked it. She hit the disconnect button on the dash and grabbed her bag. She jumped out of the car, slamming the door as she bolted for him. Her blouse flew open like a cape as she ran, and she slammed into Liam's arms. His mouth crushed hers, his kisses hot and needy. She could feel his erection as he pressed it against her.

Liam slammed her up against the door, his hand gripping a breast as his tongue delved deeper into her mouth. Shae wrapped one long leg around his waist, grinding shamelessly against his manhood. He groaned.

"For fuck's sake, Shae, open the goddamned door!" he growled against her lips.

Shae whimpered and stood, pushing Liam off her so she could sort her keys. Finding the house key, she shoved it in the lock and soon had the door open. Liam wrapped an arm around her waist and lifted her off the ground. She giggled as he hauled her inside and slammed the door behind them.

Then his hands were everywhere, tearing at her clothes, sinking into her flesh. She kicked her shoes off, and her slacks dropped to the floor. Liam's eyes darkened as he took her in. She smiled, reveling in the admiration. Pushing away again, she grabbed his tie and turned, dragging him up the stairs as if he were on a leash. He followed obediently, his eyes burning two holes in her ass.

"You know what I like to see," Shae whispered when they arrived at her bedroom. Liam made a noise of protest as she slid up the bed, lying against the pillows, watching him.

"Come on, Shae," he growled.

"Do it, Mr. Kline," she said.

Liam slid his suit jacket off, standing at the foot of the bed. Slowly he undressed for her. She loved watching the cufflinks come off. It was so hot for some reason. For the last ten years she hadn't slept with a man who didn't wear cufflinks. The tie and the belt were other favorites, and her core pulsed with need as she watched.

Liam moved over her, sliding a hand between her thighs. He began to stroke, but Shae was in no mood for his fumbling tonight.

"Uuhhh! I can't wait any longer!" she cried loudly.

Liam didn't waste any more time, and soon they were both vocalizing their release, Shae a bit more enthusiastically than was technically ladylike. But she didn't care.

Shae collapsed on the bed and Liam disappeared into the bathroom to dispose of the condom. He came back a minute later and began to dress.

Shae made a little whining sound. "No round two?" she asked.

"Sorry, I have an early meeting tomorrow," Liam said, buttoning his shirt.

"On Saturday?"

"Yep," he said, doing his belt now. It was much less sexy going on, she thought. "Besides, I think that was pretty incredible," he said, coming around to kiss her.

It was good, Shae couldn't argue with that. But she was ready for more, and clearly that wasn't going to happen. She huffed out a frustrated breath.

"Call you tomorrow," Liam said, ready to go.

"I'm taking my parents to Bolinas. They'll probably want to stay the night," she pouted.

"Oh, well, then I guess let me know when you're free. I've got several cases going to court soon, though, and I'll be working a lot of nights and weekends."

Shae grumbled. That didn't sound like a good thing for her sex life.

"You're adorable," Liam said, kissing her again. "And absolutely amazing."

"Thanks," she said, grabbing his tie again. "Sure you don't have one more in you?"

"Don't make me feel bad, babe," Liam laughed. "See ya."

He disappeared out the bedroom door. A few seconds later Shae heard the front door close.

Chapter 2

What kind of neighborhood had he moved into? Aiden shook his head as he watched the old man disappear into the house two down from his new residence. What a dick.

Aiden only had his moving truck in the driveway for ten minutes before his new neighbor approached him. Aiden smiled as the older man strode over, thinking he was going to welcome him to the neighborhood. Instead, the man laid into him about cleaning up the trash in his driveway. It wasn't even his trash. The previous residents left it there when they moved out.

Aiden was angry for a moment, but he didn't believe in letting negative emotions have too much space in his life. He shook his head again and concentrated on moving his heavy equipment inside. He really should have taken Gabe's offer to help him move tonight. But Tabby would have killed him if he'd given Gabe an out from dinner with her parents. And he didn't want to get in the way of Gabe's happiness. Tabitha was the perfect woman for his best friend, even if the rest of her family were troglodytes.

Aiden had managed to get his table saw and huge tool chest into the house when an ostentatious Mercedes pulled into the driveway next door. A man in a suit stepped out with his cell phone glued to his ear. Aiden hated it when people ignored the hands-free law while driving. That's how people got killed.

Aiden wasn't looking forward to living next to that guy. Two for two on terrible neighbors so far. He hefted his air compressor in one hand and dragged the pressure washer down the truck ramp with the other. He didn't suppose the suit would offer to help him. When he came back out the guy was still standing in front of the door talking on his phone.

Ten minutes later he was *still* standing there. Aiden thought about going over to introduce himself, see if the guy needed some help, but then another car pulled into the driveway and Aiden's jaw dropped to the ground. He froze halfway up the truck ramp and stared as the most gorgeous woman he'd ever seen stepped out of the little hybrid and ran to the front door.

Chestnut hair flowed down her back and over her shoulders in shiny, bouncing waves. Her blouse flew open as she ran, revealing a set of luscious tits barely contained in sheer lace. Aiden closed his mouth and swallowed as the woman jumped the man in the suit, practically attacking him. He watched for a second, wondering if they were going to go at it right in the front yard. But they disappeared inside a moment later.

Aiden shook his head again, this time trying to get the image of those soft, creamy breasts out of his mind. He pulled the last box out of the truck and locked it up, heading inside. Taking a deep breath, he surveyed the scene before him.

It was nasty. This was probably going to be the most ambitious job he'd ever taken on. That was a good thing. He was getting bored with his projects lately. When he'd seen this house pop up last week, something about it had drawn him in. He drove by right away. The neighborhood was decent, not too hoity-toity for him, but the houses were well-maintained, and the yards showed pride of ownership. Just his kind of place.

Aside from his new house, that is. This house was a garbage pile. He looked at the buckled floors. He'd have to replace the entire subfloor, and the drywall. It was just as well. These tract homes tended to have all sorts of problems it was easier to take care of if you stripped it down to the studs. At least the upstairs was in decent condition.

Aiden trudged up the stairs with his one box of personal belongings. Aside from that all he'd brought was his bed, a folding chair and table, and his tools. He would bring more later, but not until he replaced the nasty carpet upstairs with some high-grade laminate. He already had a color in mind. The third bedroom upstairs had a hole burned right through the carpet in the middle of the floor. He didn't even want to know how that happened.

He flipped the chair open and set the box on top. First thing he was going to have to do was open all the windows. Mold had probably already started. The weather was dry enough right now that some airflow would chase the stagnant smell out of the place. He set about opening the upstairs windows.

"Uuhhh! Just fuck me already!" a woman moaned, followed by some other enthusiastic noises. Aiden stopped by his bedroom window and looked out. The light was on in the window across from his, but the curtains were closed. He couldn't see what was going on in there, but he could hear everything, whether he wanted to or not. Lucky for him, he wanted to.

Damn, she sounded like she was having a very good time and didn't mind letting her partner know. Aiden appreciated that. He liked to know when he pleased a woman. He imagined the woman with the chestnut hair and legs like a giraffe sprawled on the bed beneath him. She cried out and he knew she was cumming. Hard from the sounds she was making. His cock throbbed and he turned away from the window, setting himself to the task of putting his bed together. It only took a few minutes, though, and he went back to the window.

To his surprise it was quiet already. He stared at the window, then noticed how bright the stars were in the sky. This row of houses was built right along the edge of the town. The other side of the fence was open space as far as the eye could see. No city lights to block out the dark sky. It would be perfect for the rooftop deck he had envisioned as soon as he saw the place.

The suit emerged from the front door down below and got into his prig-mobile. Aiden snorted. That was awfully fast. Didn't even stick around for a little cuddle. Or seconds. Aiden couldn't imagine leaving a woman like that after one round. Maybe he should go over and offer his services to her. As a friendly neighbor, of course. He wouldn't charge her. A woman like that wouldn't need to pay for companionship.

And like he'd willed it to happen with his thoughts, his phone rang. Not his personal phone, his business phone. The number only his clients used. He checked the screen. Cherise. Well, well.

"Hi there," Aiden answered.

"Hi handsome," Cherise breathed into the phone. "You busy?"

"Never too busy for you, darlin'," he drawled. Cherise liked to play cowboy.

"What are you doing?"

"Just sittin' here listenin' to my neighbors go at it like deer in rut and wonderin' what I'm gonna to do with this massive hard-on." Aiden laughed to himself. That was crude, but Cherise liked it that way.

"Oh, you poor thing! Why don't you come over and let me help you out with that?" she purred.

"Well now, that is mighty kind of you, ma'am. But what kind of gentleman would I be if I didn't take care of you, too?" Aiden teased her.

"Oh, yes, come over now," she moaned.

"On my way, ma'am," he said, clicking off. Well, duty called. Couldn't leave a damsel in distress, after all.

Aiden grabbed the soap and towel from the box and hit the shower. He skipped shaving the two-day scruff he had going. Cherise liked it rough, in more ways than one. In ten minutes, he was out the door and in an Uber. His truck was still at the rental place. He'd needed to rent a moving van for all his equipment. He wanted to take it all at once. No sense in making ten trips across town.

"Thanks, man," he said to the driver as he stepped out in front of Cherise's estate. He keyed the code into the little gate by the driveway and walked up the path to the front door. He rang the bell and stood there with his hands in his pockets.

Cherise opened the door wearing denim, fringe, and hip holsters. Giddy-up!

AIDEN WOKE WITH THE sun the next morning. Cherise was still asleep beside him. Damn, what a wild ride she'd been. He smiled, loving his 'job'. He rolled out of the bed as stealthily as he could. He'd love to spend the whole day in bed, but he was itching to get started on this project. Besides, he couldn't sleep once the sun was up, and Cherise wouldn't be riding any more broncos for a few days at least. He slipped his pants on.

"You're going?" a sleepy voice said.

"Yeah, you just go back to sleep, darlin'," he whispered, running a hand over her hair.

"Alright. Thanks, cowboy," she mumbled and turned over. Soon she was breathing deeply again.

Aiden dressed and slipped out, walking down the street. It was only about a mile to his favorite coffee shop, and there weren't a lot of rides for hire before six on a Saturday morning. The walk was pleasant, and the tea was even better. He sat at a table outside and had a scone while he waited for the one brave soul driving people around at this hour. He'd finished his tea by the time the car pulled into the parking lot.

As he climbed in his phone rang. It was his mother. She was the only one who would call him at this hour.

"*Bonjour Maman*," he answered.

Mom jumped right into everything she wanted to tell him, firing French at him as if it were her native language, which it wasn't. She was a plain old Midwesterner who'd transplanted to California sometime in the eighties when she'd been offered a postdoc position in the French department of the most prestigious university in the Bay Area. She was now head of the department. She insisted he always speak to her in French. Aiden humored his mother.

"*Oui, Maman. Non, Maman*," he answered as she asked him questions. "*À demain. Ciao.*"

By the time he got off the phone he was back at his house. He thanked the driver and stood on the sidewalk looking at it. It looked a lot worse in the daylight. Well, no sense in standing around when he could be doing something about it. He went inside and changed quickly into work clothes and began loading the rental truck with garbage. Might as well make the neighbor happy, assuming that grouch could ever be happy.

After the driveway was cleared there was still a lot of room in the truck, so Aiden ripped the carpets out upstairs and loaded those in, too. He felt so much better already. The truck was full now, and he threw a broom in the back and closed it up. He'd have to sweep it at the dump before he returned it.

It was already getting hot this morning. A late May heat wave. He lifted the hem of his t-shirt and wiped the sweat from his brow. When he looked up, Chestnut was standing in front of her car staring at him. He raised his arm and waved at her, taking a step forward to introduce himself. She gave a little wave back and scurried into her car. He wondered if *any* of the neighbors were friendly.

He made his dump run and picked up his truck, then ran by the flooring store and ordered his floor. He was sure about the color now- chestnut brown would be stunning. When he got back he started on yard maintenance. Mowing, power washing, trimming, and weeding. He would have preferred to take a torch to the front yard. It would have been easier. But he had a feeling Grumpo down the street would throw a fit. By the end of the day the trash and the jungle were gone, and the driveway was washed, at least. If it didn't look nice, at least it looked a little more respectable.

He eyed the crab grass crawling over into Chestnut's flower bed. Those were some damn pink flowers. He would never have planted pink flowers, but they really worked with everything else she'd done. Her house was a big reason he bought his. It looked good and would definitely increase the resale value.

He knelt down and started pulling the grass out of her beds. The soil was rich and well-tended under the layer of black mulch. He'd made a terrible mess of it by the time he finished. The border on his side of the property was an atrocity as well. He needed to make a run to the hardware store for supplies anyway. He was going to rip out the master bath as his first project, he decided. Lay tile to replace the plastic shower surround, new cabinets, new sink, new everything.

But the first thing he did was install a new flower bed border and lay fresh black mulch. It looked better than it had before. He'd done a wave design in black and soft red adobe pavers that would complement both their yards. That is, it would when he'd ripped out the lawn and put in the butterfly garden and painted the house a butter yellow. It would look great next to her moss green. The house on the other side was a neutral beige, unremarkable and wouldn't affect resale value.

For a second Aiden considered keeping this one. This was his thirteenth home in six years and the first he could actually see himself staying in. But a shiver ran through him. Settle down? That was never going to happen. At least not while he could swing his hammer. Or get an erection without Viagra. When that stopped working maybe he'd think about settling down and going back to teaching.

Maman had been harassing him again this morning about returning to academia. She didn't get it. He hadn't been happy there. She complained he never gave it a chance, only working as a professor for two years before throwing it all away to be a *gigolo*. That was just a side gig, though it paid handsomely and had excellent benefits. Building was his passion.

Teaching architecture and creating it with your hands were disparate experiences. He'd felt stifled at university. His designs were brilliant (and that was not ego, he had the accolades to prove it), but he found himself wanting to see the projects through to the end, hammering the nails in himself. His mind was always working, thinking, creating. The only time he could make it quiet was when he worked with his body. It was the curse that came with his genius IQ.

Yes, Aiden Love was a certified genius, a fact his parents brought into conversation as often as they could without being impolite. They were exceedingly polite. Sometimes Aiden wondered what barbarian ancestor's DNA had survived the centuries to reemerge in him. He knew his parents wondered.

Having two academics for parents, Aiden began his elite education at birth. He was given every opportunity in life to succeed, and succeed he did. He promoted through two or three grades a year. He outpaced his tutors quickly, and in one instance became his tutor's tutor after grasping the concept of physics so quickly that the young woman had asked for his help with her final exams. Among other things.

Aiden had his first taste of sex that year. He was seventeen and Layla was nineteen. She had a brilliant mind and was a bit of a sapiosexual. In other words, she got hot for smarts, and damn had she ever been turned on when Aiden announced he'd read through all three texts for a year of university level courses over a three-day weekend.

His mother was furious when she figured it out. She blew up in front of both of them in his room where she caught them making out half-naked. She'd screamed in French that she wasn't paying for his sexual education and that he should be getting paid since he was now tutoring Layla in physics.

Layla didn't speak French, though she got the gist easily enough. She laughed when he told her what his mother had said about paying him. She told him it was true. He was wasting his talents in school. He could make millions with the way he used his hands.

Years later her words came back to him as he sat in his office one day, drawing and thinking. The dean's wife came in, locking the door behind her. She'd been hinting at him for months, flirting every chance she got. Every school function he attended he got his ass squeezed at least once.

"Hello, Professor *Love*," she said, emphasizing his name in the lascivious way she unerringly did.

"Good afternoon, Mrs. Strauss," he answered.

"You work so *hard*, you know that?" she asked, coming around to sit on the desk. She placed her ass right on his sketch pad, forcing him either to jump back, dropping everything, or cup her ass. He opted for the latter, mostly out of curiosity to see where she would take this. "You know what they say about all work and no play?" she asked, her eyes hooded as he cupped her.

Watching her face, he squeezed, and her breath rushed in. "No dull boys around here, I assure you," he said quietly.

Dean Strauss' wife was younger than her husband, but still at least thirty years older than Aiden at the time. She was an attractive woman, and Aiden learned that day in his office that wisdom did indeed come with age. And some things you didn't learn in the lecture hall.

That was his last year as an academic. Word got around and his services were soon in demand. Somehow, he'd established a 'rate' that would show up in his Venmo account after every date. Of course, his parents eventually found out through the grapevine, but being the progressives they were it made little difference to them.

What shocked and devastated them was his exit from academia. That summer Aiden's favorite pet project was reaching fruition. It was a city project and one he was immensely proud of. When last minute changes were made, approved, and acted on by the city council without involving him, he'd snapped. They'd ruined it. He didn't want his name on it. He wanted to take a hammer out there and fix it, but it was too late.

In a fit of temper, he typed and sent his letter of resignation. The very next day he hit the real estate market. That's where he met Cherise. She sold him his first house and had been an excellent customer ever since.

His first project didn't go as smoothly as he'd planned. Swinging a hammer took a lot more practice than he'd assumed, making him feel like an ass indeed. He'd been taught to look down upon manual labor his entire life. Now he appreciated the skill it took to do it right. He managed to create a decent home eventually and sold it for a mint. Twelve houses later he was a master at his craft, and he'd never looked back.

The sun was low in the sky as Aiden carted the last piece of garbage down the stairs from the master bath. He threw it on the growing pile in the living room. The dumpster wouldn't come until Monday. He was sure Grumpo wouldn't be happy when that was plunked down on the front lawn. It wouldn't be there so long, though. Demo was always fast and easy. It was the build that took time and finesse.

Aiden showered in the downstairs bath. He would tackle that last of all. It was the nicest room in the house at this point. He breathed deeply as he thought about the amount of work he had before him. He was glad to have a party to go to tonight.

It was the monthly Mensa Mingle night. Not a party in the traditional sense, though there was food and some alcohol. Most members didn't drink much, preferring not to dull their senses. Mingle night was a chance to stretch your mental muscle and connect with others who may or may not share your views.

That was what Aiden loved about it. Everyone was brilliant, but in so many different ways. He'd learned over the years that IQ didn't equate to every type of intelligence. There were many aspects to human nature that couldn't be measured, and he loved the variety he found at 'The Club'.

He pulled one of his favorite joke t-shirts over his head. It was a test of sorts. Some people would get the pun but dismiss it, and some would laugh because they knew it was supposed to be funny, but Aiden sought out those who understood the joke as well as laughed at it. He had no time in his life for uptight assholes.

There were plenty of them in 'The Club', and that was what Aiden didn't enjoy about it. That, and the ingrained elitism that allowed clubs like this to exist. They were all entitled, mostly wealthy, mostly white. It made him uncomfortable. At the same time, he needed the mental exercise. Sex and work were great, but his mind needed stimulation, too.

He glanced in the bathroom mirror, running a hand through his hair before heading out the door. He was appropriately scruffy-looking. He liked to keep people wondering about him. As he unlocked his truck, he glanced next door. No car in the driveway, no lights on inside. She must still be gone. Aiden wondered if she worked weekends.

"ALCOHOL IS ALWAYS A solution," a tiny blonde read from his shirt. She giggled a high-pitched, squeaky sound. It was cute. So was she.

"Son, I don't think that's very funny," Basil Wentworth said from his left side, placing a word into the game circle. Damn, he pulled past Aiden with that play. "You shouldn't encourage drinking. Dulls the mind. Case in point." Basil pointed at Aiden's beer. Aiden picked it up and gulped it down, sighing contentedly.

"It's not meant to encourage drinking," Aiden said, placing his word. He looked at Basil with a satisfied expression as the man took in his play and realized Aiden had just bested him. "What's your excuse?"

Basil just sneered at him. "Well played, young man," he said, standing and leaving the table. The blonde immediately took his place.

"I think it's funny," she said, nodding toward his chest. He watched her eyes rove over him before returning to his face.

"Yeah?" he asked, allowing his eyes to travel as well.

"I'm Hestia," she said, holding out her hand. Aiden took it, giving it a few firm pumps.

"Hestia? Who are your parents, Kronos and Rhea?" he asked, giving her a rye look.

"I know! I should change it, really, but they think it's the best name ever. I mean, she wasn't even one of the very famous goddesses. But she was the one who kept her promise to Zeus, and that's why my dads picked it. They can be so old-fashioned."

"And tell me, Hestia, have you kept the promise? Have you remained forever pure and undefiled?" Aiden asked, leaning in and looking into her eyes.

"You know your mythology," she said, smiling wickedly. "And let's just say I really should change my name."

Aiden laughed. "No, don't. I think that's perfect. Hestias of the world unite! Change the brand!"

"What's your number?" Hestia asked.

Aiden cringed inwardly. He knew she wasn't asking for his phone number. She wanted his IQ score. Why did she have to go and ruin it? He was enjoying talking with her.

"Don't you think that's all just a bunch of bullshit?" he asked.

"Oh," she said, looking down her nose at him.

"Guess not," Aiden said, answering his own question when she didn't. "Listen," he said, leaning to whisper in her ear, "it's a *big* number. It's too *long* and *hard* for most people to handle."

Hestia sucked in a breath as he brushed her ear with his lips. He grinned, checking the laugh that wanted to roll out of him. Sometimes it was too easy. He straightened his expression and pulled back to look into her eyes. Her pupils were dilated so much, only a sliver of blue surrounded the black centers.

"I, uh," she coughed, clearing her throat. "I think I could handle it," she said quietly.

Leaning in he whispered into her ear again, "The last woman I gave it to screamed, Hestia. Do you want that?"

She was panting next to him. "Yes! Yes, I want it, Aiden."

He stiffened. How did she know his name? "Tell me, Hestia," he whispered in her ear again, moving his breath down the side of her neck. She trembled. "What do you get when you cross a mosquito with a rock climber?"

The only sound was her heavy breathing. She didn't answer. Aiden pulled back to look at her. Her lips were parted, her eyes hooded. She met his eyes and closed her mouth.

"I don't know," she said at last. "What?"

"Never mind," Aiden sighed.

"Come back to my place?" she breathed.

"Sure," he said, standing. It was late and the place had mostly cleared out anyway. When Hestia stood, she was at least a full foot shorter than him.

"You're huge," Hestia said, glancing up and down his frame.

"I usually don't hear that until later," Aiden laughed. Hestia's eyes went wide, and she grinned.

"You're cocky. I like it. We'll see how hyperbolic you are, won't we?"

"OH! OH! OH! OH! OH! Oh! Oh! Oh!" Hestia screamed as she rode him. Her squeaky voice was starting to grate on his nerves.

She fell back, sliding off him and making squeaky panting noises. He found the bathroom and tossed the condom.

"You weren't exaggerating," she moaned as he came back and gathered his clothes. "You're incredible."

"Thanks," Aiden said, gauging her mood. Did she want him to stay?

"I hope you don't think this is rude, but I have to get up early for church tomorrow, so…" she said a bit sheepishly.

"Church, really?" Aiden laughed. "That's your excuse?"

"It's not an excuse," Hestia objected. "I go to The City every Sunday for church with my dads. I told you they're old-fashioned. Well, for San Francisco anyway."

"Say no more. I'll be out of your hair momentarily. Have fun at church." Aiden winked at her as he zipped his jeans. "Don't mention my name at confession, though," he laughed.

"I'm not catholic," Hestia said, slipping a robe on. She followed him to the front door and kissed him once more before he left.

It wasn't unusual to get laid at a Mensa meeting. Not in his experience, anyway. But it wasn't why he went. He felt good now that he'd given his brain and body a workout. He might be sore tomorrow after hitting the house the way he had today, though. No matter, he could go easier tomorrow. That was the benefit of being your own boss.

As he pulled into his driveway, he noticed there was still no car next door. Maybe she was at her priggish boyfriend's house. Aiden wondered why he was thinking so much about a woman he'd never met and had only seen briefly twice. He didn't even know her name. But he planned to find out.

Chapter 3

Flax granola, chia granola, pumpkin seed granola, granola with probiotics. Shae added mental tick marks to the types of granola tally in her head as she followed her mother down another row of booths. She was up to twenty-five.

"Oh, look at these!" her mother gushed. Shae looked over and her guts twisted in horror. Her mother held up a pair of baby booties, wiggling them in Shae's face. "Aren't they adorable? I remember when your feet were this tiny. What are these made of?" her mother asked the vendor.

"Hemp. Those are dyed with avocado pits," the vendor answered. Shae stared in dread at the pink things in her mother's grip.

"That's great, Mom. Let's go. Thank you, sir," Shae said, shuffling her mother along.

"Honestly, I don't know why you're so uptight about having a baby. Children are the most wonderful gift. You really should have that experience," her mother said, taking her hand.

"I don't know if you remember how it works, Mom, but I can't do it by myself. I need a man, which currently I do not have." Liam didn't count. He was sexy and successful, but he'd be a terrible father. He was barely around for Shae.

"You only have to do it once, Shae. Surely you could open your legs long enough for that," Mom laughed.

"Mother!" Shae choked.

"Do you need some instructions? We can go through *The Art of Tantric Sex* when we get home. You need to slow down and enjoy yourself. You're always so focused on the end goal that you forget to stop and smell the roses."

Shae just groaned, knowing any response she gave would encourage her mother to continue the topic at hand. Her mother loved to talk about sex. And while Shae had inherited her mother's healthy libido and open mind, she didn't enjoy discussing the topic at length with her.

"Oh, look at this!" Mom jumped to a rack of brightly colored fabrics and pulled a piece out. "This would be gorgeous on you!"

Shae looked at the... she supposed it was a dress. The colors were quite pretty, but she'd never wear it. It wasn't her style. She preferred classic lines. Something she could wear a bra with. "I don't know," she said.

"Oh, come on, humor me. You can wear it to dinner at our house if you don't want to wear it wherever else you go," Mom said, holding the fabric up to Shae's body.

"Ok," she said, pulling her wallet out. If this was all she had to buy today she'd be getting off easy. She paid for the dress and shoved it in her large purse.

Dad caught up with them and they shopped a while longer. Shae enjoyed watching her parents in their element. They chatted with people and smiled and kissed each other, holding hands like teenagers. It wasn't her scene, but she went with the flow, enjoying the happy energy around her.

The night activities began with the sunset ritual. The rituals were always different but the same. Burning incense, sage, and of course, weed. That had been going all day. Drum circles, dancing, lots of breasts on display. Thankfully her mother didn't encourage her to do that. Not that Shae had anything against baring her breasts. She did it all the time at home. But she preferred to save that treat for one special person at a time, not a park full of them.

The night was warm, and Shae sat on the beach in a circle with a dozen other people who felt like being quiet. She stared into the fire and let the rhythm of the drums rock her body. Her mind drifted and memories of River filled her consciousness.

"What's wrong?" River asked, sitting next to her on the tiny couch in the van.

Shae was crying. It was seventh grade, and she wasn't fitting in at the public school. "I'm so stupid," she cried, her face in her hands.

"You are not," River said.

"Yes, I am. And everyone hates me!"

"How could anyone hate you, little firecracker? You're the best person I know."

"What do you know? You don't have any friends, either," she said, lashing out. She wished she could take it back as soon as she said it. It wasn't true anyway, River had lots of friends. He just didn't bring them around her.

"Trouble making friends?" River asked gently.

"The popular girls threw rocks at me today," she cried, burying her face in his shoulder. Beside her River made an angry sound and wrapped an arm around her. "They laughed at my bell bottoms. I wish I could buy my own clothes!"

"Why do you care about that shit, Shae? You look fine. Cute, even," River said, poking her in the ribs.

"I don't want to be cute to *you*, I want to be cute to J.R.," Shae whined. River laughed.

"Who is *J.R.*?" he asked, wrinkling his nose at the name.

"He's the new boy at school. He talked to me today. And I said a bunch of stupid stuff because I'm stupid!" Shae cried again.

"Hey," River said softly, hugging her into his shoulder.

"All the popular girls crowded around him. I'm sure he likes them more than me. I just want one pair of designer jeans! They laughed at me in front of J.R."

"Some people are mean," River said quietly. "You don't need them."

"I do if I ever want to have a life," Shae sighed.

"Let me pick you up from school tomorrow," River said, an impish grin on his face.

"Why?" Shae asked. "You don't even have a car!"

"I'll borrow one. Just make sure J.R. and all those girls are around, alright?"

River showed up in a cherry red convertible after school the next day. He'd shaved and combed his usually unruly hair into a fashionable style. He wore a denim jacket that was all the rage at the time. He leaned against the car, his arms crossed on his chest, looking like the coolest cat that ever lived.

Shae made sure to follow the popular girls out that day. They were fawning over J.R. as the whole group walked toward the loading zone. Shae almost tripped when she saw River. She knew girls threw themselves at him all the time, but she'd never thought of him that way. He was her brother and best friend. But today she could see why he got so much attention.

River raised his arm, waving to Shae. "There's the cutest girl at Wilson Junior High," he said loudly. In front of her the girls stopped, thinking (or more likely hoping) he was speaking to one of them. Shae rushed past them, and River wrapped his arms around her.

"Hi River," she said, beaming.

"You look good today," River said, smiling at her. "I love a woman with her own sense of style. These your friends?" he asked as the group walked slowly by, still gawking. "Hey, I'm River."

Shae watched as River shook hands with the girls, each one blushing and giggling. He grabbed J.R.'s hand last, shaking it firmly. Shae held her breath.

"Any friends of my Shae are friends of mine," River said. "Come on, little firecracker, we've got things to do. It was nice to meet you, ladies." River opened her door and shot the group a bright smile.

Shae watched their faces as she pulled away, her hair blowing in the breeze. J.R. watched her back and she tingled. She giggled.

"Where did you get this?" she asked when they were safely away from the school.

"I borrowed it from a friend. Nice, huh?" River said, raising his eyebrows to her.

"Thank you," she said quietly. Tears pricked her eyes.

"Don't thank me yet. We're gonna have to walk home after we drop this off. And it's three miles," River said, smiling at her again.

Shae smiled back. She knew no matter what, River would have her back. She thought maybe she didn't care so much anymore what the popular girls thought about her.

"Shae, honey?" her mother said, gently shaking her shoulder.

Shae came back to the present and wiped the tear that spilled down her cheek. "Hey, Mom, you guys ready to go?"

"Yeah, Dad's tired. You ok?" Mom asked, looking at her face.

"Yeah, yeah. These things just make me think of River, you know." Shae stood and her mother wrapped her in a hug.

"Me, too."

They walked along the sand, finding Dad and headed to the car. Shae drove them to the hotel, and they all collapsed into bed. Her parents had insisted they share one room and Shae didn't mind. It was bigger than most of the places they'd lived growing up.

Her parents fell asleep quickly, but Shae was restless. She thought about calling Liam, but it was an hour's drive. That was a long way to go for a quickie in the backseat. They could always have phone sex. He wasn't bad at it. But she wanted the real thing.

The real thing had been playing in her head all day, and she wanted to make it stop. The image of hard, glistening abs glimpsed from under the lifted hem of a tight t-shirt permeated her thoughts. That mover she'd seen this morning next door had to be the most extraordinary example of maleness she'd ever set eyes on.

He was tall with messy sandy-brown hair and a light beard that looked like he hadn't shaved in a few days. She squirmed, imagining the feeling of that rubbing between her thighs. She let her fantasy go a little further, watching him remove his shirt in her mind's eye, revealing a sculpted chest.

She'd watched him for a few seconds before he spotted her and waved. That was enough to send her scurrying. He looked like he wanted to talk to her. She couldn't imagine what he would have to say, other than to hit on her, and she wasn't up for that so early in the morning. He wasn't her type anyway.

Shae drifted off to thoughts of sandy hair and tan skin.

SHAE PULLED INTO HER driveway after breakfast with her parents and she stopped so fast her body lurched forward, the seatbelt cutting painfully across her chest. Someone had changed her flower bed!

Stepping out of the car she surveyed the new border that separated her front yard from the neighbor's. It was gorgeous. She walked over and dug down into the black mulch. It was deep. Someone had added mulch, too. Next door the moving truck was gone, replaced with a big, shiny black pickup. The house had been transformed in a day. No garbage, no weeds, no dirt or cobwebs on the exterior. Wow.

Shae took her bags inside and unpacked, throwing a load in the wash. Then she settled in with a cup of tea and the Sunday New York Times. She read through the news, skimming most of it. She thought it was important to stay up on current events, but it depressed her sometimes. If she were honest with herself, she just wanted to get to the crossword. She saved it for last as a reward every week. She settled in at the kitchen table and clicked her pen open.

As she worked and sipped, she thought about how much fun it used to be doing this with her brother. He wasn't as good as she was at it, but he made it fun. She'd had a few boyfriends over the years who would do it with her. She picked up her phone and texted Liam. Maybe he would come over and help her finish it. Dinner with him sounded nice. Her phone buzzed as she finished loading the dryer.

Sorry, buried in work today. I might be able to get away for an hour tonight. You want me to come over?

Gee, every woman's fantasy. Shae didn't mind booty calls in general. She enjoyed them, in fact. But she needed some connection with the person, and lately Liam had been spending less and less time with her. He'd been much more attentive in the beginning. Now work seemed to be his sole focus. She understood the drive to be excellent at what you did, but she wanted at least a few of his thoughts to be about her.

No worries. Call me when you have time

Liam responded with an emoji and Shae went back to her puzzle. The sun was low in the sky by the time she looked up. She stood and stretched, tossing her pen on top of the paper. She supposed she should move a little. She'd walked what felt like a hundred miles yesterday, but her legs were stiff from sitting all day today.

She slipped on her comfy shoes and headed out the front door. She decided to do a loop around the cul-de-sac. It was fairly long, almost a mile, maybe. Enough to whet her appetite for dinner.

She stopped at the other end of the street to admire the house there. It was the craziest, coolest front yard she'd ever seen. The house was bright burnt orange. Two copper metal palm trees about ten feet tall graced the center of the yard, a hammock strung up between them. There were plants Shae couldn't name tucked in among the black and white zebra striped rocks that ran from the house to the street. It made her think of Gilligan's Island, only set in some future time where the cast consisted of robots. Shae laughed and decided she was glad there wasn't an HOA in this neighborhood after all.

As she returned to her house, she saw the lights on in the house next door. She glanced up as she opened her front door and a figure moved from the upstairs window, but not before she got an eyeful of toned, tanned muscle. He wasn't the mover then. He was the new neighbor. And he looked even better without a shirt in person than he did in her dreams last night. Damn.

Chapter 4

"Hey, you wanna get a beer, man?" Gabe asked as they fixed the last piece of drywall to the studs.

"Um, yeah, sure," Aiden agreed. Gabe would want to go to a sports bar, of course. What was it right now? Baseball maybe? Aiden didn't follow sports. He could tolerate them in small doses since that was what his friend enjoyed doing, especially since Gabe had spent his entire Saturday helping him hang drywall. But he found watching a ball fly back and forth mind-numbing, and not in the good way.

"Can we go up to the roof?" Gabe asked, surprising him.

"I suppose so. It's rough though, I'm warning you. Maybe I should have you sign something releasing me from liability in case of death," Aiden laughed.

"I'll take my chances," Gabe said. "I wanna see what you've done up there."

"Alright. I have some beer in the fridge," he said, stepping out of the living room into the kitchen.

"Damn, I wanted to tell you this place is looking good. I think it's your best yet," Gabe said, taking the beer Aiden handed him.

"Thanks, I've been happy with it." Aiden led the way up the stairs. He'd had to take out a hall closet to fit the spiral staircase, but he'd added another closet in some dead space, along with adding storage to both bathrooms, so now there was more than before. He climbed the curving stairs with Gabe following behind.

As he emerged, he was awed at the view yet again. The sun set over the dark hills; the country spread out before him. On the other side the lights of the town twinkled in the gathering darkness.

"Damn!" Gabe said as he came up. "This is incredible!"

"Just don't go near the edge, alright? Here, sit in the chair. I'll feel better. I haven't put up any of the rails yet." Aiden motioned to one of the chairs he'd placed up here. So far he'd been the only one up here, and it was nice to share it with someone.

"The fireworks are going to be epic from here!" Gabe said.

"Oh yeah. Probably be able to see two different shows from here." Next week was the fourth of July and he planned to have the deck completed before then. Should only be two more days of work. Then he could have people up here without fearing for their safety. He sat next to Gabe, and they cracked their beers open, facing the sunset.

"The chicks are going to dig this," Gabe said.

"You know I don't bring my work home," Aiden laughed.

"You know, you might meet someone someday who isn't a job," Gabe said.

"Women are all a job, man. Relationships are work. Might as well get paid for it."

"That's a little pessimistic, don't you think?" Gabe asked.

"I consider it to be disillusioned. Don't expect someone to be there when you need them, and you won't be disappointed."

Gabe took a swig on his beer and sighed. "That's kind of what I wanted to talk to you about," he said, looking straight ahead.

"Oh, shit, man. I didn't mean all relationships. Just mine. You and Tabby have a good thing going." Aiden backpedaled wildly, feeling like a heel.

"No, no, it's fine. I mean, it's not fine, you really ought to get some therapy or something." Gabe paused, taking another long pull from his bottle. "Tabby left me."

"Fuck," Aiden breathed. "Why?"

"Apparently I haven't been putting in the work. She said I don't appreciate her, I always put my needs ahead of hers, and I'm not home enough. Those last two are bullshit. What does she want from me? I work hard so I can give her the life she deserves. If that's not putting her needs ahead of mine, what is?"

Aiden took in everything his friend had just said, watching the sun sink completely below the horizon. "You want her back?" he asked after a few minutes.

"Yeah, I do," Gabe admitted.

"Alright, no problem then," Aiden said.

"Oh, no problem? Maybe I didn't explain it right," Gabe said.

"No, you explained it well. You have a simple communication issue, that's all. Women need to be told how you feel about them. It's not enough to show them. Like I said, it's work. I'll send you some stuff. She'll be back in your bed tomorrow."

Gabe just stared at him, then he laughed. "You really think you're hot shit, don't you?"

Aiden laughed. He knew the kind of woman Tabitha was, and he knew he could help his friend fix this. They'd only been married a year. This was just growing pains. He knew their marriage was going to be one of the good ones. The fact that Gabe was having this conversation with him proved that.

"What in the hell is your neighbor doing?" Gabe said, leaning forward in his chair to peer over the side.

"What?" Aiden asked, looking down. One side of the deck looked directly down into Chestnut's yard. He considered it one of the nicer features of this deck. Although so far, he'd yet to catch her sunbathing in a bikini, maybe untying the little strings in the back. He'd imagined it plenty of times, though.

Down below in the fading light, he could see her, spinning in a circle. Her long, chestnut-colored locks flew out around her, matching the sway of her flowing, colorful skirt. She performed some graceful movements, raising her arms to the sky, then throwing them to the ground.

He and Gabe watched, amused and astonished as she stretched and twisted her lithe body. Then she froze and howled. She howled like a wolf. Aiden started to laugh, but the hills around them erupted with the howls of coyotes and he was so startled his smile dropped.

Aiden looked to the hills and saw the full moon rising up, big and bright. He remembered there was a super moon tonight, and it was a magnificent sight. When he looked back down, Chestnut flipped herself into a handstand of sorts and her flowing dress dropped from her body, pooling around her shoulders on the ground. Every inch of her creamy skin was revealed as she wasn't wearing anything underneath. Her taught breasts hung full and round in the moonlight, and he couldn't help but notice the puckered nipples. Or the dark V between her thighs.

Aiden choked, sucking in a breath, and Gabe chuckled. Aiden shoved him back in his seat with a flat hand against his chest.

"We shouldn't be watching her," Aiden growled.

"Whoa, dude, fine. You don't have to get handsy. Nice neighborhood you picked, though. I wish my house had a view like that," Gabe laughed.

"Shut up, she'll hear you!" Possessiveness surged through Aiden and his chest burned. He didn't want Gabe to look at her. "Let's get off the roof," he said.

Back in the house he gave Gabe a crash course on seduction and promised to send him an email with a foolproof strategy. At first, he thought it would be fun to play Cyrano de Bergerac for his friend, but right now he wanted him out. He needed to process what he'd just seen.

"Later, man," Gabe said as he was shuffled out the front door. "And thanks for listening and everything."

"Yeah, yeah, no problem. You know you and Tabitha are my favorite couple. Don't worry," he said, giving Gabe a little wave before closing the door.

Christ.

His mind and body almost went into overload as his brain sent the message from his eyes straight to his cock. Like some feral animal instinct, his whole body pulled toward her. As crazy as it should have seemed, the howling only turned him on more. He wanted to hear her do it again. *He* wanted to make her howl like that.

She had the most incredible body he'd ever seen. Pale skin against dark hair. Full hips that you could sink your fingers into. In the bright moonlight he even noticed her toes, painted black or a very dark red. It was sexy as fuck, whatever it was.

She was different than he'd thought. The few times he'd seen her coming or going, or taking walks down the street, she'd been so buttoned-up. Preppy, like her boyfriend. There was something old-fashioned about her. He put his finger on it. She could have been one of those pin-up girls from the WWII era. The thought of that sent a throb to his dick.

But tonight, she was wild. Like a witch or a fairy, or some Bacchanalian goddess. Maybe there was more to her than he'd given her credit for. He'd been able to minimize his interest in her by telling himself she was everything he wasn't looking for. A social climber who wanted a corporate husband and a couple of rug rats as soon as possible and a boring, suburban life. But what if he was wrong?

He should probably tell her that he could see into her backyard. It wasn't kind of him to peep on her. Before he built the deck no one would have been able to see her performing her moonlight ritual. He resolved to go over the next day and introduce himself. It was ridiculous that they'd been neighbors this long without finding out each other's names at least.

Excited by his plan, Aiden found he couldn't sleep. He set to work taping the drywall. He'd finished the entire job before he realized it. He'd been lost in thoughts about her. His body was finally tired, though, and after a hot shower he fell into a deep and dreamless sleep.

AIDEN WOKE TO THE SOUND of someone laughing. He opened his eyes to bright sun streaming in through the open window. He left all the windows open most of the time. The smell of paint, drywall mud, and whatever else he was working on was too strong otherwise. He realized he was hearing children playing outside. He glanced at his phone. Eleven? Seriously? Half the day was gone. That's what he got for staying up until four in the morning.

Stretching, he got up and padded down the stairs, admiring the shining retro ebony stair treads he'd added. Aside from the rooftop terrace, the upper level of the house was done. New paint, new flooring, new bathrooms, and new stairs. The lower level was still a bit rough, aside from the kitchen, which he'd completed this week. Aiden went in there now, straight for the coffee pot. His head was foggy, and he felt much better when the steaming mug was in his hands.

Heading back up he decided he'd take his coffee to the roof. The sun was already beating down when he got up there. It was going to be a hot day. Sipping his coffee, he looked over the side into her yard. It was quiet. He couldn't see the front of her house, or the street from the terrace since he'd built it behind the peak of the roof. He'd wanted the view of the hills, but now he couldn't see if her car was there or not. Suddenly he needed to know. He trotted down the spiral staircase to his bedroom and looked out the window. He could just see the edge of her driveway from there. Yes! Her car was in the driveway.

Finishing his coffee, Aiden brushed his teeth and pulled on jeans and a t-shirt. He combed his hair, taking extra time in front of the mirror until he realized what he was doing. He should be working today. Why was he so fired up to impress this woman? He blew out a breath through his lips. "Pfft. Get it together, man," he said to his reflection.

He had a hard time taking his own advice, though. He practically ran down the stairs and out the door, feeling that wild draw inside again. The pink flowers made him happy as he walked up to knock on her front door. He banged harder than he meant to, the loud sound reverberating inside the house. He winced, wishing he'd pressed the doorbell instead.

"Yes?" she said abruptly, swinging the door open.

Hot. Damn. Words failed him as she locked large, hazel eyes on him. She stood there, pink and flushed, her lips parted slightly as she breathed hard through her mouth. Her hair was pulled back in a messy ponytail, tendrils escaping here and there. His eyes dipped for a fraction of a second to the opened buttons of her blouse before he dragged them back up to her face. He swallowed hard, his mind a complete blank for the first time in his life.

"Oh, just get in here!" she growled, grabbing his t-shirt in a fist, and dragging him inside. She pushed the door shut and spun around, pulling him at a run behind her. He followed, taken aback by the greeting.

"I've gotta say, this wasn't the reception I was expecting, but I'm not complaining," he said, finding his voice. For a moment he dared to hope she was taking him to her bedroom, but she led him into the kitchen. Several large pots were boiling and steaming on the stove. There were glass jars spread out over one entire side of the long counter.

"Here, stir this, quickly!" she said, shoving a large spoon into his hands. He did as he was told and she poured a bowl of what looked like cloudy honey into the red, bubbling pot. "Mix it quickly so it doesn't clump."

He stirred vigorously as she grabbed a fat, squat pair of tongs and extracted more jars from one of the boiling pots, setting them on the towel on the counter next to the rest.

"Ow!" he yelped as some of the red substance bubbled up and splashed onto his hand, burning him. He dropped the spoon and stuck his hand in his mouth.

"Oh! I'm so sorry!" she said. "Are you ok? I should have turned this one off!" She grabbed his hand and inspected it. "I'll get you some ice."

"No, no, it's fine. Just startled me, that's all," Aiden said, flashing her a smile as she held his hand. She looked up into his eyes and he was frozen again.

"It looks alright," she said, dropping his hand. Turning her back to him, she grabbed the spoon and stirred, inspecting his work.

Aiden found his voice again now that those eyes weren't on him. "Is this some sort of witch's brew you have going here?" he asked.

"It's strawberry jam," she said, tapping the spoon on the side of the pot. She picked up a ladle and began transferring the contents of the pot to jars. "I'm sorry you got burned. You caught me right at the critical point. I had to get the pectin in quickly. Mind telling me why you were pounding on my door like the apocalypse was nigh?"

Aiden sucked on the side of his hand again as he watched her back. As long as she didn't turn those eyes on him again, he seemed to be able to speak. He cleared his throat. "I, uh, wanted to come over and introduce myself. Since we're neighbors. Howdy, neighbor," he said, thinking that just because he could speak didn't mean he should. Clearly half his brain cells had decided to leave the building. "I'm Ai-" he started to say as she swung around and pierced him with a look again.

"Howdy?" she said, the corner of her mouth turning up as if she were trying not to laugh. He smiled mutely at her. "My name's Shae," she said, holding her hand out to him. "Nice to meet you, A."

"It's Aiden, actually," he managed as he took her hand to shake it. He'd never been so much on the backfoot with a woman before. "I saw you last night. In your backyard," he blurted out.

Shae didn't move her gaze from his, continuing to look him in the eye. "Oh?" she said, raising one eyebrow. She shrugged as if it were interesting, but of no consequence. She turned back to her ladling.

"Yes, I just thought I should come over and tell you. I didn't look. I mean, I stopped looking when you did the handstand. I... oh, god." he said, mortified. He wasn't explaining this properly. "I built a rooftop terrace, and it looks into your backyard. I just thought I should tell you."

"I saw that going up," she said, her back still to him. "It looks nice. I bet the view is great from up there."

"It is!" Aiden stammered. "You should come over sometime. Check it out." Shae continued her work and Aiden shoved his hands in his pockets and rocked back on his heels, not sure if he should just leave. But he didn't want to leave. "What were you doing last night, if I may ask?"

"A lunar love ritual," Shae answered. Aiden waited for an explanation, but she didn't give it.

"You have me at a disadvantage, I'm afraid. What is a lunar love ritual?" he asked, intrigued.

"It's used to harness the energy of the moon. It's tied to feminine cycles." She was screwing lids onto the jars now, then placing them in a huge pot. She finished and placed a lid over the pot, turning to face him again. She leaned against the counter, and he crossed his arms in front of him, gripping his own biceps to stop himself from reaching out to touch her.

"And the howling?" he asked.

Shae gave him a little smile. "Do you really want to know?"

Aiden nodded.

"I'm a red moon woman. The howling is a way to get closer to the earth and the creatures of it. A way to call the power of the moon to gain deeper insight into my natural rhythms and how my divine flow guides me to have greater control over my mental and emotional well-being as well as harness the full potential of my creativity, and strength."

"A red moon woman?" Aiden asked, thinking of little green men from Mars. Did she think she was an alien?

"There are two types of women. A white moon woman, which is the more common of the two types, will menstruate around the darkness of the new moon and ovulate by the light of the full moon. A red moon woman will menstruate with the full light of the full moon and ovulate with the darkness of the new moon. I'm a red moon woman. Guess I gave something away there," she said, smiling wryly at him.

"Well, if you expected me to be put off by that, I'm afraid I'm not," he said, chuckling. He was shocked, yes, but not by the fact that she just told him she was menstruating. It was the entirely open and honest way she told him. She completely owned her body to an extent he'd never seen before.

"I should hope not," she said. Then she motioned to his t-shirt and laughed. "*Is it solipsistic in here or is it just me?*" she read. "That's funny."

"Oh, yeah, I like funny t-shirts." He smiled. She got it *and* she laughed. Check, check.

"So, listen, I was just about to sit down to lunch," Shae started.

"Say no more. Sorry I barged in on you like this. I really just wanted to say hello and warn you about the new deck. I'll get out of your way."

"You're welcome to stay if you like," she said, holding her hand out toward the dining table. "I made a lot. I'll just be taking the leftovers to work tomorrow anyway. There's no way I can eat this much."

Aiden felt excitement rush through him. "I'd like that, thank you. I haven't even had breakfast yet."

"Well, then you're in luck. I made scones for lunch. They should be delicious with this fresh strawberry jam." She placed a large basket piled with scones on the table along with a jar of jam that had escaped the boiling pot. She turned and he took a seat at the table, watching her bend to take things out of the refrigerator. Damn, his fingers itched to run over her soft curves.

"You made these?" he asked as she turned back, setting a bowl of something white in front of him.

"Yep. I made all of this. I like to bake. Don't get to do it often, at least not the way I like to. It's only me here, and I'd be as big as a house if I baked as much as I want to. I cook for my parents, but they're vegan, and it's just not as good if it's not butter, you know?" She set a plate and utensils in front of him and sat down, placing a scone on his plate.

"Clotted cream?" he asked, inspecting the contents of the bowl.

"Sure is. See what I mean about the vegan thing? I mean, I don't eat meat, but I can't give up dairy. Just can't do it. Ohhhh," she moaned, a most indecent sound, as she bit into the scone with jam and cream. "That's so good!"

Aiden's mouth watered watching her, but not for the scone. He quickly diverted his eyes from her mouth and set about preparing his own food. He hoped he could quash the erection straining to get out before he had to stand up from the table. He shoved the scone in his mouth and immediately made his own moan of approval.

"Outstanding," he groaned as the creamy, buttery, strawberry-sweetened goodness melted on his tongue. "That is ambrosial."

"Wow, food of the gods, really? That's quite the compliment," Shae said, smiling.

"And well-deserved, I assure you. I happen to be a scone connoisseur," he said.

"Oh, really? Well, in that case I apologize for the temperature of the cream. I should have taken it out earlier, but someone distracted me."

Something in her voice shook him. He looked up and her eyes rested on his. The look she gave him was deep and sultry, like her voice as she'd said those last few words. The food caught in his throat, and he covered his mouth, coughing a little.

"Oh, I'm the worst host," she said, standing. "Let me get you something to drink. Was the scone too dry?" She filled a glass with water and set it in front of him. He took a long drink, washing the food down.

"No, no, it's really delicious. I just swallowed the wrong way."

"I've got water on for tea." She rushed around pouring tea and nudging a creamer toward him.

"I'm ok, really," he said. "I think I'll survive." He flashed her his patented panty-melting grin and the worried crease between her eyes relaxed. She looked down and fell into her chair, fixing her eyes on her teacup. Maybe he could affect her after all because she seemed to be refusing to meet his eye now.

"So, what do you do, Aiden?" she asked, looking at her scone.

"I build," he answered simply.

"Houses? Like your house?"

"Yep. I buy less than desirable houses and turn them into comfortable homes."

"Less than desirable," Shae laughed. "Your current project certainly fits that bill. Thank you for the flower border, by the way. At least, I assume that was you, unless there's a landscaping Santa Claus roaming the neighborhood."

"A landscaping Santa Claus?" Aiden laughed. "As much as I would like to see that, it was me. And you're welcome. It was nothing."

"It's beautiful," Shae said, reaching out to place her hand on his arm. Heat radiated from her touch, and he started to lift his other hand out to place on hers but stopped when she continued, patting his arm. "Don't ever belittle your work."

It wasn't what she said that made him stop. It was the way she said it. Patronizing, as if she were speaking to a child. She looked at him now and there was something about it that put him off.

"Well, thanks," Aiden said, moving his arm from under her touch and reaching for his teacup. He took a sip. "Thank you for lunch, but I've taken too much of your time already." He stood and pushed in his chair. Shae stood as well. Aiden suppressed a sigh of frustration as he reacted to the sight of her unfolding her long body.

"I look forward to seeing that deck from the top side," Shae said, but then looked like she wished she hadn't. Aiden couldn't figure out what was going on with this woman, or why he was reacting this way. Every time she looked at him, his mind froze.

"Yeah, sure, I'll have you up some time," he mumbled as he made his way to the door.

"It was nice meeting you. Thanks for coming over and introducing yourself," Shae said.

"Mmm-hmm," was all he could manage as he left, nodding to her as he turned to walk back to his house.

He was frustrated and infuriated, and fucking turned on. It was the most confusing mix of feelings he'd ever had. On the one hand Shae (even the name) was the most intoxicating, beautiful, alluring woman he'd ever set eyes on. And she was smart and open, and he guessed she didn't take any shit from anyone. On the other hand, she treated him like he was somehow below her. It wasn't anything she said exactly, just a feeling he kept getting. Maybe she was the social-climbing type after all. In which case a lowly construction worker wouldn't do for her at all, now would it?

Aiden growled as he walked in his front door. He needed to get his mind off of her. He stomped upstairs to his office and plunked himself down in front of his drafting table. He had to finish this project, anyway. Maybe he could channel his frustrations into work. People were counting on him, after all.

He took up his pencils and worked furiously. The project came together almost seamlessly. He could see it now. The whole town rebuilt after the hurricanes. Disaster relief housing should offer dignity to its occupants, inspiring them to build for the future. This design could be added to over time utilizing locally sourced materials. He drew on sustainable and green building techniques for this particularly fragile ecosystem.

Though he would never get paid for this work, or have his name on it, these were the most satisfying projects he did. Aiden realized after the city building debacle that he wasn't focused on what really mattered in life. He was focused on collecting praise and recognition from powerful people. But what did that really amount to in the end? He'd been told his whole life that it was important. But it wasn't. Not to him.

Now he volunteered for organizations that built in some of the poorest parts of the world. He put his knowledge to better use, he thought, than locking himself away in some rarefied ivory tower. This project would provide homes with running water and electricity to people who really needed it. And the carbon footprint would be low, making as little impact on the planet as possible.

Aiden leaned back and sighed. He'd done something good here. He assembled everything to send off to the project manager. They'd be happy to get these designs a week early. The sense of accomplishment he loved having at the end of each project came over him now.

He heard his work phone buzzing from the bedroom where he'd left it when he went next door. He walked in and picked it up off the nightstand. A number he didn't recognize flashed on the screen. Normally he'd let it go to voicemail, but he was already bored now that the project was complete, and he didn't feel like working on his house tonight, so he answered.

"Hello?"

"Hi, Aiden?" a high-pitched voice asked.

"Yes, hello Hestia," he said, recognizing her immediately. She sounded like a baby chipmunk.

"How did you know it was me?" she asked.

"Recognized your voice. How did you get this number?" Aiden asked. They hadn't exchanged numbers, or much else besides bodily fluids.

"I, uh, I got it from a friend. I, um, wanted to make sure you got the Venmo I sent. For Friday night, you know," she stammered.

"Oh, that was you. I was wondering. Listen, Hestia, I wasn't working Friday night. I didn't realize you knew me."

"Oh? I was kind of hoping you'd say that," she said quietly.

Oh, shit. He didn't mean to imply he wanted more. "Yeah," he laughed. "It was fun, right?"

"Yes. Do you maybe want to do it again sometime?"

Aiden sighed internally. He'd thought they were on the same page. Just two people blowing off some steam. "I enjoyed spending time with you," he said gently, "but I'm not looking for a relationship. You know this is my work line, right?"

Silence hung on the line between them before he heard her take a breath. "Of course," she said, sounding artificially chipper.

"I'll send your money back," he said. "I don't want it to be weird if we see each other at The Club."

"No, no, it won't be weird. And keep the money. I mean, maybe I'll call you for a date sometime."

Aiden was about to object when she hastily cut him off.

"Alright, Aiden. Take care. Bye." And she hung up.

Aiden hated it when his personal life and his work life collided. It usually didn't happen, thankfully. He wondered who'd given Hestia his info. He didn't think anyone at The Club knew about his side gig. At least she had sounded ok with everything. He didn't think having her as a client was a very good idea, though. There was a reason most of his clients were older women. They were less likely to be on the hunt for the future father of their children.

Aiden thought about having a child but dismissed the idea. Someday, in a future he couldn't quite see yet, yes, he would love to have children. It was a theoretical desire, though, not one he felt the need to fulfill at present. Right now, he had plenty to keep his life interesting. And, if he was being honest, he'd never met a woman he could envision as the mother of his children. That woman would have to be someone extraordinary, and he wasn't sure she existed.

Chapter 5

S hae stood in her front doorway and watched Aiden disappear into his house. She couldn't see his face, but something in the way he carried himself, his back straight, his stride long, told her he was upset. She went over their conversation in her head and couldn't figure out what could possibly have upset him. Maybe he was expecting her to offer to pay him for his work on the flower border?

She shook her head, realizing he'd gone inside at least a minute ago and she was still standing there. She took one last glance at the door and went back inside. Her breathing was still slightly labored.

Aiden.

Just his name was doing things to her now. The man must be emitting prodigious amounts of male pheromones. It had to be something. She ran a hand over her breast, feeling the tightened nipple through her thin shirt. She groaned a little, squeezing her breast and closing her eyes, imagining his hands on her.

Rough hands, from working with them. How would that feel when he grabbed her? When he ran those hands down her sides? Up her thighs as he spread her apart? Shae moaned now, her body going into overdrive. How could she be so attracted to someone so wrong for her? It had to be pheromones.

Or those piercing, dark blue eyes. God, those eyes. They were like the sky at twilight, after the reds and oranges have faded, just before the blackness takes over. A deep navy that she could lose herself in. She almost had. She'd started to flirt with him before her better judgement could stop her.

When she'd touched his arm, it had taken everything she had not to fling herself across the table and into his lap. But that would have been a mistake. He was the homey type. He'd want a nice little wife to cook and clean for him while he drank beers and watched football. That wasn't what Shae was looking for at all. She needed someone who was her intellectual equal.

But, god, she would like just one night with someone that looked like him. Sun-kissed skin taught over hard muscle, tousled, sandy brown hair, and lips that tempted her to lean in and take a nibble.

It wasn't like Liam was chopped liver. He was attractive in the corporate way Shae always went for. He kept fit by playing racquetball, and he was always immaculately groomed. If James Bond had a blander brother, Liam could be him. The thought of Liam had her grabbing her phone. She was about to explode, and he hadn't called her in a week.

"Yello," Liam answered. She knew he would only answer the phone in that silly way for her, and it annoyed her for some reason. She didn't want silly Liam right now.

"Hey," Shae breathed, almost panting. "Where are you?"

"At the office."

"It's Sunday afternoon!" she complained.

"Yes. Did you call me to inform me of the day and time?" Liam joked.

"No. Can you come over?"

"Sorry, I've got meetings until late tonight. I shouldn't even be on the phone now. I miss you, though."

"Do you?" Shae asked petulantly. "Do you really? Because it's been over a week, Liam. I need a release."

"I'm sorry, Shae, I have to go. My next meeting is here. I'm really sorry, believe me."

Shae sighed loudly. "Fine." She hung up, flinging her phone onto the couch. She would just have to take care of things for herself before she exploded.

She tried to think of Liam as she laid down on the couch and unzipped her pants. Flinging a leg up over the back of the couch, she slid her hand down into her panties, her fingers sinking into her soaked center. She was beyond wet.

Shae stroked herself, her breathing coming faster. A few more circles and she was close, climbing to the peak at breakneck speed. Dark blue eyes flashed through her mind. Aiden's hands on her. She gripped a breast and cried out as her orgasm hit her, "Aiden!"

Her arched back relaxed into the cushions and she caught her breath. She was going to have to go change her panties now. Sweat trickled down her neck, tickling as it went. She sighed at herself. She needed to get this man out of her head.

"RRRRGGGHHH!" SHAE GRUMBLED, stabbing at her laptop keys. It took her three tries to enter the data correctly and she cursed under her breath.

"Hey, what's got you so riled up?" Deja asked, strolling over to Shae's desk.

"It's this damn report. I can't make it right." She punched at the keys again.

"Come on now, don't kill it," Deja laughed. "Here, let me." Deja gave the keyboard a few gentle strokes and the graph Shae had been trying for came up perfectly.

"Ugh, thank you. My head is just screwed on backwards today," Shae grouched, attacking the laptop again to save and transfer the data to another spreadsheet.

"Seems more like it's not screwed at all. Or rather, you're not," Deja said, pulling a chair up next to Shae. She leaned back in the chair and settled her eyes on Shae. "So, spill the tea, girl."

Shae wondered at how Deja always seemed to know when something was up with her. They had been close friends since college, where they were both interns at the same company they worked for now. And nothing ever got by Deja, especially if it was something juicy.

"I haven't been fucked in ten days," Shae whispered, glancing around to make sure no one could hear them. The office was mostly cleared out for lunch, so she felt ok to speak freely.

"Damn," Deja said, her eyes wide. "I mean, for you that's like a year."

"Yes, it is!"

"What happened? Liam's dick go limp or something?" Deja laughed.

"I wouldn't know. He's been so busy working I haven't seen him. I've barely even talked to him on the phone. It's not like I'm a clingy girlfriend. We're not even in a 'relationship' per say. But I have needs that must be fulfilled, and he knows that. It's not just this week, either. He's been putting me on the back burner for a couple months now."

"Damn, you shouldn't have to put up with that," Deja said.

"The worst part is, I can't even seem to care," Shae moaned. "Not since Aiden showed up on my doorstep a few weeks ago. He's all I've been able to think about, and with Liam gone all the time..."

"Sounds like you need to get your needs fulfilled somewhere else," Deja said.

"Ever the pragmatist, aren't you?" Shae said sarcastically.

Deja winked. "I have a friend who knows a guy if you're interested."

"A guy for what?" Shae asked, her mind not wanting to go where she knew Deja was going.

"For your *needs*," Deja whispered as John walked by. He nodded to the two women who smiled back, waiting until he'd rounded the corner out of sight before continuing.

"I know you're not suggesting I hire a hooker," Shae said, frowning.

"Not a hooker! Just... someone for you. Someone who will take care of what you need and won't bother you with what they need." Deja made it sound so simple.

"I'm not that desperate yet," Shae said, even though the thought did appeal to her on some level.

"Well, I hear he's hot as fucking sin and can make you come six ways from Sunday. And I almost called him once. Before I met Jalen."

Shae's mind was blown. Deja had almost called a male escort? "Who are you getting this information from?"

"My friend Brooke," Deja said. "She seriously can't stop talking about their date. I worried about her bankrupting herself or falling in love with him, but she was so satisfied she said she didn't need to go out with anyone again for a long time. Apparently, he's really good at the loving *and* the leaving. She is just happy."

Shae considered this. Brooke was an extraordinarily successful businesswoman with a good head on her shoulders. Not to mention absolutely gorgeous. Shae had met her a few times and secretly admired her. She could have her pick of any man she wanted. If *she* had called this man...

"Text me his number," Shae said before she could change her mind. She didn't have to use it, but it might be fun. "What's his name?"

"I'm not sure. Brooke always called him *Dr. Love*," Deja laughed.

"That's juvenile and a bit of a turnoff," Shae said. Dr. Love, how absurd. She pulled a protein bar out of her desk and opened it.

"I'm leaving early today. Mom and Dad are coming to my house for dinner tonight and I have to go pick them up. They haven't been over in a few months. So I'm working through lunch."

"Ah. I was going to ask if you wanted to go try that new place that opened up where the bagel shop used to be. I want to go, though, so plan on it soon. I'm going to go grab something. Have fun with the folks tonight." Deja departed and a moment later Shae got a text from her.

Dr. Love, followed by some choice emojis and a phone number. Shae smirked and went back to her work. She felt less stabby now. Maybe she wouldn't murder her computer after all.

FOUR HOURS LATER SHE'D completed her probability theory and statistical analysis reports on the adequacy of the property-casualty insurer's statutory loss reserves. Statistics and graphs had crowded her head all day. She enjoyed it, but she also enjoyed the peace and calm she felt as she headed out of the office to spend the evening with her family.

Shae made a stop at the organic market in town before picking her parents up at their house. Now they all stepped out into her driveway and Shae opened the trunk to unload the produce. She handed sacks to her parents and closed the trunk, her eyes subconsciously darting next door when she heard the sound of a door opening.

Aiden stepped out his front door and walked down the drive. He looked up as the trunk slammed and their eyes met. He raised his hand, giving her a wave, then continued on to put a letter in the mailbox. He flipped the flag up and turned back toward his house.

"Hi there!" Veronica yelled across the driveways. Shae cringed. Aiden stopped and waved again, this time to her mother.

"Howdy," he said. The corner of Shae's mouth turned up in amusement. *Howdy*? Did he always say that?

"I'm Veronica," her mother said, setting her bag on the ground and walking toward Aiden. Shae groaned internally.

She hadn't spoken to Aiden since that day he'd come over to introduce himself several weeks ago. He'd waved once or twice when they'd happened to be outside at the same time, but that was it. Hearing his voice sent a tingle of desire through her and she took a deep breath. Why did he do this to her?

"Aiden," he said, walking over and extending his hand. Veronica just reached her arms out and took Aiden into one of her signature hugs. Her mother didn't shake hands. She hugged. And once you were trapped, she didn't let go for many, many seconds.

Shae watched Aiden's face, waiting for the look of discomfort most people got when they were held for a length of time by a stranger. But he just hugged her back, smiling at Shae after a few seconds. Shae felt herself smile back.

"Well, aren't you just a handsome young man," Veronica said, pulling back to look at Aiden, still gripping his arms with her hands. "You must be the new neighbor. Shae said someone nice had finally moved in."

"Shae said I was nice?" Aiden asked, a grin on his face which he now turned on her. Shae shifted on her feet, the feeling of his eyes on her sending another shockwave through her.

"This is my mother," she spit out quickly. "And my father, Vern." Shae stepped back behind her father as he went to shake Aiden's hand. She picked up her mother's discarded bag and made a move toward the front door.

"I really should get dinner started if we're going to eat before it gets late," Shae said.

"Aiden," Veronica said, "you'll come eat with us, won't you? Of course you will," she answered for him before he could say anything.

Veronica grabbed Aiden's arm in both her hands and dragged him across the flower bed and into Shae's driveway.

"I'd love to," Aiden said. "But let me go grab some shoes." Shae looked down and noticed he was indeed barefoot. Damn, even his feet were sexy. She'd never thought that before about anyone's feet.

"Oh, tosh," Veronica said, pulling him along. "Who needs shoes?" She lifted the hem of her long skirt revealing her own bare feet. Shae thought Aiden would run now, for sure, but he only laughed.

"Tosh? I haven't heard anyone aside from my father use that word in America. Are you English?" Aiden asked, walking up the drive with Veronica as if they were old friends.

Shae shoved past them, confounded by these events, and unlocked the front door, wrestling her bags inside. She held the door while they all filed in, Aiden's eyes locked on her mother as they conversed. It was as if Shae weren't even there. It drove her mad.

"No, no, we're not English," Veronica answered. "I just have a love of languages. I speak three fluently, but Shae over there speaks five. I think she gets it from me, though my love of language stems from my interest in different cultures. Shae just likes to show off her big brain. How about you, is your father from England?"

"Yes, he is. Though he moved here about thirty-five years ago. He's been living in America longer than England at this point."

"Oh, my, come sit down over here and tell me, have you been to England?"

Shae and Dad took the bags into the kitchen as her mother began to interrogate Aiden. She knew there was no point in trying to stop it. Her mother wouldn't stop now until she'd gotten his whole life story.

"So, Dad, what's new in your life?" Shae asked as they unloaded and began prepping the food.

"Nothing much, Shaky-Bakey. Looks like we'll have a good harvest in a few months. The weather has been great this year."

While technically legal in California, her parents' farming practices would not be approved of by the federal government. Shae didn't approve of it either, so she changed the subject.

"How are you and Mom?" she asked. "Do you want me to come over tomorrow?"

"We're fine, Shae," her father said, taking her shoulders and looking her in the eye. "Are you ok?"

"Yeah, yeah. I'll be fine," she said, turning back to chopping.

"And you don't need to come over," Dad said. "Go have fun with all the other young people. Mom and I will be asleep before the fireworks even start. Go out, see a show. I'll give you some of my cookies tonight if you need to relax."

Shae wouldn't be celebrating the Fourth of July, even with some of Dad's 'special' cookies. She knew her father knew that, but even so, every year since she was sixteen, they'd tried to get her to enjoy the holiday. She didn't think she ever would. Not with everything she'd seen the night River died. It was a night she dreaded, the loud explosions bringing back vivid memories of the accident.

Changing the subject yet again, Shae began preparing the meal and chatting about work. Her father was soon regaling her with one of his funny stories and she began to relax.

"It's starting to smell delicious in here," Mom said as she and Aiden walked into the kitchen half an hour later. Shae took a breath, her shoulders tensing again when she remembered Aiden's presence.

"I'll have everything done in a few more minutes, if you want to set the table," Shae said, turning to give everyone a smile. Her face fell as she met Aiden's eyes. His gaze was locked on her, his hand gripping the back of a chair, and she sucked in a little breath. Something hot and alive seemed to move between them, pulling at her to be closer to him.

Aiden seemed to feel it, too, and he took a step toward her. Then he was next to her, and she turned her eyes back to the stove, her pulse beating in her ears.

"What can I do?" he asked quietly, standing so close his shoulder almost brushed hers. She could feel the heat of his body, see the rounded pecs that strained against his tight t-shirt, and liquid heat pooled between her legs.

Kiss me! That's what you can do! she wanted to scream. She glanced sidelong at his lower lip and every cell in her body begged her to run her tongue over it, taste him, have him. "Hand me that large bowl from the top of the cabinet up there," she said, clearing her throat. "I have to stand on a chair when I want to get that one down."

Shae watched as Aiden extended a long arm, easily reaching and grabbing the heavy glass bowl in one hand. As he stretched, the hem of his t-shirt lifted, revealing a peek at toned, tanned muscle. Her mouth watered and she dragged her eyes back to his as he held the bowl out to her.

"Could you just give it a rinse in the sink, please? I don't use it that often and it's probably dusty," she said, trying to swallow before she drooled on herself.

As she finished her prep, she watched him wash and dry the bowl. His hands were huge and square, his fingers thick. She wanted those hands on her. Those fingers inside her. "Damn it, Liam," she muttered as Aiden handed her the bowl.

"What?" he asked, looking confused.

"Nothing," Shae said quickly, a blush rising to her cheeks. She hadn't meant to say that out loud. If only Liam were coming over a little more often, she wouldn't be in this state of constant torture. She filled the bowl and began moving dishes to the table. Aiden helped her silently, his arm brushing hers once, shocking her with a bolt of fire so hot she was sure there would be a mark.

"As we come together at this special time, let us pause a moment to appreciate the opportunity for good company and to thank all those who have helped to bring it to our table, and vow to respond in turn to those in need with wisdom and compassion. Let us also wish that someday, all people on Earth may enjoy the same good fortune that we share. Blessed be our friends, our families, and all of our loved ones. Blessed be our mother earth, our father sky and sun. We receive this food in gratitude to all beings. Thank you for being with us, Aiden." Veronica finished her blessing and Shae watched Aiden, sure he would stand and run at any moment.

But he didn't. He smiled and chatted easily with her parents as if eating barefoot in her kitchen and blessing father sky were all perfectly normal to him. Shae ate in silence for the most part, unable to sort through the swarm of conflicting emotions running through her. By the end of the meal her body was restless and her mind in a jumble.

"I should get you home," Shae said, jumping up from the table as her father yawned. They'd finished dinner at least an hour ago, and it was getting late for her parents.

"Oh, we've been having so much fun," Mom said. "But I suppose we should get to bed. It was so lovely to get to know you, Aiden. I hope we'll see you again real soon."

Aiden stood and walked around the table. "I've had a lovely time, as well, Veronica," he said. Her mother wrapped him in a hug again. When she released him, Dad hugged him, too. Shae stood there, feeling awkward, wanting to run from Aiden, but at the same time wishing she had an excuse to fall into his arms.

She led the group to the front door where she and Dad slipped their shoes on. Shae shook her head at her mother's lack of footwear. Aiden hung back, speaking as Shae reached for the doorknob.

"I'll stay and clean up," he said, one hand in his pocket. He looked so comfortable standing there, his feet bare, wearing another one of those ridiculous joke t-shirts. For a moment she could almost imagine he belonged there.

"No, that's not necessary, I'm sure you have work you need to do," Shae began, but the lopsided grin Aiden gave her stopped her.

"It's the least I can do. And I do have work, a lot of it. But nothing that can't wait. That is, if you don't mind me being here while you're gone. I promise I won't snoop," he said in a manner so sincere Shae believed him at once.

"Oh, how sweet," Mom said. "Such a nice neighbor."

"You really don't have to," Shae said.

"Oh, let him. He's a nice young man. Don't be so distrustful," Mom scolded her.

Shae pressed her lips together into a thin line. No matter what she did now she wouldn't be happy. She didn't want to let Aiden think she didn't trust him, because despite logic, she seemed to trust him implicitly. But having him in her house, touching her things... It felt so... intimate.

"Thank you, Aiden," she said, deciding it was easier to give in than to fight everyone. "It'll take me about an hour to get them home. I guess just lock the door handle when you leave."

A flash of disappointment crossed his face but was gone before Shae could be sure she'd seen it. He smiled again, saying goodnight as they went out the door.

Shae drove her parents home quickly, making sure they were safely inside before driving back even faster. Her body raced with anticipation that she refused to acknowledge in her conscious mind. Still, her actions revealed what she really wanted- Aiden.

She found the handle locked when she got to her front door and a feeling akin to panic settled in her. When she opened the door, she found the house quiet. Only one light was on in the living room. She went straight to the kitchen, flipping the lights on.

Everything sparkled. Not a dish was out of place. It was like she hadn't even used the place. Even the stove and sink had been scrubbed and dried until they shined. But Aiden was gone. Her chest squeezed uncomfortably, and Shae let out a long sigh. She couldn't deny now that she had been hoping he would be there when she got back.

But why? Pure animal lust, that was why, she told herself. She reached for her phone in her pocket, then stopped, staring at the screen. Liam was out of town for a week. Another week without touch. At least. Who knew how busy he would be when he got back? He was always swamped after he got back from trips. And when she thought about him, it left her flat. When had that happened?

Shae bit her lip as she contemplated what she was thinking of doing. But she couldn't stand it anymore. Before she could think better of it she sent a text.

Hi, Dr. Love, I'm looking for a date tomorrow night. I heard you might be free?

She tossed the phone down as if it bit her the minute she sent it. Was she crazy? Was this really what her life had become?

"Fuck," she muttered under her breath and picked the phone up again, starting another text.

Liam, I know we never discussed our relationship, if you can even call it that, but it's not working for me. I don't think we should see each other anymore. I enjoyed our time together.

There. She was not about to 'cheat' on Liam, whether they had discussed being exclusive or not. A minute later her phone rang, and she stared at the screen. Liam. She dismissed the call, sending a text back instead.

I'm not in a place to discuss this right now. Call me when you're back in town if you like

She honestly didn't know if Liam cared whether she was in his life or not at this point. He'd barely acknowledged her existence the last few weeks. And when he had it had only been to bang her and run. She felt a little lighter now. Freer. Her phone buzzed in her hand, and she looked down, expecting a text from Liam. Her pulse pounded as she read the words.

You do realize tomorrow is the Fourth of July?

Well, that seemed like a snarky reply for someone who was supposed to be the master of seduction. She typed:

Yes. I don't celebrate, but we can have an early dinner if you like

Shae waited a moment, wondering if dinner was part of the package, or if they were just supposed to meet in a seedy motel room. Her phone buzzed again.

Just to get business out of the way first, I'll need to know who referred you and your name

Brooke Hammond gave me your number. My name is Marley Mitchell

Shae threw out the two names before thinking. She had to use Brooke's name, since he probably had no idea who Deja was. And she used her middle name, not wanting to give a stranger her real name. What if he were some kind of stalker? She could always block his number if he turned out to be a weirdo.

6pm, cocktails at Antonio's. Meet me at the bar. I'll be holding a blue carnation

See you then, Shae typed, her hands shaking with nerves. She couldn't believe she was going to do this. She thought of Aiden again and her thighs clenched together. Oh, she was doing this. She had to get that golden-haired hunk out of her head and her system.

If it had worked for Brooke it could work for her. Couldn't it?

Chapter 6

S hae tugged the bottom of her tight dress down her thighs. The material stretched, but was still six inches above her knees. And now the front dipped too low. Her breasts were practically falling out of the blue satin. She wondered if *she* looked like the escort tonight.

She'd pulled out every stop when dressing tonight. Full makeup, stilettos, musky perfume. She was dressed for sex, and it wouldn't take much seduction to get her on her back tonight. As she walked into the restaurant several people glanced appreciatively in her direction. Maybe she shouldn't be paying for this *service* after all.

The bar was dark after the brightness outside. This time of year, the sun would still be beating down for a couple more hours. Her eyes took a moment to adjust to the low light and she scanned the figures at the bar, landing on a man in a black suit. His broad back was to her, but the cut of the suit made her mouth water. That had to be him. She marched boldly up to the bar and slid onto the stool next to him.

Shae's stomach dropped to her feet in the next second as navy blue eyes met hers. She glanced down to the blue carnation in his hand, disbelief gripping her as Aiden's soft lips curved into a smile.

"Shae, what a surprise," Aiden said, grinning at her.

You have no idea, she thought. "*Dr. Love?*" she asked, incredulously.

Aiden's smile dropped and he swallowed, then cleared his throat. "Marley?"

"Yes," Shae said, then began to laugh. Aiden looked at her, confusion in his eyes, but then he began to chuckle.

"I guess this is for you," he said, handing her the flower, which somehow matched his impossibly blue eyes.

"Thank you," she said, taking the flower and raising it to her nose. Carnations were her favorite flower, and this one had a deliciously spicy fragrance. She inhaled, watching Aiden's face.

"Normally, I would buy you a drink," Aiden said.

"Please. Let's not be weird about this. Just treat me like any other client. Pinot Grigio," Shae said when the bartender caught her eye.

"Alright," Aiden said cautiously. Shae's drink arrived and Aiden raised his glass, tilting it to hers. "Cheers."

"Cheers," she said, clinking his glass and taking a long sip. The heat of the alcohol spread from her stomach up her chest. She looked at Aiden and the heat became a fire that spread through her.

"So, Marley Mitchell?" he asked.

"It's my name. Shae Marley Indigo Mitchell," Shae answered, drowning in his eyes. "So, *Dr. Love?*" she said, smirking.

"It's my name," Aiden answered, mirroring her tone. "Aiden James Love."

"Guess we could have avoided this if we'd exchanged last names," Shae said, licking her lips and leaning in toward him. "But I can't say I'm completely unhappy about ending up here."

Aiden cleared his throat, sitting up straighter and gulping his drink. If she didn't know better, she'd think she was making him nervous. Shouldn't it be the other way around? Shouldn't he be trying to put her at ease?

"Shae, uh," Aiden said, sucking in a breath. "I normally wouldn't ask this, and you can tell me it's none of my business, but do you do this often?"

"Do what? Go out with escorts?" Shae laughed. Aiden seemed even more nervous.

"Yes. It's just, the man with the Mercedes who comes to your place, is he? I don't want to get in the middle of something with you living next door, and..." Aiden trailed off, tugging at his tie.

Shae laughed. "Liam is not an escort. He's a lawyer. And he's not my boyfriend, either. We're not currently seeing each other. And to answer your first question, no. This is the first, and probably the last time I'll do this."

Aiden seemed to relax at that. He finished the rest of his drink and pulled at his cuffs, adjusting them. Shae spied the silver cufflinks at his wrists and heat shot through her.

"Can I tell you something?" she whispered, staring at his hands.

"Of course," he mock-whispered back, his eyes twinkling with laughter. His soft voice sent tingles along her spine.

Shae leaned in until her lips were at his ear. For a moment she lost her mind as his scent enveloped her. He was spicy and masculine, the smell of freshly cut wood mingled with a light cologne. Her breath rushed out against his neck, and she swallowed, stopping herself from running her tongue over his ear. "It's been so long," she breathed, closing her eyes, frozen there next to him.

A low laugh sounded in her ear. Aiden's hand skimmed down her side, so feather light she almost couldn't feel his touch, only the heat from his palm. He settled it on her waist, giving her a squeeze. Liquid heat pooled between her legs and her core spasmed. She'd never been so hot for the smallest touch in her life.

"We both know that's not true," Aiden whispered, the laughter still present in his voice.

Shae opened her eyes, pulling back in surprise. Aiden gripped her waist, his thumb running down to roughly stroke her hip bone. A shiver ran through her, but she forced her mind to work through the growing haze of lust.

"What do you mean?" she asked.

"I mean, you leave your bedroom window open a lot. It can't have been more than a couple of weeks since I last heard you orgasm."

Shae wasn't easily flustered. Not with the way she grew up. But somehow, knowing Aiden had been listening to her sent her reeling. She was abashed yet aroused at the same time. The way he said *orgasm*, especially referring to her, sent her pulse flying.

"Two weeks is an eternity," she told him, trying to convey how very much she meant it.

Aiden looked at her appraisingly, his smile dropping, and he nodded. "Dinner?" he asked simply, raising an adorable brow at her.

"To go?" she asked, finishing the rest of her drink.

Aiden nodded again and stood silently. She watched him walk to the hostess, speaking to the woman who seemed to be hanging on his every word. Shae couldn't deny that he wore a suit like he'd been born to it. Everything about him tonight screamed sophistication. She'd be tempted to fall if she didn't know the truth.

But that was for the best. Tonight, she could live in a fantasy. She could imagine Aiden was an educated, world-travelled businessman who fell madly in love with her the moment he set eyes on her. They would go to gallery openings on Saturday night and do the crossword together on Sunday. He would whisper to her in some foreign language while he made love to her, and he would never get enough.

Aiden turned back to her, his dark eyes meeting hers and she almost melted to the seat. She let herself remain in the fantasy as he took his seat on the stool next to hers again. He reached out, lifting her hand to his lips and gently brushed her fingers, his gaze locked on hers. The touch of his lips on her skin stormed her senses and she almost swooned, swaying on her seat.

"Whoa!" Aiden exclaimed as she tilted to the side. He pulled her hand to his chest as his other arm came around her waist, holding her upright. The motion brought her closer to his chest and the smell of him surrounded her again. "Have you eaten enough today?" he asked, worriedly.

"Yes, yes, I'm fine," she said, still lost in his eyes. They were so close now, his lips only inches from hers. Her eyes began to flutter closed and she leaned in, but Aiden released her, settling her back on her seat and pulling away.

"Should only be a few minutes," he said, clearing his throat. "So, I suppose that begs the question, Shae, your place or mine?" He smiled as he said it, and Shae laughed despite her disappointment at not being kissed.

"Yours," she said decisively. "I want to see this terrace you've built."

"I dare say that's only fair, considering the view it affords me of your backyard," he laughed.

"You *dare say*, do you?" Shae smiled, enjoying his use of the term. It was better than *howdy*, that was for sure.

"Yes, I do," he said, running a finger around her wrist, then slowly up her arm, watching his hand as it moved. "I dare to do a lot of things." His eyes darted back to hers and her breath froze in her lungs.

"Ah!" Aiden said, standing and breaking the spell he'd cast over her. Shae shook her head as Aiden took a large cloth bag from the hostess. "Thank you," he said, and turned back to Shae. "Shall we?"

Aiden offered her his free arm and Shae slid her hand around his elbow reflexively, allowing him to guide her out the door. The brilliance of the evening sun outside brought her back to reality and she dropped her hand.

"Did you drive?" Aiden asked.

"Um, yes, I did," Shae said, trying to shake the fog from her head.

"Good, I Ubered here. Lead the way," Aiden said, smiling as if all this were normal. Shae's stomach twisted uncomfortably. She turned down a side street and stopped at her car. Without looking at Aiden she opened the door and sat behind the wheel.

For the first time in her life Shae had a hard time looking at someone. She'd learned from a young age to not care what people thought of her, at least on the outside. Deep down she did care, though she put on a good show most of the time. Right now, at this moment, for reasons beyond her comprehension, she cared a whole lot what Aiden James Love thought of her. And that feeling had her looking straight ahead, focused on the task of driving home, afraid to look over and see what he was thinking.

Because it was bad no matter what it was. If he judged her for hiring him, she would be too humiliated to look him in the eye ever again. If he gave her another one of those smoldering looks, she would probably pull the car over and jump him on the side of the road in broad daylight. But worst of all, if she looked over and he gave her that sweet, goofy, lopsided grin...

Shae pulled into her driveway and parked the car, jumping out and closing the door, leaning against it with her back to Aiden. She heard him get out and close his door. Then he was standing in front of her. She kept her eyes turned to the ground. He had really nice shoes, she thought.

"Shae, you alright?" Aiden asked.

"Yeah. You have great taste in shoes," she said, her mind spinning. What was he doing to her?

Aiden laughed. "Shae, this isn't getting weird, is it? Why don't you just come over for dinner. Just friends. Forget this whole thing. I think you need to eat."

She didn't need to eat, she needed... What? What did she need? She thought she knew, but now... She looked up into his face and he smiled. A gentle, friendly, open smile that shot her right in the chest.

"You're right," she heard herself saying. "I probably need food. I'm not feeling myself."

Shae took his hand and led him across to his front door. It felt like ten miles. Her hand quivered in his as she touched him, and the quiver had spread all the way up her arm by the time they reached the front door.

Aiden stopped, turning so they faced each other, and laced his fingers through hers. The quiver turned into a full-blown earthquake as he grinned at her again.

"A warning before you enter. I haven't finished the downstairs yet. Maybe I should blindfold you until we're upstairs," he laughed.

Shae stilled the trembling in her body, a task that was made infinitely more difficult by his mention of a blindfold. Oh dear. She smiled weakly and he slid his hand out of hers to unlock the door. She rubbed her palms together, already missing his touch.

Inside Shae froze. This couldn't be the same house. It was the same floorplan as hers, but she'd never recognize it. Even without floors or paint on the walls it was gorgeous. She took in the dark wood on the stairs that matched the new fireplace mantle with a marble surround. Hers was still brick.

Aiden took her hand again and pulled her up the stairs. Her heart raced as they got closer to where she knew the master bedroom was. But then her attention was diverted again by the winding spiral staircase that rose up from an alcove between the second and third bedrooms. She'd wondered how he got to the roof.

Aiden led her there now, but she stopped him. "Give me the tour?" she asked. Aiden hesitated, then nodded, setting their dinner on a step and leading her to the bedroom on the end.

"I have my office in here," he said as he pushed the door open. Shae peeked inside and her jaw dropped. Whatever she was expecting, it wasn't this. A long table dominated the space, a drafting surface at one end with drawings clipped to it. There was a large board in one corner with more drawings. A couple computers and tools Shae had no names for sat here and there on the table.

Aiden backed out, motioning her to the middle room. Shae knew it was the smallest and wondered what he'd done in there. She almost fell over again as he swung that door open.

"You have a baby?" Shae gasped.

"No, no," Aiden laughed. "It's just for show. I've already staged this room for sale since I won't need to use it. I thought this might appeal to a nice family who would take care of the house after I put so much work into it."

"Oh, that makes sense," Shae mumbled, still trying to get over the surprise. She followed Aiden along the hall, her heels clicking on the shiny, dark floors. They were beautiful, too. A hall bath was next, which shined, and had also been staged in a children's aquarium theme.

"Master bedroom," Aiden said, holding the door for her. Shae stepped inside and her heart almost stopped as Aiden stepped up behind her. He stood so close she could feel the heat coming off him.

The room looked like a spread out of Architectural Digest. There was so much going on, Shae could hardly take it all in. Crown moldings, a stunning rug, built-ins, the most gorgeous gauzy curtains she'd ever seen. Another step and she could see into the walk-in closet that had been left open. It was the closet of her dreams.

She spun and headed into the bathroom, keen to see what he'd done in there. Shae fell onto the bench that was built into the corner under the windows, across from the walk-in shower. A double vanity, a soaking tub, beautiful black and white tile with sapphire blue accents. "Beautiful," she whispered, her eyes wide.

She looked around and remembered where she was. Emerging from the bathroom, she smiled shyly at Aiden, who stood with his hands in his pockets, leaning his back against a dresser.

"What do you think?" he asked, pushing away from the dresser and standing.

"It's absolutely incredible," she said, meaning it. "I never would have thought..."

"Yeah, it was a surprise to me how well it turned out, too," he laughed. Then he shrugged off his suit coat and hung it on a hook on the wall. "You don't mind, do you?" he asked. "It's rather warm on the roof today."

Shae watched as Aiden grasped a cufflink between his fingers and twisted, releasing it and setting it on the dresser. In a second, he'd done the other one and set it next to the first. An ache set in deep inside her and she flew into his arms, no longer able to hold back the tidal wave of desire that had been building in her for weeks now.

"Shae," Aiden gasped as her body hit his.

"Aiden," she moaned, wrapping her arms around his neck, tilting her head to offer her upturned lips to him.

His eyes burned, dark pools of desire as he looked into her eyes, then down to her mouth. Then he took her, his full, soft lips finally, finally pressed to hers. Shae whimpered as his arms came around her, pulling her into him. She could happily stay in these arms forever.

His kiss was like warm honey, a thick heat spreading slowly from her lips down her body, until every inch of her felt warm and heavy. He deepened the kiss, coaxing her lips apart, tracing his tongue along the seam until she opened to him, and he slid into her. A low rumble emanated from him as he tasted her, slicking his tongue over and around hers in a sensuous dance.

Shae slid her hands down his chest, pressing her palms against the hard planes of his pecs. Her fingers wrapped around the knot in his tie, tugging it loose until she could pull it off. His lips never left hers, his arms only holding her closer as if he were afraid to let her go. Finding the button at his throat she slipped it open, then the next, her fingers playing lightly against his skin.

His hot, slightly stubbled skin. Pulling her lips away from his, she moved to his jaw, kissing him on the sharp angle below his ear, then down his neck. Aiden gripped her even tighter, until she gasped for breath. Her chest was heaving, and she cried out as he dipped his head and bit her neck. A spike of pure ecstasy shot down her body, making her clit throb as his mouth closed around her. His teeth grazed her a second longer before his tongue, hot and smooth, swirled against her sensitized skin.

"Uuunnnggghhh!" she moaned out, low and loud, unable to control her reaction. No one had ever bitten her before, and it was the most erotic thing she'd ever felt.

"God, Shae," Aiden moaned, his face buried in her neck, his lips working her toward delirium. "You taste incredible."

Shae tore at his shirt, forcing him to release her to slide it down his arms. She yanked at the hem of his undershirt, pulling it off, but his arms were back around her before she could admire the view. Now his flesh was against hers, the tops of her breasts heaving with every breath against his chest.

Aiden lifted her entire body, tossing her to the bed as if she weighed nothing. He followed, falling onto her, his mouth on hers again. He slid his arms under her, around her, pulling her body into him and buried his face in her neck. His teeth grazed down her neck, down until his lips brushed the tops of her breasts.

"Oh, Aiden!" Shae cried, carried away by the lust and her own fantasies. "I've wanted this for so long!"

Aiden stilled his ministrations, his face in the valley of her breasts. He inhaled sharply, his large hands sliding down her sides to pull her against his chest. "As have I, Shae," he said quietly. "Beautiful Shae."

"I need you inside me, Aiden. Now!" she moaned. She couldn't take another second of this torture. Her body ached for him. She reached down to pull at her skirt, but Aiden's hand gripped hers.

"So impatient," he teased her, sliding his large hands up the sides of her thighs until his fingers gripped her panties. He pulled them down, raising up to kneel before her as he slid them off, tossing her shoes aside as he ran his hands down the length of her legs.

Shae bit her lip as she took in the glorious sight of him. Up close she could see the light dusting of golden hair on his chest, running down the beautifully blocked ridges of his abdomen. He reached for his belt and Shae felt a spasm so strong in her core she thought she might cum right then.

"You are so fucking beautiful," she moaned.

Aiden grinned that lopsided smile at her. "That's supposed to be my line," he laughed. "You like to watch, don't you?" he asked, stepping off the bed to stand at the foot. He toed his shoes off as he undid his belt slowly, his eyes never leaving hers.

"I do," Shae breathed, her body on the verge of total combustion.

Aiden grinned as he dropped the rest of his clothing. Shae's stomach leapt into her throat as his very impressive erection slapped against those hard abs with a dull smack. She whimpered, licking her lips. Sitting up she pulled her dress off, flinging it aside, leaving her in a black satin bra.

Aiden's eyes blazed as he looked down at her, stalking her around the bed. When he got to the side, he moved like lightning, gathering her into his arms and dragging her up to her knees as his mouth crushed hers. Shae's breath rushed in as her bra was whisked from her body.

Then there was nothing between them. Nothing but a burning desire that threatened to eat her alive. Aiden's smooth skin pressed against her, and she cried out again, "Inside me, now!"

Laying her down gently, Aiden began to slide down her body, but she was done with the seduction. She wanted him now. Using one of her favorite martial arts moves, she wrapped her legs around his waist, locking her ankles, and flipped him onto his back. The look of surprise on his face gave her a rush.

"Where are your condoms?" she asked.

Aiden flung an arm out to the bedside table, pulling the drawer open and grabbed a foil packet. She snatched it out of his hand, tearing it open and sheathing him quickly. But then she hesitated. Slowly she leaned down, kissing him gently on the lips. Something in his eyes made her stop.

"Is this ok?" she asked, unsure of what she was seeing in the intense look he was giving her.

"Yes, Shae," he said quietly, wrapping his arms around her until she felt as if every inch of her were touching every inch of him.

Looking into her eyes, he shifted his hips until he pressed against her slit. She was slick with need, and the broad head of his cock easily slipped between her folds, parting her open as he pushed into her inch by inch. The air was forced out of her lungs on a low moan as he entered her, filling her until she thought she couldn't take anymore.

She closed her eyes, savoring the hard, thick length of him as he eased the aching need inside of her. When he was fully seated, he rolled his pelvis against her, and she sucked air into her lungs as pleasure shot through her body. Aiden pulled back, sliding out of her only to grip her hips, holding her down as he thrust up into her.

"Ohhhhhhhhhhh!" she groaned as the tip of him brushed the very back of her, sending a shiver of delicious sensation through her. Below her, Aiden made his own growl of pleasure, bringing her closer to the edge of nirvana.

"Shae," he sighed, biting and sucking at her neck. His thrusts grew longer and harder and Shae cried out as every muscle in her body tensed at once.

Wave after wave after wave of glowing, golden bliss washed over her. She gripped Aiden's huge shoulders as she rode the tidal wave until it brought her to the peak, and she screamed. Her body spasmed of its own will, moving against his body, taking what she needed, until she couldn't take any more.

From somewhere Aiden's voice came to her, groaning her name, sending another shock of pleasure through her. Then she felt him, so big, so deep already, thrust into her until she thought she might split in two. But her pleasure was only heightened as he came with a throbbing burst that sent her own core pulsing anew.

Shae collapsed against Aiden, her breath fast and shallow, her arms and legs too weak to support her. She could hear his heart beating in his chest as she laid her head against him. It was so loud. She slid a hand up his chest, his neck, feeling the outline of his cheek, until her fingers landed on his lips. She felt them curve into a smile, and her own lips turned up in response.

They lay there until their breathing slowed; Shae lulled by Aiden's steady heartbeat. She thought about never moving. Just remaining there until sleep took them. But Aiden stirred.

"Shae?" he said quietly.

"Mmmm..." she mumbled.

Aiden chuckled, his chest bouncing her slightly. "Condom," he said, sliding his arms off her to grip her and lift her up. She felt like a ragdoll in his grasp.

"Oh, right," she said, smiling lazily down at him. He beamed back up at her.

"You look happy," he said.

"I am," she said, rolling off him and flopping onto her back. She sighed a contented sigh. She felt Aiden leave the bed as her eyes fluttered shut. She wasn't really sleepy, just completely relaxed, and she basked in the feeling.

"Now there is a beautiful sight," Aiden said, coming back into the room. Shae opened her eyes and watched him watching her. She stretched, giving him the best possible view of her body. She knew her body drove men to distraction, and she was delighted now as he swept over her with a carnal gaze.

Aiden laid beside her, his eyes still hungrily taking her in as his hands joined them to run over her skin. His palms were rough as she had imagined them to be, and the calluses sent little shivers through her.

"Dinner is probably cold by now," Aiden whispered against her neck as he nuzzled her, running his nose down to her shoulder and kissing her softly there. She ran her hands through his hair and down his broad back.

"Oh, I'm starving," she moaned, and her stomach rumbled. She giggled. "What did you get?"

"You'll see," he said teasingly. "Why don't you get dressed, and I'll heat it up, and meet you on the roof?"

"I think I'll go next door and get something more comfortable to wear," she said, not wanting to strap herself back into the satin number.

Aiden tensed beside her. "No, here," he said, jumping up. He disappeared into the walk-in closet and came out a few seconds later wearing shorts and a t-shirt. Shae stuck her lip out, pouting at the covering of that magnificent chest. Then he handed her a folded square of fabric.

"Two women walk into a bar and talk about the Bechdel test," Shae read as she unfolded the t-shirt. Then she burst out laughing. "You have the most absurd sense of humor."

Aiden smiled. "You think so?"

"Yes, I do. What are the women's names?" she asked.

Aiden looked at her. "What?" he asked.

"Their names. The fictitious women in the fictitious bar. Your shirt doesn't pass the Bechdel Test unless they have names."

"Oh!" Aiden said, letting out a breath and running a hand through his hair. "Sylvia and Janice," he said, laughing again.

"Sylvia and *Janice*?" Shae laughed. "Well, I suppose I can wear this, then." Shae slipped the shirt over her head. It was large on her, but shorter than her dress. Her long legs were still mostly uncovered. She liked it, though, as Aiden's eyes strayed down them again.

"Are you comfortable?" Aiden asked.

"Very," Shae said, standing and striding over to him. She wrapped her arms around his neck and kissed him languidly. He responded, one hand sliding down to grip her ass firmly. Her stomach grumbled again.

"I'll go heat dinner. You can head up, check it out if you want," Aiden said, pulling away. Shae didn't miss how he adjusted himself as he turned. Damn, he was already hard again. For her.

She left her panties on the floor as she slowly walked out of the room, watching Aiden jog down the stairs with the bag. She swung onto the first step of the spiral staircase, hanging on the center pole. Slowly she ascended the steps. When her head popped out at the top her mouth dropped open. This man had more surprises up his sleeve than Houdini.

The sun was setting over the hills in front of her, casting deep red shadows across the green and golden countryside. There was a grill up here, a table with six chairs, and a comfy-looking double lounge chair. She walked to the railing and peered over the edge.

Yep. Quite a decent view of her yard. Other than that, she couldn't see any of the neighbors, or the street. You could only see her yard if you were next to this edge, but she didn't enjoy the thought of strangers buying this house and being able to spy on her whenever they pleased. She didn't mind Aiden watching her nude moon rituals, but she wouldn't want some creeper up here.

She settled herself on the large lounger, stretching out in the warm summer twilight. A breeze had picked up, and the night would be cool as they always were in this little county just north of San Francisco. Shae reached her arms over her head and closed her eyes, smiling contentedly.

Chapter 7

A iden's heart sped up as he came up the steps and spied her there, stretched out on the lounger, a Cheshire cat grin on her face. Her long, bare legs beckoned to him, begging him to run his hands up their smooth expanse. As his eyes moved up her body they froze on her hard little nipples, poking through the thin t-shirt.

He tried to move quietly, wanting more time to admire the stunning figure before him. But as he set the food on the table, she opened her eyes, turning them to him. He could get lost in those eyes. They were beautiful, every shade at once swirling in her irises. Hazel seemed too ordinary a name for the color. They sparkled as her smile widened, and he dared to hope he'd had a hand in bringing that twinkle to her eye.

"I'm starving!" she said, bringing her long legs under her to stand. She looked better in his shirt than he ever had.

"Please," Aiden said, pulling a chair out for her at the table. She fell into it, diving into the food he set before her. He smiled. "Good?" he asked, taking his own seat.

Shae looked up sheepishly. "Sorry!" she said, setting her fork down and wiping her mouth with her napkin. "I usually have better table manners. It's just that I've worked up quite an appetite." She looked at him then with desire in her eyes and he felt her hand slide up his thigh under the table.

Aiden nearly jumped out of his seat. He'd been hard since she'd kissed him in the bedroom and now another rush of blood headed south. He couldn't remember anyone affecting him as strongly as Shae did. From the first time he saw her, he'd been drawn to her by some invisible force. Now he could barely sit still and eat his meal as she slipped her fingers under his shorts and caressed his thigh.

"How did you know Alfredo was my favorite?" Shae asked, her voice low and sultry.

"I took a guess. Also, there are only two vegetarian options on the menu at Antonio's. The Alfredo, and the primavera," Aiden said, pointing to his own plate.

"Ooohhh! I love primavera, too!" Shae said, her fork sneaking over to his plate. "Do you mind?" she asked, already spearing a zucchini.

"I don't mind at all," Aiden said, relishing her enthusiasm for the food. "But maybe you'll allow me?" Taking his own fork he lifted a bit of penne and tomato to her lips, watching them close around the utensil. Damn. He stiffened more.

"Like a bite of mine?" Shae asked, holding her fork out to him. He took the food, thinking there was something else of hers he'd like a bite of more.

He'd barely been able to explore her body and it was driving him mad now. He would have liked to go slow with her, tease her, taste every inch of her. But she needed it fast, he could see that, and he was powerless to refuse her. His own desire overtook him, and logic and reason left the building. All he'd felt was pure, carnal instinct, and it was glorious.

"The view is beautiful up here," Shae said, looking toward the hills. Aiden rested his chin on his hand, his elbow on the table and gazed at her.

"It sure is," he said.

Shae turned, caught him staring, and laughed heartily. "I know you DID NOT just use that line on me!"

"I did, and I won't apologize. Dessert?" he asked, looking down at her empty plate. She'd polished it off before he could blink.

Shae hesitated before answering, "Don't you have plans or something? I don't want to keep you from whatever Fourth of July plans you have. It's getting dark."

"This is the only plan I have. I was hoping you might want to spend the evening with me. Break in the new deck watching the fireworks?"

Something flashed across Shae's face, some emotion he couldn't read, but then she smiled. It didn't seem quite natural. "Sure, I suppose," she said.

"You mentioned you weren't doing anything," Aiden said, "but if you have plans..."

"No, no. No plans. What's for dessert?"

"Triple chocolate cake. I hope you're a fan." Aiden revealed the cake with a flourish, watching Shae's face for a reaction. She frowned for a moment, then shook her head. It was the tiniest movement, and he would have missed it had he not been staring at her.

She rubbed her hands together. "Yum!"

"Are you just saying that?" he asked, unsettled by her reaction.

"Oh no, it's my favorite! I just have this silly thing with men and chocolate cake," she mumbled, her cheeks pinking. Was she blushing?

"What silly thing?" Aiden asked, his curiosity peaked.

"I can't tell you," she giggled nervously. "It's too ridiculous. I don't know why I said that."

"Well, now you have to tell me," Aiden said jokingly, though he was sitting on the edge of his seat. "If it has to do with eating it off each other, I'm in."

Shae laughed. "No. I just think of men as chocolate cake. Different layers, and all that."

"And let me guess," he said, only half-joking, "the richer the better?"

"Oh my god, Aiden! No!" Shae objected, and he breathed an internal sigh of relief. At least she wasn't that shallow. "That never even occurred to me!"

"Tell me more, then," he said, leaning in.

"Well," Shae said, stabbing her fork into the cake. "He has to have substance, the cake part of the cake. Not too fluffy, but not too dense, either. The cake part is the bare minimum a man has to have for me to be interested."

"Okay," Aiden said. So far, so good. He had substance, he hoped.

"Then there's the frosting. He should be sweet, and kind, and make me better by being there." Shae brought a large bite of the cake to her mouth and moaned as her lips closed around it. "This cake right here would be my dream man!"

"The cake and the frosting aren't enough?" Aiden asked. "What else is there?"

"The chocolate mousse filling. Oh, god, this is good," she moaned, taking another bite.

"And what does a man have to have to be the chocolate mousse?" he asked, his mouth watering, but not for the cake.

Shae looked up at him and a wicked smile spread across her face. "Well, it doesn't hurt if he looks good, too. Like you."

Aiden's heart swelled in his chest. She thought he looked good.

"And if he's good in bed, that's a bonus, too. Though I don't mind teaching. But to be the dream, he'd already know what he's doing. And he'd have to want it as much as me, of course." Shae turned her eyes back to the cake, scooping up another piece. "I told you it was silly."

Shae held the fork out to him, and he took the sticky chocolate bite. His mouth was dry as he hung on her words, and he swallowed the cake with a gulp of water before he even tasted it, waving away the next bit she tried to feed him. He watched her devour the rest, unable to turn away from the beautiful site.

"Would you like a drink?" he blurted. "Wine, I mean. Or beer?"

"Ok, sure," Shae said, looking at him like he was a little off his rocker. That was how he felt. Off-kilter.

"I'll be back in a jiffy, then," he said, jumping from his seat and loping to the stairs. "Which one?" he called from the top step. "Beer or wine?"

"Surprise me," Shae laughed.

Aiden ran down the steps to the kitchen. He grabbed a cold bottle of pinot grigio from the wine fridge and two glasses and padded back upstairs. He stopped on the landing, turning to open the hall linen closet. He pulled out his fluffy winter comforter, hefting it under one arm as he held the bottle and glasses in the other hand. He squeezed himself up the spiral staircase somehow, wishing there'd been room for regular stairs. Getting large items up spiral stairs was a pain in the ass.

As he reached the top, he caught Shae just as she finished washing the dishes in the little sink he'd installed up there. She'd cleared and tidied everything and lit the candles on the table. Her pale skin glowed in the light of the candles and the string lights he had up around the top of the pergola.

"You didn't have to clean up," he said. "I would have taken care of that."

"I know you would have," Shae smiled, walking over to take the bottle and glasses from him. "You do an amazing job of cleaning up after dinner, as I know. But I would rather enjoy this evening with you, than watch you wash dishes. Although, I'm sure it's a very nice site. I'm sorry I missed it last night."

Aiden dropped the blanket on the lounger as a zing shot through his chest. "I'd be happy to come over and wash dishes for you anytime," he said, reaching out to snake an arm around her waist and haul her up against his chest.

Shae murmured in surprise and her eyes shot to his mouth. He could almost taste her desire. He knew she wanted him to kiss her, and god he wanted to taste her again. Her body was so soft against him as he tenderly took her lips. Unable to stop, he slid his hand down to palm the soft flesh of her backside, forcing her closer against him where she would surely feel everything she was doing to him.

She tasted divine, the faint hint of chocolate lingering to mix with her own sweet flavor. Shae mewled as he held her, and he slid his hand up her side, skimming her breast through the soft shirt. It was his turn now, and he wanted to take this nice and slow.

Releasing her, he reached for the bottle of wine. Shae made a little whimper of disappointment, and he hid his smile as he walked over to grab a corkscrew. "Don't worry, sweetheart, I'll have the wine open soon enough," he teased her.

Shae looked at him and rolled her eyes. "I don't need wine to get me in the mood, *cupcake*," she said snarkily.

"Humor me," he said, filling a glass and handing it to her. He walked over and unplugged the lights, then blew out the candles. They were bathed in darkness. Overhead the stars twinkled brightly in the clear sky.

Aiden picked up his own glass and raised it to her. "To you, beautiful," he said.

Shae giggled and clinked his glass. "Right back at ya, handsome."

Aiden set his glass on the table and proceeded to spread the comforter on top of the lounger. He motioned for Shae to sit. She sauntered over, crawling onto the makeshift bed on her hands and knees, the t-shirt barely covering her. Aiden groaned.

Picking up his glass he climbed in next to her and pulled the blanket around them both. Now she was trapped against him, and he pulled the blanket tighter until she was forced to press the length of her body to his.

"Thought you might be getting cold," he whispered, watching the starlight twinkle in her eyes.

"Certainly not a problem now," she breathed, her breath washing over him, spinning his head.

"I was going to invite you over tonight, you know. Before you so conveniently turned up," Aiden whispered. "That's why I don't have any plans tonight. I wanted to show this to you." He motioned to the sky.

Shae knitted her brows together for a moment, then looked to the sky. "Why, Aiden?" she asked quietly.

His confidence faltered. Didn't she want this? Didn't she want to be here with him? "I thought you might like it, that's all," he said, sighing.

Shae turned to him, running her hand over his cheek. "I do like it," she said, looking into his eyes. "I like it very much." Then she smiled a shy smile and Aiden's heart pulled in his chest. "You must have had quite a good view of me a few weeks ago, though."

Now Aiden laughed. "I did. But I promise I didn't look."

"Why not?" Shae asked, sliding a long leg over him, and pressing her breasts against him. "Didn't you like what you saw?"

"Damn, Shae, it was the most beautiful sight I've ever seen," he groaned. "But I didn't have your permission."

"I give you my permission, Aiden," Shae said, and she sat up, stripping the shirt off and tossing it aside.

Her beautiful, perfect body rose up before him, her skin milky white like a marble statue in the starlight. Her dark hair fell around her shoulders and over her firm, heavy breasts in thick waves. Aiden sucked in a breath at the sight.

"Do you need written permission, or is oral enough?" Shae asked, looking down with dark desire in her eyes.

Aiden sat up and ripped his own shirt off, then his shorts, probably breaking the world record for fastest removal of clothing. He reached his arms around Shae, sliding his palms over every inch of skin as he pulled her down and laid her under him. He took her in; hair spread across the white blanket, lips dark and plump and begging to be tasted.

"Oral is perfect," he whispered, lowering his head until his lips brushed hers. "I prefer oral." Then he kissed her. Softly, slowly, the way their first kiss should have been if not for the mad desire they elicited from one another. Shae groaned and opened to him, her tongue slipping out and wrapping around his.

Fireworks exploded around them. They both jumped, Aiden gripping her tightly as if he needed to shield her with his body. Then they started to laugh.

"That was some kiss," Aiden said, chuckling.

Shae laughed nervously, gripping his arms and pulling him to her. "Please, Aiden, don't stop. I'm terrified of fireworks. Make me forget."

Aiden looked down into her eyes and she did indeed look frightened. "Should we go inside?" he asked, worry filling him.

"No, it doesn't matter. Just, give me something good to focus on, please," she almost begged.

"Shae," he soothed, "it's alright. I'm here."

He held her in his arms and her lips found his. The need in her kiss pulled at him, and he kissed her back with a fiery passion that burst forth from somewhere deep inside. He kissed her until her lips began to swell, nipping and sucking and still never getting enough.

"Aiden," she panted, and he moved down her body, laying kisses against her soft neck, inhaling her sweet aroma.

Her hands moved over him, so soft as they glided over his back and down his arms. With his own hand he grasped a breast, feeling the weight of it as he brought the pebbled bud to his mouth. Shae cried out her pleasure as his tongue swirled over her. It was so perfect, so tender, her flesh hardening even more under his touch.

He lavished attention on her breasts, feeling her growing arousal as she wriggled under him. She made the sounds he loved to hear, and his dick ached for her. He knew now that being inside of her was the only place he ever wanted to be, and it was sweet torture waiting. But as he moved to lay kisses down her soft belly, he smelled her arousal, and he needed to taste her.

Aiden pulled the blanket over his head, covering Shae as he moved lower so she wouldn't be cold, but she tore it off and looked down at him with fire in her eyes. Her hands gripped his hair and he bit into her inner thigh. She whimpered, throwing her head back and arching up, her breasts thrust skyward. Aiden almost couldn't wait another moment.

Her pussy already glistened as he got closer. He admired it for a moment as he ran a finger down her center, splitting her open. That's where he wanted to be. That was home. Her clit was swollen as he spread her lips apart, and he ran his tongue softly over the little nub, tasting her for the first time.

Shae moaned, a deep sound coming from her belly. He loved it; loved that he could make her feel this. He flicked his tongue over her again, this time circling around and around. Moving his fingertips to her entrance he pressed against her, two fingers slipping in just enough to feel her pulse and spasm as his tongue circled.

Another cry from her and he knew she was close. Gently he pushed his fingers in deeper, pressing more insistently against her clit with his tongue. Oh god, how his dick ached to be inside those silken walls as they clenched around his fingers. Fireworks exploded- Bang! Bang! Bang!- but Shae didn't tense. The rocking of her hips didn't falter. She was lost in the sensation, and he wanted to take her all the way.

Curling his fingers inside her, he pressed up and stroked the round bundle of nerves as he slid in and out of her. He flicked up and down against her clit, faster now. Shae cried out, her fingers digging into his scalp. She gripped his head, bucking against him, until her whole body tensed, the walls of her pussy so tight he could barely move his hand.

Warm cream covered his fingers and he stroked her as she thrashed and cried out, never letting go of his hair. He must have heard her cum at least a dozen times. But being this close to it was an entirely new, spectacular experience. He slid his fingers out of her, replacing them with his tongue, scooping into her to feel her pulsing against his mouth.

She was the most responsive lover he'd ever had. Her body guided him, told him what she wanted. Every sound she made drove him wild, brought him closer to his own peak. He moved his mouth to kiss her hip, then her lower belly. He loved the soft rise there, so feminine, so sensuous.

He moved back up her body, sliding off her now to reach down for the condoms in his shorts pocket.

"Come back here," Shae moaned, trying to pull him back on top of her.

"I don't dare, babe," he laughed. "There's no moon tonight, and you already told me what that means. You've got me so turned on I'll probably cum the second my cock gets close to your sweet..." He inserted one finger inside her, and she groaned. "Creamy..." Another finger, stroking along with the first. "Center."

"Uuuhhhh!" Shae cried out, riding his hand. He quickly pulled out of her, and she turned a pouty lip to him.

"Condom," he said, finding the packet in his shorts and holding it up triumphantly.

Shae took the packet from him with one hand and grabbed hold of his erection with the other. "Let's just see how close you are," she said, smiling lasciviously at him.

Before he could say a word, she slid down his body and he felt the tip of her tongue swirl around the swollen head of his cock. Now it was his turn to groan, which he did, as a sensation so intense he thought he might pass out hit him. Holding him, she stroked up and down as her tongue danced lightly across the sensitive underside of his glans. She ran up and down the fat vein and he felt everything tighten as his body readied to spurt into her clever mouth.

But fuck if that was happening. He grabbed her wrist and gently pulled her up. "Put the condom on," he ordered.

Shae looked defiant for a moment but grinned at him as she ripped the packet open and rolled the condom on. God damn even her fingers felt incredible. He grabbed both her wrists as soon as she had it on him and threw her back against the cushions, shoving a knee between her legs and spreading her open for him.

Dipping his head down, he took her mouth, harder this time, deeper. He released her wrists to run his hands down her arms, her sides, around her, holding her tight as he found her wet heat and drove into her in one long thrust.

"Ohhhhh!" Shae screamed, her pussy already squeezing around him. It was going to take everything he had to last more than a few thrusts.

"Yes, Shae," he groaned in her ear. "Tell me you want it. Tell me you need me."

Shae cried out again as he impaled her, driving deeper into her. "I want you Aiden! Oh, god, I want you!"

Aiden squeezed his eyes shut as sensation rocked his body. He buried his face against her neck, his chest tight, his breathing shallow and rapid. He could feel her ecstasy building beneath him. He knew they would reach their climax together. He knew it would be better than anything he'd ever known before.

Shae's walls closed around him, and she gripped his back, her nails digging into him. He slowed, drawing out the last seconds as they climbed to the cliff together. Suddenly Shae howled, the sound striking him and echoing through his body. She spasmed, jerking his cock inside her, and he was gone. He came in her with a howl of his own, spearing in deep, filling her body with his seed.

The world seemed to light up around them, the sky bright and loud as they clung to each other, the pleasure so intense he wanted to cry. Moving into her one more time, he stopped, his body beyond spent. He slowly opened his eyes, realizing it was dark and quiet again, the faint smell of smoke hanging in the air. The fireworks were over.

Under him Shae sighed long and low, her body still pulsing gently around him. She opened her eyes and gazed at him with hazy satisfaction. He grinned back, loving the sated look on her face. He stroked her cheek, brushing a stray lock of hair away, before laying a soft kiss on her lips.

Rolling off her, he stood and tossed the condom in the trash bag, then tied it shut. He turned back to Shae and offered her his hand. She glanced admiringly at his still erect shaft before standing wrapped in the comforter and letting him lead her down the stairs. He was careful to keep the blanket from tripping her up. He led her to the bedroom, and they collapsed into the bed.

Aiden reached for her, dragging her into his arms and kissing her temple as she scooched her ass against him. "Shae?" he whispered.

"Yes?" she said sleepily.

"What do you get when you cross a mosquito with a rock climber?"

She turned her head to give him a wry look over her shoulder. Then she sighed and laughed a small, quiet laugh. "Nothing, silly. You can't cross a vector and a scalar."

She sighed and her breathing became slow and deep as Aiden lay there grinning behind her. He never thought he'd fall in love. And never like this. Not so fast and hard he could hardly keep his head on straight. But he had, and no matter how much he thought he'd prepared himself for it, or how much he'd read on the subject, there were just some things you couldn't learn in school.

Chapter 8

Shae felt consciousness seep back in slowly. She was warm and floating, her body fuzzy and relaxed. She held onto the edges of sleep as long as she could, not wanting this feeling to go away. She stretched languorously, taking a deep breath through her nose.

The scent caused her eyes to fly open. Where was she? The smell of sawdust mingled with freshly brewed coffee and something distinctly male. Beside her the source slumbered peacefully, lying on his stomach, his large arm slung across her belly.

Oh, god! She wasn't supposed to sleep over, for Christ's sake! How much was this going to cost her? Did he charge by the hour, or by the act? She didn't even know how she was supposed to pay him. Leave a stack of hundreds on the nightstand? She really should have gotten more information from Deja. Fucking Deja! She always seemed to get into trouble when she listened to her. Half a dozen incidents from college flew through her mind and Shae cringed.

Turning her head, she looked over at Aiden. He seemed to be sleeping deeply. Maybe she could extricate herself and sneak out without disturbing him. But her eyes refused to leave his face. He certainly was beautiful. A lock of golden hair fell across his forehead, and he looked so content.

It really was too bad it could never work between them. She needed more. She needed real substance. A real doctor, not a fantasy. Reluctantly she lifted his heavy arm up and moved it to the side. Damn, he had a lot of muscle. She thought about having those hard arms wrapped around her again and a thrill ran through her. That wasn't supposed to be the deal.

She was supposed to get him out of her system. Love then leave. That's what Deja had said. Instead, it felt like her system had been inundated with him. She rolled onto her side and studied his face again. Those lips called to her like a shiny lure, and she was the fish. One bite and she'd been hooked.

Her eyes travelled down his broad back. The blankets were up over his hips, and her fingers itched to reach over and pull them down. She hadn't gotten a good look at his backside last night, but she'd bet it was magnificent based on everything she'd felt. She sighed, feeling sexual energy surge through her. The opposite of the effect she was hoping for this morning.

Aiden shifted, rolling from his stomach to his side, his arms reaching out. Finding her, he pulled her against him, and she let him. He was still asleep, his eyes closed and his breathing even, but she could tell he was waking. Throwing her better judgement out the window she leaned in and placed her lips against his.

Oh! They were soft! And full and perfect! Shae felt something inside as Aiden slowly responded, his arms tightening, pulling her tighter, his lips moving fervently. It wasn't sexual desire, though that was almost strong enough to drown out the other emotion. It was a warmth that spread through her chest as he held her. She'd felt it last night.

Memories of last night sent a shiver through her. Aiden had held her to him, just like he held her now, his large, strong arms feeling so protective and comforting. She hadn't been scared of the fireworks. Not once those arms had come around her. It was the first time in years she hadn't cried on the Fourth of July.

And even now, as memories of River came to her, she didn't feel quite as melancholy. She hardly had time to acknowledge her feelings, much less sort them, though, as Aiden's lips pressed against hers more insistently. A soft whimper issued from her before she could stop it.

"Oh, Shae," he mumbled against her lips, his hands skimming over her even as he held her fast. One large, roughened palm skated over her backside, and she shivered in pleasure. His hands felt even better than she'd imagined.

There was no resisting when he rolled her onto her back with his large body. His hand gripped her thigh, forcing her legs to part as he nestled between. Shae's breath rushed in, then caught in her throat as Aiden buried his face against her neck, then buried his cock deep inside her. Every inch of her skin came alive as his slow, deep thrusts struck home.

Shae caught her breath, moaning out his name, trying to tell him something. Ecstasy enveloped her and she lost her thought. "Aiden!" she cried, twining her legs with his, bucking against him.

Aiden growled into the hollow of her neck as his mouth moved over her skin, hot and wet and probing. His tongue swirled against her, and the world spun. Her body moved with him, taking what he gave her until a torrent of fire burst from her and she cried out.

"Aaaahhhh!" she screamed as rapture blazed through her. Aiden bucked into her, and her mind cleared enough to remember. "Aiden! Condom!" she panted as lights flashed behind her closed eyes.

"Fuck!" he growled, pulling out of her, and tearing out the bedside table drawer. It crashed to the floor, but he'd managed to grab a packet before it did. Rolling it on, he pushed back inside her, and her body took him, grabbing him and milking him as if it never wanted to let go.

Aiden held her more gently now, rocking her body as she came down from the searing high of her climax. He kissed her softy, then opened his eyes, gazing down at her. His eyes blazed and his hand tightened around her waist, holding her down as he slid deeply into her and came with a shudder.

His body tensed, his brow furrowed, and a low sound came from him. Shae's gaze was locked with his and she held him firmly to her. A heat filled her chest and she pushed back the intense wave of emotion that forced tears to prick at her eyes. Slamming her lids down, she found Aiden's lips and kissed him until she couldn't breathe. She shouldn't cry! Why did she want to cry?

"God, Shae," Aiden whispered against her lips.

The awe in his voice made her smile, and she felt his lips curve up against hers. He chuckled, and the sound filled her with joy. She giggled, and soon they were both laughing wildly. Aiden pressed a soft kiss against her lips, caressing her cheek with his palm. She leaned into his touch and was lost in his eyes. The dark navy rings glowed as the morning light hit them, and Shae sighed.

"Would you like some coffee?" Aiden asked, nuzzling the tip of his nose against hers.

Shae hesitated; the happy feeling inside replaced with butterflies that danced in her stomach. "Sure," she said, wishing he would give her a few moments to gather her thoughts. Emotions swarmed her mind, and she couldn't think.

Aiden grinned at her and pecked her on the lips, jumping up and disappearing into the bathroom. Shae kicked at the blankets trapping her feet and swung her gaze wildly around the room. Where was her purse? She finally spied it sitting on the chair in the corner, her dress flung over it. Scrambling on her hands and knees, she crawled off the bed and dug her phone out, jumping back in just as Aiden strolled back through in all his naked glory. Shae couldn't tear her eyes away as he walked out the door. Yep. He looked just as good from behind.

Deja! SOS!!! I need to know more about Dr. Love right now! I'm currently in his bed, and I don't know how to proceed. Help! This is all your fault, btw

She'd better answer, Shae thought, and soon, or she'd never speak to her again. A few seconds later her phone buzzed.

Ooooohhhh! I can't believe you did it! Sending you the Venmo info. How was he???? Are you fulfilled?

There was no way she could adequately explain the situation she found herself in with a text message.

Can't explain now. He's bringing me coffee. I'll call you later

Shae jumped up and hid her phone back in her purse, pulling the blanket back up to her chin as she heard Aiden's footfalls on the stairs. He appeared a moment later, two mugs in his hands. He set the mugs on the bedside table and lifted the covers, sliding in next to her, his lips at her throat and his hands in her hair before she knew what was happening.

"Shae, you're incredible, do you know that?" he whispered in her ear as he laid kisses up her jaw.

"Ohhh," she moaned, her heart fluttering.

"How do you take your coffee? I forgot to ask." Aiden pulled back and gazed at her. His eyes were so soft and sweet she wanted to cry again.

"Just black," she squeaked, clearing her throat. Her heart was in serious danger, she realized. Every touch, every word he spoke pulled her in. Did he know what he was doing to her?

"That makes it easy for me," he said, turning to hand her a mug. "I would have gone back down to fix it for you if you wanted cream or sugar, but I'd much rather stay here where I can look at you."

Shae sipped her coffee and gave him a weak smile, not knowing what to say. He watched her, that sweet, crooked smile on his face as he drank from his own mug.

"Are you hungry? I could make you breakfast, or we could go out. It's Sunday. Do you have any plans today?" he asked.

What the actual fuck was going on? Was this still part of the seduction? Shae couldn't take it anymore. "Aiden, I don't know how all of this works, and I'm sorry if I'm being tactless, but I only wanted one night. I can't afford to hire you for a whole weekend."

Aiden's smile fell and she hoped she hadn't offended him. He was doing a very good job at all of this, after all. It had been an eternity since a man had made her feel as special and as treasured as Aiden did, but she had to stop it now before she really fell for it.

"Shae, I told you to forget about it. Just friends, remember?"

Oh, he had said that as they left the restaurant, hadn't he? She'd been so nervous, she'd forgotten. So, if he wasn't working, why was he being so sweet to her?

"I have to tell you something," Aiden said, and Shae stiffened. "I've wanted you since the first time I laid eyes on you. The night I moved in here."

"You saw me the night you moved in?" Shae asked, astonished.

Aiden smirked. "Yes, I saw you. A lot of you." He reached out to cup her breast, tenderly pressing her flesh. "These beautiful breasts, for a start."

Shae's breath caught as heat flashed through her. His touch was electric, and it had her moaning softly despite herself. "How did you see my breasts?" she asked, breathlessly.

"You were practically going at it against your front door," he snickered, dipping his head so his mouth could join his hand. He sucked on her nipple and her moans grew louder. "I've never seen such beautiful breasts. Or heard such libidinous noises. You drive me insane."

Aiden's hand moved into her hair, pulling her to his mouth. He kissed her long and slow, his other hand sliding over her curves as if he were mapping every contour. Her flesh hummed with every touch, and she fell back onto the pillows, giving in to him completely. After all, if he wanted to make love to her all day, she wasn't going to object.

"I don't seem to be able to stop now that I've got you in my bed," he whispered against her lips, eyes smiling into hers. "Just give me a shove when you've had enough."

Shae's entire being thrilled at his words. How could she ever have enough of this? It was pure bliss. Aiden moved down her body, lavishing kisses along her neck and collarbone, his cunning tongue skating over her nipples until the throbbing started inside her again. Then he moved lower, teeth grazing her hips, her stomach as he caressed her. Oh, those hands!

"I'm enamored with this part of you," he said, softly kissing below her bellybutton. He ran light fingers over her flesh, and she quivered. "So soft."

A surge of pleasure washed over her. His words were more sensual than any dirty talk. Knowing he appreciated her body turned her on immeasurably. She sighed and ran her hand through his thick hair, enjoying the slide of it through her fingers. His warm mouth closed on her, and he sucked, moving lower.

Shae didn't think she'd ever cum so much in less than twenty-four hours before. Her sexual fantasies were coming true, and she could hardly believe it as Aiden took her again. The man was a machine. He locked eyes with her as she straddled his lap, riding him slowly. He was sitting up against the headboard this time, one strong arm wrapped around her as his other hand fondled her breast. He rolled the nipple between his thumb and fingers, and she came with a long, low moan. Aiden joined her, his arm tensing around her, forehead pressed to hers.

Shae was lost for a moment in his eyes. So deep, so dark. There was something in the depths of his eyes that drew her in, made her want to stay and gaze at him forever. Something that made her want to know more.

"You have the most beautiful eyes," Aiden said, causing Shae to nervously giggle at how close his thoughts mirrored her own. "I love watching you cum."

She shivered and her body spasmed in response. "Well, I love cumming, so we're a good match," she laughed.

"If you keep talking about it you're going to get me started again."

"You're the one who started it!" Shae laughed. Aiden's smile was wide and bright, and he kissed her softly.

"It must be almost noon by now," he said, taking her lips again.

"Past, I think," Shae mumbled, not caring one iota.

"Let's go for a walk," Aiden said, surprising her.

"A walk? Why on earth would we do that? Aren't you enjoying yourself in here?" she teased, giving his cock a squeeze.

"I've never enjoyed myself more in my life," Aiden said earnestly. "But I'm worried you'll lose your strength soon if I don't feed you."

Shae's stomach growled as soon as he mentioned food. "Oh, now you've done it," she said, sliding off his lap. "Now you've awakened my other desire, and she won't be quieted down easily."

"I would like to fulfill all your desires," Aiden said, pecking her on the cheek and standing from the bed. "So, have lunch with me. I'm happy to share the shower with you." He gave her a wicked smile and she wondered just how many times he could pleasure her in one day.

"I think I should go home and get some clothes. Or I *could* walk around the neighborhood in your t-shirt and my stilettos, I suppose," she teased.

Aiden growled and leered at her in the most adorable way. "I'll pick you up in half an hour, then," he said. "Wear something comfortable that won't make my dick hard the second I see you. I suppose it's too hot for a parka and overalls?" He laughed and headed to the bathroom. "Never mind, you'd probably be sexy in that, too," he threw over his shoulder.

Shae heard the shower turn on and walked over to grab her dress. She threw it on, grabbing up her bra and panties along with her purse and shoes. At least her walk of shame was only twenty yards long.

Should be fast enough to avoid nosy Mr. Greene down the street. That guy was always up in everyone's business.

As she stepped out the front door, she was so busy looking for anyone that might impede her escape that she nearly tripped over the newspaper. She bent to pick up the huge bundle. The NY Times? She glanced over and saw her copy sitting on her porch. No one she knew still got a paper, and if they did it was a local paper. Hmm.

She turned and set the paper on some big construction machine. She wasn't sure what the thing did, but Aiden should see the paper there. She slipped out and made her way across the lawn and into her house without incident. She headed straight for the shower. Twice last night and three times today, and she was a sweaty mess. Not to mention sleeping in her makeup.

The shower revived her skin and she opted to go without any makeup, only towel-drying her long hair. It took forever to blow dry, and it was so warm outside that it would be dry in a few minutes anyway. She idly wondered where Aiden was going to take her, and immediately the butterflies were back in her stomach.

Just the thought of him had her going mad. She'd never felt this way before, this nervous excitement. A new affair was always exciting, but the little bolts of electricity that zinged through her arms and made her stomach clench were entirely new. No wonder Dr. Love had such an excellent reputation. If only she could bottle and sell this feeling, she'd be a millionaire.

A little pang of guilt niggled at her. Aiden was nice, and sweet, and a fuck of a lover, but what if he wanted to be more than friends? Shae couldn't imagine they had much in common, and he wasn't her type, not for a long-term thing, anyway. Maybe she shouldn't do this. Maybe she should just stop now. She should be able to go a while on all the orgasms he'd just given her, shouldn't she?

But just the thought had her running a hand over her breast as she looked in the mirror. Damn, the look of hungry desire on her face told her she wasn't anywhere near done with this. A knock on the front door made her jump. She tried to wipe the sex-kitten expression off her face as she ran down the stairs. She was so eager she could hardly believe herself.

She swung the door open, and the zings shot through her again, only this time they were full on bolts of lightning. Aiden stood there smiling at her and she lost her mind. She jumped him, wrapping her arms around his neck and her legs around his waist. She planted her lips on his, drinking him in as if it had been months since she'd last kissed him, not minutes.

Aiden responded, his hands holding and caressing her, one large palm firmly gripping her backside. "Miss me?" he mumbled against her lips, giving her a nibble.

"Yes," she said before she could stop herself. "I mean, I'm hungry," she covered, lowering her legs back to the earth. But Aiden held her against him, even as she tried to pull back, and the lightning struck again.

"Then let us be on our way, by all means," he said, taking her hand in his. Shae closed the door behind her as he led her down the driveway. "You look gorgeous, by the way," he said, glancing up and down her body out of the corner of his eye as they walked.

"I tried not to," she laughed. She'd decided on a pair of vintage slacks and a blouse that didn't even show any cleavage. She thought it was plain enough.

"I can't figure you out," Aiden sighed. "Your parents I get. And the whole moon ritual thing with you makes sense after meeting them. As well as that dress you were wearing that night, the flowy thing with all the patterns. But every other time I've seen you, you've been dressed like Bettie fucking Paige and it drives me crazy."

Shae was blown away. "You know who Bettie Page was?"

"Of course I do," Aiden laughed. "She was only the sexiest pin-up girl in history, and you remind me of her. Except you're even sexier," he said in a low voice.

Shae's hand tingled as Aiden gave it a squeeze. Deep flashes of heat coursed through her belly. "She's always been an idol of mine," she admitted quietly. "Well, her early work anyway."

"Really..." Aiden said bawdily.

"Oh no," Shae laughed. "I'm not into all the bondage stuff, so don't get any ideas."

"Me either," he said, grinning. Shae gave him an 'oh sure' look and he laughed. "I swear! I was kind of in love with her when I was younger, though."

"Hmm," Shae said, considering this. "Well, maybe a blindfold once in a while."

Aiden raised an eyebrow at her, one corner of his mouth quirking up. "Hmm," he said, looking forward again.

"Where exactly are we going and will it take much longer because I really might faint," Shae said dramatically.

Aiden stopped abruptly and before Shae knew what was happening her feet were scooped out from under her. She clung around his neck, squealing in surprise. Her heart pounded and her breath came in short little gasps, partly from being startled and partly because Aiden held her pressed against his massive chest and he smelled like clean soap and sexy man.

"We can't have you losing consciousness," Aiden said, pecking her on the lips. "We're almost there."

"Put me down. You're ridiculous," Shae said, but she loved every second he held her. He barely seemed to be exerting himself. He made her feel feminine and petit, which was unusual for her since she was five foot nine.

"I'm ridiculous?" Aiden asked, his face stricken. Shae's smile dropped and she began to say she didn't mean it like that when

Aiden's face cracked into a grin, and he laughed. Shae smacked his shoulder.

"You are ridiculous. I stand by my statement," she said, her fingers playing on his chest. He was so hard under the thin t-shirt. She walked her fingers up, over his collarbone, then up his neck, until she spread her palm against his cheek. He looked down at her as he walked and she sighed, nestling her head against his neck.

Aiden stopped and Shae smelled something wonderful. He set her on her feet and motioned toward a diner. "Here we are," he said.

"I've always wondered about this place, but I've never tried it," Shae said.

"Oh, it's good." Aiden pulled the door open for her and her eyes widened.

From the outside the place looked like your ordinary corner diner. Boring, greasy, not worth a second look, Shae thought. But inside it was adorable. It was like they'd stepped eighty years back in time. There was a real soda fountain, buckets of homemade ice cream, a checkered floor, and a bar with stools lined up in front of it.

Aiden led her to one of the booths that lined the windows opposite the bar. A stack of old-fashioned candy and gum sat on the counter next to a vintage cash register. Shae's head swung back and forth taking it all in. Then she cocked her head listening. "Old radio shows?" she asked.

"Yep," Aiden answered. "Aren't they fun? They have all the old ads in them, too, about how good cigarettes are for you and how much prettier you can be for your husband if you buy this or that."

"Well, I could do without that part of the good old days," Shae said, rolling her eyes.

"Agreed," Aiden laughed.

"Good afternoon, folks, what can I get started for you?" a waitress asked, setting two glasses of ice water in front of them. "Oh, how are you doing, Doc? I didn't notice that was you sitting there."

The waitress had her eyes locked on Aiden now and Shae felt a burning in her chest she didn't enjoy. Jealousy? Was she really getting territorial? That wasn't her usual modus operandi.

"Hey Candy," Aiden said in the open, friendly way he always had about him. Right now it made Shae narrow her eyes slightly. "Give us a minute, please. This is Shae's first time here."

Candy turned her eyes on Shae and gave her a curt smile. "Sure, can I get you some coffee?" she asked, her tone saccharine.

"Shae?" Aiden asked.

"No, thank you. Do you have tea?" Shae asked. She wasn't a big coffee drinker and she'd already had a cup at Aiden's.

"Sure, two teas, then?" she said, turning back to Aiden, her smile genuine now.

"Yes, thanks," Aiden said, passing Shae a menu as Candy left. "The eggs Florentine is excellent. They make it without meat. It's my usual. Plus a scone. Though I won't recommend that since yours are exponentially better. Don't tell Candy I said so."

"Hmm, whatever you say, *Doc*." Shae glued her eyes to the menu feeling angry. She had no right to, she knew it, but logic was not steering the boat at the moment.

As she perused the menu, she heard Aiden chuckle. She looked up and he was watching her and laughing.

"What's so amusing?" she asked sharply.

"You. You're quite a little firecracker, aren't you?" Aiden said, his eyes dancing with amusement.

Shae dropped her menu, upsetting her glass of water which she barely managed to keep from tipping and spilling everywhere. She pulled at the napkins in the silver metal holder on the table and dabbed at the mess. She felt tears prick her eyes.

"I'm sorry. I'm so clumsy," she mumbled, eyes fixed to her task.

"Shae," Aiden said, his hand coming down on top of hers and stilling the movement. "It's dry. Are you ok?"

"I'm fine, just uncoordinated." She pushed the wet napkins aside and took a sip of her water. She still couldn't look at him. Why had he called her that?

"Here's your tea. Have you decided?" Candy's voice came down from above as mugs and silver teapots were set in front of them.

"Eggs Florentine," Shae said without thinking.

Candy began to ask her about potatoes and toast and how hard she wanted the eggs, but Shae just shook her head.

"Just bring us two of my usual," Aiden broke in. "Thank you."

She heard Candy step away and she tried to clear her head. This was ridiculous. "Get your shit together," she whispered to herself. She looked up to see Aiden watching her, a crease between his brows. She tried to smile and plucked a mint tea bag out of the container Candy had placed on the table.

"She's not one of my clients," Aiden said, the worry lines deepening on his face. "I apologize for laughing. I forget that not everyone is as comfortable with what I do as I am."

"Oh, it's not that, please don't think I'm that small-minded," Shae said quickly. "I did try to hire you after all. I like to think I'm less hypocritical than that. I will admit to being a little jealous, though." She gave a little shrug and a small smile to Aiden who visibly relaxed.

"You don't need to be," Aiden said hastily. "Candy and I don't have a relationship. Never have, never will. She knows me through my mother."

Someone might want to tell her that, Shae thought. She picked up the teapot to pour hot water into her mug. "I'm just a klutz, don't worry about it."

Aiden's hand shot out and his fingers closed over hers on the handle of the teapot. "Perhaps I should do this," he said, smiling softly at her. She set the pot down and Aiden took over.

"So, you're a tea drinker as well?" Shae asked.

"Yes, blame my father. My mother will never forgive me for being converted to his side. She loves her café, but my father doesn't touch the stuff. I prefer a happy medium. I always set the coffee pot to be ready in the morning. The caffeine is especially helpful when I've got a day of hard physical labor. Coffee in the morning, tea in the afternoon."

"My parents never touch coffee," Shae said. "But they drink every manner of tea. I guess that's why I prefer it. Although I usually stick with the more mainstream stuff. You wouldn't believe some of the strange Chinese teas my mother would feed to me as a child. And of course, gallons of kombucha. I can't stand the stuff!" Shae laughed.

Aiden smiled and the tension left her body. He was so easy to be with. He didn't balk at her unorthodox upbringing, quite the opposite. He seemed interested and entertained by her family's antics. Most men she went out with wouldn't be able to handle her free spirit, but she felt she could be open with Aiden.

"That stuff is nasty," he laughed, reaching over to place his hand on top of hers. The gentle caress of his fingers sent a tiny shiver through her. "That, and apple cider vinegar." Aiden made a face and Shae had to laugh.

"I know! It smells like hot garbage!" Shae said. "My mom used to make me drink some every day."

Candy delivered their plates without glancing once in Shae's direction. She only had eyes for Aiden. But it didn't bother Shae anymore. She already felt silly for being jealous at all. Because Aiden only had eyes for her.

Shae devoured the huge platter of food, moaning a few times, earning a fiery gaze from Aiden. She could hardly react to him, though, the food was so delicious. She wished she could unbutton her slacks by the end of the meal as her belly strained to contain everything she'd just put into it.

"Oh, that was amazing," she groaned, leaning back against the booth. "I can't believe I ate so much!"

"You must have needed it," Aiden said, playing with her fingers again. "I really like this color." He ran his fingertips over her long nails.

"Thank you. It's called 'Blackest Black', and I almost didn't buy it because the name is so dumb. I mean Vantablack is the blackest black. This is more of a chocolate brown." Shae looked up at Aiden, wondering if he knew what Vantablack was. "Scientists at MIT created Vantablack using carbon nanotubes. They're carbon atoms arranged in cylindrical layers, joined by covalent bonds in hexagons, so they form a hollow tube a few hundred nanometers in diameter. They're very small. Microscopic," she explained.

Aiden just continued to caress her, which was driving her further and further to distraction now that her hunger had abated. He probably didn't understand what she was saying anyway. She should stop babbling about carbon nanotubes over lunch.

"Can I get you anything else?" Candy asked, and Shae jumped, pulling her hand away and placing it in her lap.

"No, just the check, please," Aiden said. Candy handed him a slip of paper and placed her hand on his shoulder.

"Say hi to *Maman* for me," she said, running her hand up and down Aiden's arm. Shae felt a twinge of jealousy return.

"Alright, thanks," Aiden said. Candy moved on to the next table and Aiden turned his eyes back to Shae. "Are you ready to get out of here?"

"Yes," Shae said almost too enthusiastically. She would have loved this place if not for Candy. Maybe she'd come back sometime when Candy wasn't working.

Aiden stood and took her hand, helping her up. They paid at the old-fashioned register and Aiden held her hand as he opened the door for her. They walked along in comfortable silence for a few blocks, their fingers entwined and the sun on their shoulders.

As they neared their street, the butterflies in Shae's stomach began their fluttering again. What was supposed to happen now? Should she invite him to her place? A smothering feeling crept over her, and she was relieved when Aiden's phone rang.

Chapter 9

Aiden fished his phone out of his pocket and looked at the screen. *Maman.* He sent it to voicemail and put it back in his pocket. He was enjoying himself too much to ruin it by talking to his mother right now.

"It's Mom," he said, giving Shae a smile. "I'll call her back later."

"Oh," Shae said with a nervous smile. "Maybe you should see what she wants."

"She calls every Sunday. It's not an emergency." But his phone rang again. As he looked at the screen Shae's phone rang as well.

"Now it's my mom," she said. "I really should talk to her. I'll see you later?"

Shae answered her phone, waving him away and turning to march up her driveway. Aiden was momentarily bereft as he watched her go. His phone rang again, and he picked up as he opened his own door.

"*Bonjour Maman,*" he answered.

"Why did you not answer my call?" his mother demanded in her perfect French.

"I was otherwise engaged," he returned in equally flawless French. "But I am free now. Is everything ok?" he asked, slightly irked. His mother had a way of speaking to him as if she owned him. It had been that way his entire life and it got under his skin.

"Everything is fine. I wanted to know if you were coming for dinner tonight?"

"I, uh," Aiden hesitated. He'd rather have dinner with Shae, but he didn't know what she was thinking when she left so abruptly. "I won't be able to make it tonight."

His mother made and exasperated noise. "I wish you would inform me of these things. I wanted to discuss the Annual Faculty Club Dinner on Saturday."

Now Aiden sighed. Yes, the dinner was for current and retired or former faculty, but he'd only been on the faculty for two years. He doubted anyone cared whether he was there or not, aside from his parents. He'd never hear the end of it from his mother if he didn't attend, however.

"I'll be there," he conceded.

"Good. And will you be bringing anyone special?"

What in the world? His mother had never inquired about a date before. And no one brought dates to this dinner unless they were married or ex-faculty themselves.

"I am planning to come alone," Aiden said, a question in his tone.

"Not seeing anyone special? I just want you to be happy, *honey*," his mother said, lapsing into English when she called him honey.

"I'm perfectly happy. Why are you asking me these questions?"

"I just thought you may have met someone recently," his mother said mysteriously.

Aiden shook his head, wondering what she was on about. But then he smiled, thinking he really had met someone, and he wanted to tell the world. "I may have. It's still early days, so don't get your hopes up."

His mother squealed with joy, a sound he wasn't used to hearing from the typically staid woman. "Oh! I knew it! I can't wait for you to introduce her! It's about time you settled down and thought about starting a family."

A family? "Jesus, Maman, I don't plan on knocking anyone up anytime soon."

"Language, Aiden!" his mother scolded. She hated it when he spoke roughly.

"Sorry. Listen, I'm going to go. Say hi to Dad for me and I'll see you Saturday."

His mother seemed satisfied and said her goodbyes, but something about that conversation didn't sit right with him. His mother had gone from never mentioning his love life to encouraging him to have children in the near future. Talk about zero to sixty.

He glanced around the room and spotted his newspaper sitting on the tile saw. He grabbed it and took it to the kitchen table, spreading it open. The front page depressed him, so he dug through for the comics. His phone caught his eye where it sat on the table, and he picked it up and typed.

Hey, you want to grab dinner later?

He set the phone down and read a few pages of comics. When it buzzed indicating a text he dove at it, eagerly swiping it open.

I don't think I'll need to eat for a month! I should get ready for my week. Sunday is my prep day. Maybe tomorrow?

Aiden sighed in disappointment. He really, really wanted to hold her again. Just the thought of burying his hands in her soft hair and kissing her plump, red lips... He needed to stop this. It was only going to torture him.

I'll hold you to that. What time do you get home tomorrow?

He sent it, hoping he didn't sound too eager. But damn, he was.

I should be home by 6. Mondays are always brutal, and I usually stay a little after everyone's gone home.

Only twenty-five more hours. He could wait that long, right? He spent a few moments convincing himself he wouldn't die without touching her. Then he made himself a cup of tea and started on the Sunday crossword.

AIDEN FLIPPED THE BASKET of vegetables on the grill and gave them a final brush of olive oil. They smelled delicious and he hoped Shae would be home from work sooner rather than later. His mouth was watering, and he was hungry for more than just food. He hadn't been able to stop thinking about how hungry he was since yesterday.

Damn this woman called the beast out of him. All day as he worked, he had to distract himself from thinking of her since he didn't much care for working with a massive erection getting in his way. He was onto the mindless task of painting. It was going quickly, and he'd be able to lay the rest of the floors this week, but it didn't occupy his mind the way he needed it to. Shae was still in there far too much.

He'd thought about going over last night, showing up on her doorstep and inviting himself in. He barely stopped himself. She said she needed time alone and he didn't want to crowd her. He got the feeling she was skittish and the last thing he wanted was for her to run. He couldn't understand her hesitation.

Aiden knew he was falling for her fast. Every fantasy he'd had about her over the past weeks as he watched her life in glimpses from afar had been eclipsed by the reality of being with Shae. She was brilliant, kind, beautiful, and just his type of quirky. The only problem was she kept giving him the cold shoulder. One minute he was sure she was on the same page with him, the next she was distant. And that whole lunch at the cafe had just been strange.

But maybe he was attracted to strange. He wanted to know more about her. Everything about her. What made her tick? What did she want in life? He gathered the dinner he'd prepared, placing everything in cloth sacks. As he cleaned the grill and shut it down, he heard tires crunching to a stop. He looked over the fence and saw Shae's car in the driveway. Perfect timing.

Grabbing the bags, he bounded down the front steps and across the weedy lawn, running up behind her just as she unlocked her front door. He dropped the bags and wrapped his arms around her waist from behind, nuzzling through her long hair until his lips found her neck.

Shae squeaked in surprise and her breath rushed out as he kissed her. It was a sound he loved to hear.

"Hey, little firecracker," he whispered against her skin, nipping at her earlobe. Shae went stiff in his arms. Stiff and cold as stone. She broke away from him, pushing the door open and fidgeting with the cases she was carrying.

"Hi, Aiden, come in," she said, her back turned to him. It seemed every time he came to this house the welcome was not what he was expecting.

"Don't mind if I do," he said, trying to infuse his tone with levity.

Shae continued into the kitchen, then the downstairs bedroom. He followed along, setting the bags on the table. He came through the door and saw she had the room set up as a cozy study. Shelves of books lined the walls and a TV sat in a cabinet surrounded by plush furniture. She had dark curtains on the windows, lending the room the feel of an old library.

"I love what you've done with this room," he said from the doorway. "I think I might do something similar with the room in my house. I was thinking of moving my office down there, but this is really nice."

"I need somewhere quiet to unwind sometimes. I like to read a lot," she said, setting her cases on the sofa and turning to him. Her eyes were large and sad as she searched his face, and he wondered what she could be looking for.

"Everything ok at work today?" he asked. "How are Vern and Veronica?"

Her face cleared and he breathed a sigh of relief. Whatever was bothering her it must not be her family.

"They're good, thank you for asking. Mom couldn't stop talking about you. I think she loves you. What did you two talk about the other night, anyway? She wouldn't tell me." Her smile was genuine now and Aiden felt a warmth in his chest as he watched her.

"Nothing really. She asked me a lot of questions. I don't remember ever talking so much about myself before. Guess I passed her test," he said, waggling his eyebrows at her.

Shae laughed. "I'm sure you did, though Mom doesn't test people. She loves to see into your true soul, and she lives by the old cliche of variety being the spice of life. She has an infinite capacity to enjoy people in all their variety. But I'd say whatever she saw in your aura she particularly liked."

Aiden liked hearing that. He'd enjoyed his conversation with Veronica more than he'd enjoyed talking to anyone in a long time. And Vern had been so funny in a quiet way. They'd both made him feel almost like part of their family right off.

It was different from his parents who were loving, but in a much less demonstrative way. And they sure as hell didn't love variety in people. They had one kind of people they appreciated and looked down their noses at everyone else.

"I'm glad," he said. "I liked them a lot, too. I made dinner." Shae's eyes lit up and Aiden chuckled to himself. The woman sure did love to eat.

"Oh, I'm so hungry! I didn't eat dinner last night. I was too full from our late lunch. But I've been ravenous all day. What did you make?"

"Come on, sit down and close your eyes." He led her to a chair and gently pressed on her shoulders until she sat. She closed her eyes without question, which made him smile. She was so trusting. "Open your mouth."

Shae's lips curved into a wicked grin. "What are you going to fill my mouth with?" she purred. Aiden's cock jerked and a tingle started at the base of his spine.

"No meat for you," he teased. "I think you'll like this, though." He took a fork from her utensil drawer and filled it with the grilled vegetables, dipping them in the creamy sauce he'd made. Gingerly he placed it against her tongue and watched her lips close around his offering, thinking about her wrapping those lips around him later.

"Mmm!" Shae moaned as she chewed and swallowed. "That's incredible! Can I have more?"

Aiden laughed. "You make everything sound sensual, Miss Mitchell. Open your eyes."

Shae opened her beautiful brown eyes flecked with blue and gray and he leaned down, his hands on the armrests on either side of her. Lowering his head he kissed her softly, savoring her supple lips. He fell back into the chair behind him and ran a hand through his hair.

"Damn, I like kissing you," he admitted shyly. It was a lot for him to admit. He wasn't sure she understood what that meant for him. He didn't kiss women, not like he kissed her.

"Well, you'll have to do it a lot more then, won't you," she said, fire in her eyes.

"Oh, yes," he murmured, standing to get plates and another fork. "How was work today?"

"Good. I've been working on an actuarial valuation. It's a type of appraisal of a pension fund's assets versus liabilities, using investment, economic, and demographic assumptions for the model to determine the funded status of a pension plan. The assumptions are based on a mix of statistical studies and experienced judgment. Since assumptions are often derived from long-term data, unusual short-term conditions or unanticipated trends can occasionally cause deviations from forecasts. I've been having a hell of a time trying to figure out how to compensate for that with the bear market that seems to be developing."

Aiden began serving the dinner, smiling as he listened to her. She was enthusiastic as she explained, and he really liked it when she got like this- completely wrapped up in her subject. He could listen to her for hours. She made whatever she was discussing interesting by virtue of her exuberance.

"I'm boring you," Shae said, picking up her fork.

"No, not at all," he began.

Shae cut him off. "No, I am. No one is as interested in actuarial tables as I am. I forget that sometimes. What were you working on today?"

"Today I painted. All day. Tomorrow I'll put the second coat on and then the floors can go in. After that it's just a few finishing touches and *voila!*"

"*Voila?*" Shae laughed. "You speak French now?"

"Yep," Aiden laughed. "It smells pretty strong over there right now, though. I could camp out on the terrace, unless there was some kind soul with a soft bed that would be willing to take me in for a couple nights?" He gave her his biggest puppy dog eyes and she laughed.

"Babe, if you want to spend a few nights in my bed, I am more than willing," Shae said, leaning in to throw one arm around his neck and stroke his cheek with the other. "I will need to get *some* sleep, though. Just enough to function at work."

Shae pressed her lips to his, gripping his neck then running her hands over him. He almost shook with anticipation. He'd never met a woman with such power over his mind and body. He wanted her with everything that he was. Shae broke the kiss, leaning back in her seat and continuing her meal, that same Cheshire cat grin on her face she had after the first time he'd taken her. That smile did things to him.

"I'll try to restrain myself," he gulped out, his voice more strained than he'd tried for. "Tell me more about work. I really am interested."

Shae talked and he watched her. The oven dinged, signaling that dessert was ready. Aiden jumped up and brought the hot cakes to the table, placing one in front of Shae.

"You know, you're going to spoil me," she said, her pink tongue darting out between her lips as she eyed the lava cake.

"Is that a bad thing?" he teased.

"Never!"

"I was wondering what your take on chocolate lava cake is. As relates to your theory of men and cake, that is. This is a different kind of cake, after all."

Shae shot him a lustful gaze, her lips curving up. "I'd say," she said, standing and moving her plate next to his, "that when you see this big hunk of chocolate, you know you're going to enjoy it." She straddled his lap, sinking down and pressing her breasts against him.

Aiden looked up into her eyes. She broke the cake open and scooped up a spoonful. "But when you finally get a taste of that hot, liquid heaven inside, you wonder if you'll ever be satisfied with plain old regular cake again." She placed the spoon in her mouth and pulled it out slowly, her eyes closing on an "Mmm...".

Aiden watched her until she opened her eyes and looked into his. She tasted of dark chocolate as she kissed him, her tongue playing against his. His cock pressed against her sex as it swelled and she moved her hips, rubbing against him.

"Do you want to finish your cake?" he asked, gripping her thighs as she continued to move.

"Later," she whispered against his neck as she lightly ran her tongue over his skin.

Aiden held her legs to his hips as he stood, lifting her with him. She wrapped her legs around his waist and crushed his mouth.

Blindly he made his way to the stairs as she plunged her tongue into his mouth, holding his face to hers.

He slid one hand under her bottom and reached between them to undo her pants. By the top of the stairs, he had his hand inside her panties, his fingers searching for her center. He found it and sunk two fingers into her deep. She huffed out a groan as he entered her body and he pulled out to slide over her clit.

"Damn, Shae, you get wetter than any woman I've ever known," Aiden growled as he fell on top of her on the bed. He gripped her to him and sunk his fingers into her again.

"It's all your fault," she breathed, then moaned loudly as he slicked over her clit again.

Aiden gave her a squeeze before sliding his arm out from under her, both hands moving up to her blouse now. He kissed her softly as he unbuttoned one button at a time. She was wearing another one of those satin vintage blouses that drove him crazy, and he knew he would have to force himself to go slowly.

"Aidennnnn," she moaned as he nibbled her neck, spreading her blouse open.

He reared up to see her breasts barely contained in the little lace bra. They spilled out in soft mounds that made his mouth water. He covered one with his palm, lightly squeezing the tender flesh. It fit perfectly in his hand.

"Your lingerie drives me insane," he murmured as he snapped open the front-hooking bra. The bra sprung open, and her tits jiggled free for him. He took them in his hands reverently, moving his mouth down to draw a nipple between his lips.

"Your *mouth* drives me insane," Shae moaned as he worked her nipple. The soft bud hardened, and he gave her a gentle nip. Her body pulsed beneath him.

Sliding a hand behind her back, he lifted her until she could slide her shirt and bra off. He ran a hand through her hair and looked into her eyes, loving the desire he saw there. He pushed her back down with his body, kissing her until her breath rushed out. She worked her pants off and now he could feel the heat coming from her core.

"Take your damn clothes off," Shae breathed, tugging at his shirt. He pulled it over his head and she grabbed the waist of his jeans, opening them and pulling him out.

Before he could react, Shae performed a ninja move and had him on his back. She shimmied down his body, wrapping her hand around his shaft. Looking up at him she ran her tongue from base to tip, with a wicked smile for him before she sucked the tip of his cock and swirled her tongue around it.

Aiden's eyes closed as the pleasure overtook him. Her warm, soft mouth moved over his sensitive head, her tongue lightly teasing him as she stroked him up and down. She flicked back and forth, up and down, bringing him closer with every little lick. Then she took him in, and he felt the back of her throat. She swallowed, squeezing the head of his cock until he growled with pleasure.

"I want you to cum in my mouth, Aiden," she said, breaking away from him with a soft pop. "I want to taste you."

Aiden had never had a woman say that to him before. His cock twitched as Shae took him in again, rolling the underside of her soft tongue against him. Holy fuck!

"Fine, babe, but you have to bring your sweet pussy over here, then." There was no way he was going to cum before she did.

Shae smiled up at him and sat up, sliding his pants the rest of the way off. She turned around and straddled his face before attacking him again. His eyes rolled back in his head as he buried his tongue inside her. He slid his tongue over her clit and sucked it into his mouth and her movements faltered. She dropped him for a moment to moan in ecstasy and he grinned.

Sliding two fingers inside her, he began to stroke in rhythm with her. She was dripping wet, and her pussy clenched around his fingers.

He wished his dick could be in two places at once. As he circled her clit with his tongue, he felt her getting closer. Juices ran down his chin and she spasmed. He lightly scraped her clit with his teeth, and she came.

She screamed out her release, her pussy almost crushing his fingers, pulling at them to the point that it would have taken some effort to extract them. He pressed against her clit, and she took him deep and swallowed again, stroking his balls until he couldn't hold back any longer. She sucked hard and he shot into her mouth. She sucked and stroked him, drawing out his orgasm until he relaxed back against the bed. She rolled off him, collapsing on her back next to him, her hand idly caressing his hip.

Aiden watched her chest rise and fall rapidly, her rounded breasts moving up and down, then slowing as she came down from her climax. She opened her eyes, and when she saw him watching her, she smiled. She crawled up next to him and laid her head against his chest, her arm thrown over him. He ran his hand up and down her back, resting his cheek on top of her head.

"Shae," he mumbled into her hair, "you are absolutely incredible."

He felt her laugh as her soft body pressed against his side. "I was just thinking the same thing about you." Shae stroked his chest, her fingers exploring his skin, raising goosebumps on his arms.

"I mean it, Shae," he said, trying to convey what he was feeling, but having a hard time deciphering the new feelings himself. "Not just the outstanding sex. You."

"Aw, you're such a sweetie," she said, laying her lips on his chest. She kissed him and popped up. "I really want that chocolate cake now."

Aiden didn't want to let her out of the bed. His arm tightened around her involuntarily and he forced himself to release her. She felt too damn good in his arms. He could forget everything else in the world when he was holding her. He watched her as she threw on shorts and a huge sweatshirt. Her long legs looked incredible.

"Shae, would you like to accompany me to a party on Saturday night?" he asked suddenly, surprising himself. He hadn't planned on taking anyone, but now he wanted to take her.

"What kind of a party?" she asked, looking skeptical.

"It's a thing for staff and alumni where my parents teach. My mother would like me to bring a date." He cringed as he said it. He made it sound like he was only asking her because his mother wanted him to. He felt like a fish out of water. He was used to doing the seducing, but Shae always had him on the backfoot. He wanted her so badly he couldn't think about seduction, only getting another taste, another hit of Shae.

"Oh. Come on, get dressed," she said, eyeing him lying there.

Aiden stood and pulled his clothes on. "It's black tie," he said, thinking that might entice her. Shae grabbed his hand and yanked until he followed her down the stairs. When she had her mind on food he was learning not to stand in her way.

"Oh, come to mamma!" she said, scooping up her cake. "So tasty," she moaned, devouring the chocolate. "I need to write down where you got this so I can try more of their stuff."

"I made it," Aiden said.

Shae looked at him. "God! Could you get any better?"

Aiden felt his face heat. He was fucking blushing, now? He turned away and picked up his dessert and began eating it. Anything to distract him. Shae set her empty plate on the table and sidled up behind him. She wrapped her hands around his waist and rested her head on his shoulder.

"You want some of mine, don't you," he laughed.

"I do," she admitted. "And some of your cake, too." She slid her hand over the front of his pants. He slipped a bite into her mouth.

"Your mouth isn't happy unless it's filled," he laughed. Shae smiled.

"I am so full! I really did eat too much. Your food is just too good. Let's go for a walk around the cul-de-sac." She grabbed his hand again and pulled him toward the front door.

"You walk after dinner a lot, don't you?" he asked. He already knew she did. He'd seen her plenty of times.

"Yep. I like to eat, as you know. And the only way I keep my girlish figure is to move constantly. I love to watch the sunset, too."

They slipped on their shoes, and he followed her out the door. She walked fast. Her long legs drawing his gaze. He watched her from behind for a moment before catching up to her. She took a deep breath of the cool evening air. The night was blissfully free of the acrid manure smell the whole county got from time to time when they fertilized the farm fields.

They walked in comfortable silence for a few minutes, making their way down to the far end of the cul-de-sac. Aiden had never gone down to this end before and his mouth dropped open when he saw the orange house at the end.

"What in the world happened here?" he asked.

"This is my favorite house ever, I think," Shae said enthusiastically.

"It looks like Gilligan's Island meets Lost in Space."

"That's what I always say!" Shae said in surprise. "How do you even know those old shows?"

"I don't watch a lot of television, but when I do it's usually something from the 1960s for some reason. The old stuff appeals to me more. I think this might be my favorite house ever now, too." He laughed and tickled her side. Shae yelped and jumped.

Shae grinned at him. "I love old TV. Drives my mom crazy. She thinks it's all garbage, and she might be right. Growing up we never had TV. When I was in high school, I finally bought my own little television set and I was able to get old shows with the antenna late at night."

Aiden watched her as she talked. He really could fall in love with this woman. The idea struck him, and he realized he had a few tough decisions to make.

Chapter 10

Shae looked back at Aiden shyly. The way he watched her made her nervous, but in a nice way. She hadn't felt so happy when someone looked at her since River. It was the same look, but not the same; not really. He loved her deeply. And she loved him. But there was never anything romantic between her and her brother, as much as that surprised people who saw them together.

The look in Aiden's eyes now was that same sweet, adoring, protective look River always had. Only with Aiden there was more. There was a fire so hot it burned through her blood when he looked at her. She looked away, unable to breathe. It was good and overwhelming all at once.

She couldn't help comparing them. Almost from the first Aiden had reminded her of River. Something in the kind, open smile. They would have gotten along, she thought. And then out of the pure blue ether Aiden had started calling her the name only her brother had ever used. It made her sad and happy all at once.

As they walked, she felt Aiden slip his hand around hers and the fire started in her again. His touch ignited her, and she gripped his hand. Every feeling he aroused in her was so intense she couldn't sort them, couldn't figure out what she truly felt for him. When he touched her, every thought left her head and she simply felt. It was primal and strong, but Shae had no idea where it would lead.

She couldn't see through the haze of lust that consumed her now. Her body wanted Aiden, yes. But her mind cried out that it was wrong. He was a nice guy. But could she really see herself in a relationship with an escort/construction worker? Never in her wildest dreams could she imagine that.

And now Aiden had asked her on a real date. Dinner at home or lunch in a diner was one thing. A black-tie event with his family was something else. She couldn't lead him into thinking they could be more than just friends with benefits, even if the benefits were exceptional. But he couldn't really want more from her either, could he?

He had his escort job, after all. When she thought about it her chest filled with burning jealousy. She almost choked on it. She'd never been jealous before. It wasn't the way she was. Being raised in a sexually open environment, she'd seen every kind of relationship. Free love was definitely still being practiced in the communes. Sex and love didn't have to be a package deal for her. So this strong possessive reaction to a man she didn't love surprised her. She chalked it up to the fact that the sex was the best she'd ever had, and she didn't want to share any of it.

"My parents never allowed me to watch TV either," Aiden was saying. "We had a TV, but it was reserved for arthouse films, which wasn't my deal then, and still isn't, to tell the truth," he laughed.

Shae gave him a smile, pulling herself out of her thoughts. They were coming back up to their end of the street. Aiden released her hand.

"I'll go grab some things, if you're truly alright with letting me stay," he said.

"Just come back quickly," she said, wrapping her arms around his neck and sliding her tongue into his mouth. Old Mr. Greene down the street was probably watching, but she didn't care. Let him think what he would.

"Wow," Aiden mumbled. "How could I resist?" He pecked her on the lips with a grin and ran up his drive. Shae watched his tight ass and grinned back.

Inside she cleaned up the kitchen, though there wasn't much to do. Aiden must have a mess at his place if he made all of this. As she closed the dishwasher two strong arms came around her waist and the intoxicating smell of man enveloped her. Damn he smelled good. She turned in his arms and looked up into those dark sapphire eyes.

"I should go over and help you with the dishes," she said quietly, her breath taken away a bit. "All this must have made a mess."

"Already cleaned up," he whispered back, taking her lips.

Shae's eyes fluttered shut as sensation washed over her. He kissed her slowly, tenderly, his lips brushing hers as his arms tightened around her, bringing her body against him. He tasted minty.

"You brushed your teeth," she said, keeping her eyes closed. His mouth closed over hers again, still moving slowly, teasing her. Her core trembled.

"I'm ready for bed. How about you?" he said quietly, taking her face in his hands and kissing her deeply.

"It's, ohhh," she breathed as he moved down her neck, his teeth skimming over her and sending a shiver down her spine. "It's only nine."

"I know," he whispered against her skin. "Bedtime. You have work tomorrow young lady." His hands slid down her sides and he lifted the back of her sweatshirt, granting him access to her backside. His large hands gripped her firmly and her core trembled as he kneaded her flesh.

"You are probably the best neighbor I've ever had," Shae moaned, finding his mouth again.

Aiden chuckled against her lips. "You're definitely the best neighbor I've ever had. Those scones were top notch."

Shae couldn't stop the wide smile that spread across her face. She opened her eyes and looked up. Aiden stroked her cheek with a thumb as he held her face. "*You* are funny, you know that?" she said quietly.

Aiden gave her a small smile before kissing her affectionately. He pulled back, taking both her hands and leading her out of the kitchen. The warmth in his eyes struck something deep inside her and Shae swallowed hard. What was this feeling in the bottom of her stomach? It was warm and yearning and unlike anything she'd ever felt before.

"No," Shae mumbled, shaking her head to herself. She couldn't be having real feelings for this man. Not him. Not this fast.

"What's wrong?" Aiden asked, stopping at the foot of the stairs. Shae looked up and the feeling in her stomach spread through her.

"Nothing," she said quickly, trying to stop the flush that was spreading to her cheeks. "Sorry, I was thinking of something else."

Aiden's eyebrow quirked up and his lips curved into a half smile. "Care to share? Or would you rather I just take your mind off whatever it was completely?" he asked. Shae moaned internally at how fucking adorable he was.

"The second option, please," Shae almost begged. She was definitely not going to discuss these thoughts with him.

Aiden gave her a little nod then yanked her into his embrace so quickly her breath rushed out. He hauled her up against his warm, hard chest, lifting her feet off the ground. Spinning around he headed up the stairs and she wrapped her legs around his waist, holding on.

"You sure like to carry me up these stairs," she said when she found her voice. Aiden gazed into her eyes, his forehead resting against hers. His look was intense, and her breath was gone again.

"Honestly, it took all my self-restraint not to take you on the kitchen table," he growled. "These little shorts should be illegal." He slid his hand up, his fingers inching under her panties.

Shae held on with one hand around his shoulders as the other played down his chest. Her sensitive fingertips felt the curve of his pec, hard and smooth under the tight t-shirt. "Looking like you should be illegal," she breathed, almost drooling.

Aiden sunk onto the bed holding her on his lap. He looked up into her eyes as he leaned in to kiss her. The tender touch of his mouth sent a quiver through her. Shae melted against him, stroking his strong jaw.

She felt Aiden's hands slide down her back and then her sweatshirt was lifted over her head. Aiden's eyes locked with hers and she felt vulnerable for the first time in her life. He didn't look at her body, but she felt naked before him. Nimble fingers unclasped her bra, sliding it slowly down her arms as his eyes continued to gaze into hers.

With shaking hands Shae reached down to grip the hem of his t-shirt, pulling it off. Now their heated skin touched and the feeling inside Shae erupted. A wave of emotion hit her and she trembled. Breaking eye contact, she threw her arms around Aiden's neck. His strong arms came around her and held her against him. He breathed deeply, almost crushing her, but she only wanted him to hold her tighter.

Aiden lay down, flipping her onto her back under him, finding her eyes again. She wanted to look away, to stop the mad rush of feelings that threatened to overwhelm her, but she couldn't. She could only watch as he stroked her cheek softly with his rough hand, then ran the calloused palm down her side. His fingertips swept across her stomach and her skin tightened at his touch. Her lips parted on a gasp and Aiden pressed his mouth softly to hers.

The button on her shorts was popped open, the zipper slowly pulled down. Aiden's tongue slid along her lower lip, then flicked against hers. He deepened the soft kiss, his whole body pressing harder against her now, and a flood of heat pooled between her legs. Every touch, every sensation lit up a thousand points on her skin.

She was frozen in fire. Unable to move, unable to think, the burning desire pinning her in place as this beautiful man made love to her. He was making love to her. She knew it, felt it deep inside her marrow. Aiden sighed quietly, brushing his lips across her collarbone, kissing her softly in the little divot at the center of her throat.

Her eyes closed as lips wrapped around her nipple and a hot tongue swirled the hardening bud. Strong hands lifted her hips and slid the rest of her clothing off at the same time. Aiden was in control. Shae gave herself over completely, having no choice in the matter, really. Her body refused to listen to her, responding only to Aiden's commands.

Shae gripped his shoulders, her hands running over the broad width, feeling the muscles bunch and bulge as he lifted her body. She held on as his mouth moved over her skin, bringing her closer and closer to ecstasy with every stroke of his tongue. Her breath came shorter and faster, and then Aiden's hands left her body.

She almost cried. In half a second, she would have. But then she felt him against her belly, long and hard and burning hot. His hands were back on her, and his mouth moved to hers. She gripped his back, pulling her body against him, wrapping her legs around him until he pulled his lips from her, his own breath coming hard and heavy.

Shae opened her eyes and the intensity of the dark indigo irises that met hers engulfed her. For a moment neither of them moved as they both stared, the only sound was their heavy breathing. But Shae was sure Aiden could hear her heart beating in her chest, the blood pumping in her ears.

"Aiden," she heard herself say, the small sound breathy and full of need. Aiden's eyes darkened further.

"Beautiful Shae," he sighed. Then he moved and she felt his hard shaft pressing into her. Her mouth fell open, a ragged cry escaping from her throat as he filled her.

Aiden's eyes never left hers, their intensity increasing as his body entered her. He held her tenderly, his embrace firm but gentle. Achingly slow, he took her, until his full length was seated inside her. He pushed hard and she felt him brush something deep inside. A shower of stars twinkled through her body, ebbing as he pulled back.

Aiden pressed in, a low groan escaping him, matching her cry as the tip of him sent stars exploding inside of her again. "What-" she breathed, imploring him with her eyes to do it again, to never stop. Her body tensed, anticipating the next thrust. Aiden's hand stroked down her side.

"Let it happen, Shae," he whispered, his eyes penetrating her deeper than the rest of him. "Let go. Let me give it to you."

Shae felt her body go slack at his command. She still clung to him, but something inside let go, was no longer hers. She gave it over to him and he slid into her again.

The feeling began low in her pelvis. With every slow, deep stroke it built until it was hard to breathe. Aiden laid his forehead against hers, their eyes locked, their breath mingling as they both panted. Every breath sent a tingle through her.

The throbbing fire moved up, spreading through her belly, and her body tensed against the loss of control. It was too much. She trembled.

"Let go, Shae," Aiden commanded again. "It's ok." His voice was warm, protective, and it wrapped around her.

Shae gave in to the sensation. With the next thrust every star inside went supernova. Shae cried out as the burning ache exploded from her core, spreading until even her fingers and toes burned and spasmed.

Aiden kissed her now, deep and hard and so full of passion her eyes rolled back in her head, and she only held onto consciousness by a thread. Her fingers gripped his hair, holding him to her as if she would die without his kiss.

His thrusting grew faster, his breathing more ragged as every muscle in her body tensed and released around him. He changed angles slightly, trapping her clit between them and Shae's eyes shot open. Aiden sucked her bottom lip between his teeth, nipping her and flicking his tongue over her swollen flesh.

It was all she needed. She met his thrusts now, seeking another release, the one that was already so close. Aiden rocked his hips, and her body flew. The cries of pleasure that escaped her now were raw and feral, her body pushed beyond what she thought was possible.

Aiden's entire body shuttered, and he growled against her, his arms crushing her. She held him as he emptied deep inside her, his body rocking hers, bringing her back to earth. Her eyes fluttered shut again and she savored every slow pulse as they both sank back against the soft mattress.

Shae couldn't move. She was in a dream. Floating on a cloud, sleeping beneath a warm, protective cover. She drifted, her mind blank, until the soft sounds of breathing brought her back. Aiden's slow, even breathing made her happy. She smiled, wondering if he was asleep. But then he stirred.

Raising up, he brushed a stray lock away from her eyes, stroking down her cheek. He looked into her eyes, a small smile on his lips as he caressed her face and hair.

"I've never experienced anything like that before," she said softly. She was in awe. Aiden only smiled wider, continuing his gentle stroking. She watched his mouth, the lips she craved even now.

Shae's breath rushed in, and her mouth opened wide as a giant yawn overtook her. She couldn't help it. Aiden laughed, his chest rumbling against her.

"Time for sleep," he said, giving her a quick kiss on the cheek. He slid out of her, and she sighed, wishing they could stay that way all night. Or maybe forever. He felt so right.

Aiden disappeared into the bathroom and Shae stretched. Her body felt heavy, her muscles limp. Damn, what kind of magic did that man possess? She didn't have the energy to ponder the answer to that just now. She rolled over enough to crawl under the comforter and between the soft sheets. She nestled into her pillow and sighed.

She felt Aiden slide in behind her. He pressed his hot body against her backside, wrapping one large arm around her waist. He tugged her against him, burying his nose in her hair and nuzzling her neck. Shae stroked the muscled arm.

"I just have one question," she murmured, her eyes too heavy to open.

"Yes?" Aiden laughed softly.

"When the hell did you put the condom on?"

Aiden chuckled quietly, shaking her. The warmth and the rocking of his body soothed her, and she couldn't hold on any longer. Shae drifted into a deep and dreamless sleep.

Chapter 11

Aiden woke with the sun the next morning, even though the room was still dark. Shae had heavy, purple curtains over the tall windows that ran the whole length of the room. His body knew the sun was up regardless, and his mind was already working. He wouldn't be sleeping any more today.

Beside him Shae slumbered peacefully. She was sprawled on her stomach, one long leg on top of the comforter, hair spread in dark waves over the white pillows. He followed the line of her leg from her dark painted toes to the full, firm thigh disappearing under the blanket.

Hot damn. Last night was the best night of his life. Making love with Shae... there weren't words to describe it. And Aiden loved words. He delighted in finding the perfect way to describe something, deftly employing the English language to meet his ends. But when he thought of Shae, words failed him.

When he thought of Shae his mind went still. Being here, so near to her, the torrent of thoughts, worries, and ideas that normally stormed his brain from his first waking moment was calmed. He only felt. And what he felt was peace. It was glorious.

In fact, he'd never felt as utterly content as he had while making love with her last night. He didn't have to think. It was instinctual. Every touch, every word, every look between them had come from somewhere deep inside himself; some guiding force he'd never tapped into before. It was natural with her as it had never been with any other woman.

Her responsiveness had stunned him. Her body and mind were so open to him, reacting to every little touch, every word. He could almost feel what she was feeling, and it brought him to a place beyond rapture, beyond ecstasy.

Aiden lay on his back, hands clasped behind his head. He looked down to the impressive tent he had pitched under the blanket. "Down boy," he mumbled.

He really should get to work. Only now he didn't want to. Maybe he could drag this project out for a few weeks. He wouldn't mind sleeping over for more than a few days. He'd slept better last night than he ever remembered sleeping. Holding her hand had been so nice yesterday. Walking with her... Shit! He was never going to keep his mind on work.

A soft hand slid over his stomach, followed by a long leg stretching across his thighs. He unclasped his hands and wrapped his arms around the soft, sweet-smelling woman snuggling up against him. Oh, that was good.

Shae took a deep breath and sighed it out, "Good morning," she mumbled against his chest. The brush of her lips as she spoke sent a thrill through him.

"Good morning," he said, pressing a kiss to her forehead. "I didn't want to wake you."

Shae didn't answer. Her arm stretched further across him, reaching the bedside table. He heard the crinkle of plastic in her hand as she slid on top of him. Shae's soft hand wrapped around him and he choked as pleasure surged through him.

"You're insatiable, you know that?" he groaned as she sank onto him.

"Don't play innocent with me, *Dr. Love*," Shae said, gasping as he filled her. "You'd never get any work done with that monster in your way."

"Monster?" Aiden growled, grabbing her hips and thrusting into her until she gasped again. "And I prefer Professor Love, if you insist on using an honorific."

"Alright, *Professor*," Shae laughed. "Teach me."

She had asked for it. Aiden made love to her until she screamed his name and his quads trembled from use. He left her that morning in a sweaty, glowing heap, kissing her sweetly before making his way home. He couldn't stop grinning.

"Hey!" he answered when his phone rang an hour later.

"You sound chipper," Gabe said on the other end of the line. He sounded irked.

"What's going on, Gabe? Get up on the wrong side of the bed?"

"Nothing. That's why I'm calling. You need any help at your place today? I'm off today, waiting for inspections on the solar install. God damned inspector is wasting two days of our time because he refuses to come out to the site in the morning, even though his office is five minutes away." Gabe sounded unusually upset about the normal red tape.

"Sure," Aiden said, suspecting his friend had more on his mind than he was saying. "I'm finishing up painting and floors inside. Then I'll start replacing some of the siding that's rotting. Plenty of grunt work if you want it."

"Great. I'll be over soon."

Gabe hung up and Aiden shook his head. He felt guilty for a moment, wondering if he'd been too wrapped up in Shae lately that he'd been neglecting his friend. He knew Tabitha had come back home and he thought things were going well. Maybe he was wrong.

Aiden grabbed an extra roller and a mallet, readying them for Gabe. It was nice to have someone to work with that knew what to do without being told. He never let anyone else work on his projects, unless he needed something that required equipment he didn't own, like a cement truck. Gabe was the exception.

The two men had met several times in different places. First on a jobsite, before Aiden had mastered the ins and outs of electrical work. Gabe was a top tier electrician and had helped with Aiden's first build. A few weeks later they'd ended up on a double date together with Tabby and one of Aiden's clients who was a friend of hers. It had been an enjoyable evening, and when they'd seen each other in the hardware store a few days later they'd gone for beers.

Now Aiden couldn't imagine life without Gabe. He was the brother Aiden had always wanted when he was growing up a lonely only child. Because he skipped so many grades he never really fit in with the other kids in his classes. Books were his best friends then. Now he made friends easily, but it was difficult to find people he really connected with. Gabe was smart and down to earth with a big heart. Like Shae.

And then he was off and running. Shae's eyes, Shae's lips, Shae's dry wit and caring soul. She took such good care of her parents. She rolled her eyes when she talked about some of their more eccentric qualities, but there was always a tender smile behind the snarky comments. He knew she was more like them than she wanted people to believe. He'd seen her nude moon ritual, after all.

Aiden was standing on a ladder, corner brush in hand, daydreaming about Shae's breasts in the moonlight when there was a knock on the door. He shook his head and cursed the erection in his pants. He was glad he'd locked the door and took his time climbing down the ladder and answering the door.

"Hey," Gabe said, walking in with his head down.

"Hey," Aiden responded, closing the door.

"Where do you want me?"

Aiden laughed, "That's usually my line. Take the roller."

"Very funny," Gabe groused. "You're doing corners? Good, I hate corners. You got a beer?"

"It's eight in the morning, man."

"Oh, right. I didn't sleep last night so my internal clock is a little off."

"What's going on?" Aiden asked, concerned.

Gabe rolled his brush in the paint tray and started on the vaulted ceiling. "Tabby's pissed at me again."

Aiden climbed back up the ladder and started painting, sensing his friend would rather talk while working. It was easier to get things off your chest that way sometimes. Rather than having someone staring at you.

"I don't know what's going on," Gabe said, frustrated. "One minute she's a doll, eating up all that sexy talk you gave me. The next she's crying or yelling. Last night she told me she doesn't know what she wants anymore. What the hell am I supposed to do if she doesn't know what she wants?"

"I'm surprised," Aiden said. "She never seemed like the crazy type. She's always so calm and happy."

"She's never acted like this before. It's like she's possessed, I'm telling you. I had to get out of the house today. She took the day off work, and she wanted me out. She's been tired lately, too. She got up this morning for about thirty minutes, called in sick to work and fell right back to sleep. After yelling at me, that is."

"Maybe she's sick," Aiden suggested.

"I asked her if she was going to go see a doctor and she bit my head off."

"I'm sorry, man," Aiden said.

They worked in silence for the next several hours. Aiden put music on and it seemed to soothe Gabe. When they stopped for lunch, he was in a much better mood.

"I've been talking too much," Gabe said after they'd discussed Tabby for another half hour. "What's new in the exciting life of Dr. Love?"

Aiden laughed. "I don't know," he said, suddenly reticent to talk about the events of the last few weeks.

"What is this?" Gabe asked, punching him on the arm. "You're blushing!"

"I am not!" Aiden laughed. Standing he walked over to the fridge and pretended to contemplate which beer to choose.

"I heard the great Dr. Love might have finally fallen," Gabe said, taking a sip from his bottle and leaning back in his chair.

Aiden straightened up at that. "What are you talking about?"

"In between yelling at me, Tabby told me she's been hearing rumors you've been rendering your services for free. And now you're staring into the refrigerator just so you won't have to look at me. Who is she?"

"First of all, how does Tabby know anything about my love life? And second," Aiden couldn't stop the grin that spread across his face. He closed the fridge and turned around, "her name is Shae."

"Damn! Never thought I'd see the day," Gabe said, shaking his head. "I knew there was something going on with you lately. When do I get to meet her?"

"I don't know. We're not really at that point yet."

"At what point?" Gabe asked.

"The point where you start meeting each other's friends. Can I ask your advice about something?"

"*You* want *my* advice? Do you have an electrical problem?" Gabe laughed.

"No, I have a girl problem. I think. I don't know. I asked her to go out with me to the faculty dinner on Saturday night and she kind of blew me off," Aiden sighed, running a paint spattered hand through his hair.

"Maybe she had other plans already," Gabe said.

"No, I don't think so."

"Are you trying to *date* this woman?" Gabe asked in shock.

"I think I am," Aiden answered. "Don't act so surprised. You already told me you'd heard all about it."

"All I heard was there was a woman you were shagging for free, and she was pretty damn happy about it. I've never seen you worry about a woman returning your affections."

"She's been talking about me?" Aiden asked hopefully. "Wait, this doesn't make any sense. How is Tabby hearing about all this?"

"Apparently they're friends," Gabe said.

"Seriously? Small world," Aiden said, contemplating this turn of events as he finished off his sandwich.

"You want to knock out these floors today?" Gabe asked, standing from the table. "The place looks pretty stupid with half a floor."

Gabe laughed and Aiden gave him a faux glare. "I guess so. Shae's been letting me sleep at her place while I paint over here. Fumes, you know. Would you mind not telling Tabby we're done?"

"Fumes?" Gabe laughed. "Sure, whatever you say. Not that Tabby will be speaking to me when I get home. She'll either be yelling or jumping on my dick. That's another thing! Her tits are bigger, I swear! And when she's not crying or yelling, she's been horny as hell. It has to be those sweet words of yours. I'm going to need some more ammunition, I think. I prefer the moaning to the yelling."

"Don't we all," Aiden said.

By five they had the floors done. Gabe was in much better spirits, looking forward to going home. He was like Aiden. Working with his hands always helped him settle things inside himself. Aiden thought his friends would probably figure out what he'd already guessed at soon enough. He didn't want to spoil it before Tabby told the poor man. Hopefully she'd figure out she was pregnant before they both went crazy. For a couple of smart people, those two sure were dumb, Aiden laughed.

Of course, there was always the chance that she wasn't pregnant and was actually going crazy. Aiden didn't like that thought at all. He decided to hope for the best. Sending out positive thoughts instead of negative energy. Veronica would be proud of him.

Aiden was in the shower scrubbing paint off his arms when he stopped to ponder why he was so happy at the thought of Shae's mother's approval. Shouldn't he be more concerned with his own mother? He knew *Madame la Professeure Moore* would scoff at the idea that thoughts, positive or negative, would have any effect on actual events. But he liked to think they did, and he knew Veronica would agree.

He toweled off and dressed quickly, running a comb through his wet hair. Shae would be home soon. They hadn't discussed how this thing they were doing would work. They hadn't discussed much of anything when he thought about it. He wanted to make dinner for her, but he and Gabe had worked too long and now he was out of time. He decided to pick up Chinese.

As he turned the corner coming back from the restaurant, he saw her car in the driveway. Shae was just stepping out, looking smart in a pantsuit and high heels that made her long legs look even longer. He pulled into the driveway and parked next to her.

Shae stuck her bottom lip out and narrowed her eyes at him as he stepped out, but there was mirth in her expression. "I didn't say you could move in, you know," she said sarcastically.

"Oh no? I'm pretty sure I heard you say that last night. No takebacks now. I don't care how tired you were," Aiden teased as he walked around her car. "I brought Chinese."

"Ooh," Shae said, her tongue darting out to lick her lips. Damn.

Aiden reached her and gripped her around the waist with his free hand, hauling her up against his chest. She let out a little moan as she looked up with those gorgeous hazel eyes of hers. Aiden kissed her sweet lips, and she dropped the bags she was carrying. Her arms came around his neck and she melded into him. He wanted to kiss her forever.

"You smell so good," she whispered, pulling back to catch her breath.

"Me, or the Chinese?" he asked, smirking. Shae laughed and tapped him on the arm.

"You," she said, running her hand down his chest. Fuck, his dick twitched against her.

"Come on, let's go eat," he said, wresting control from his libido. He released her and picked up one of the bags she'd dropped. Shae grabbed the other and unlocked the front door.

"It's so nice to have dinner ready and waiting when I get home," she said as she opened the door. "It gets depressing cooking for one sometimes."

"Yeah," Aiden said. He'd never thought about it, but now that he did, he found he was happy having someone to cook for. "Sorry it's only take-out. I'll cook tomorrow. I didn't have time today."

"Are you kidding? You're apologizing for bringing me dinner?" Shae laughed.

"Right," Aiden laughed. He set the bags on the table and took her in his arms again. "I do like cooking for you."

"Well, I like eating, so it works out," she grinned. "But don't worry about tomorrow night. My folks are coming over. They come over most Wednesday nights."

"I'd be happy to cook for them, too," Aiden said.

Shae's expression changed as she looked at him. "It's really too much trouble. They don't eat much anyway. Are you going to need to stay over another night?" she asked.

Aiden suddenly felt uncomfortable. He let go of Shae and leaned back against the table. "I, uh, don't need to, no." He looked at a spot on the floor feeling awkward. He'd presumed too much.

"Aiden," Shae said, stepping into him, straddling his thigh, "you're welcome to have dinner with us. In fact, my mom was adamant that I invite you. I just didn't want you to go to all the trouble."

Aiden looked up and met her eyes again. She smiled and he relaxed. "Oh, in that case I will definitely be cooking, and you are not to worry about it. Just tell me what they like and don't like."

"Fine," Shae laughed. "Can we please open that Chinese food now? I'm dying!"

Aiden laughed. Her appetites were certainly voracious. He started to move but Shae stilled him with her body. She leaned in and kissed him softly as she pressed against him. Her thighs squeezed around his leg, and she released a long sigh as she broke the kiss.

Aiden found himself frozen to the spot as Shae moved away to gather plates and utensils. Her kiss stunned him, and it was a moment before he found his breath again. He inhaled deeply, trying to bring sense back into his head. What was he doing?

"Aiden!" Shae moaned loudly. He jumped, spinning around to see her sitting and smiling, digging into the boxes. "You are a clever man!"

"What?" he asked, his heart racing from her gleeful exclamation.

"You got all my favorites! Mmm!" she moaned, stuffing a broccoli floret in white sauce into her mouth. "How did you know?"

"I didn't," Aiden admitted, taking the seat next to her. "I just got all my favorites."

"Are these egg rolls vegetarian?" Shae asked.

"Of course."

"Clever man," she said again. Aiden smiled to himself. "I like your shirt tonight, by the way."

He'd worn one of his favorites tonight, a picture of a sword with arms handing a jar of pickles to a pen with much more muscular arms.

"Thank you," Aiden said, pleased she'd gotten the joke. "I much prefer writing to fighting," he laughed.

"Do you write?" Shae asked.

"No, not really. I draw," Aiden answered.

"Pictures? Wait, let me guess, graphic novels, right? Is that what you use your office upstairs for? Video games?"

"Why would you think that?" Aiden asked, confused. He didn't have much interest in any of those things.

"I just thought, with all the computers, you were probably into gaming."

"I am, but not video games. I like board games, and logic puzzles."

"What do you draw in your office, then?"

"Plans and designs. For projects," Aiden answered.

"Really?" Shae asked, looking surprised.

"Yes, really," Aiden laughed.

Shae stood abruptly, taking his hand. "Come upstairs, I want to show you something."

"Alright hottie, but we didn't even finish dinner this time," Aiden teased.

"Don't be a pig," Shae said, glaring at him. Then she laughed. "I'm not taking you to the bedroom."

"The shower, then?" Aiden asked hopefully.

"Do you want to see this or not?" Shae asked.

"I definitely want to see it. I'll be good," he said, then pinched her ass as she climbed the stairs in front of him. Shae jumped and squeaked, and he chuckled.

"You'd better watch your back from now on, mister," Shae said sinisterly. She opened the door to the small middle bedroom and now it was Aiden's turn to be surprised.

"Um, damn, woman. You've turned the whole room into a closet."

"Yep. What do you think? Would you like to play one after dinner?"

Aiden stepped up to the shelves of board games that lined one entire wall of the room. She had every game he'd ever heard of, and some he hadn't. "I, uh, yes," he said.

"You said you liked games. I hope you didn't mean Monopoly," Shae said disdainfully. Aiden laughed.

"No, I just didn't expect this."

"Well, I know using a whole bedroom as a closet is unusual," Shae began.

"No, not unusual. I just figured it would be for shoes, not games," Aiden said, then immediately regretted his words.

"Ah," was all Shae said, her lips set in a thin line now.

"Oh, come on. I didn't mean it like that," he said, grabbing her around the waist and pulling her hips to him. "If I'd thought more about it, I would have suspected something like this from you."

Shae seemed to accept his explanation and gave him a peck on the lips. She pulled back but he grabbed her close and looked her in the eye. He only meant to gauge whether she thought he was a condescending, sexist jerk, and to convey that he respected her, but the second he really looked into those eyes his mind was lost.

Half a second elapsed and he watched in awe as her eyes softened, her pupils dilating as she looked back at him. Something inside him pulled toward her, a desire, a need he'd never felt before. Her breath brushed his cheek, and a shock ran through him.

Aiden dropped his arm to his side, releasing Shae. She looked momentarily surprised, her mouth opening and closing, but no words came out. She looked at the floor, smoothing the front of her slacks.

"I, uh, guess we should go finish dinner," she said quietly, still looking down.

Aiden couldn't meet her eyes now, either. It was too much, whatever that was. "Yes, let's."

Chapter 12

Shae glanced nervously at Aiden as he ate, her eyes darting back to her plate when he looked up. Everything was a jumble inside her head and if he looked at her again with that intensity in his eyes it was only going to make things worse.

Aiden was becoming a puzzle to her. Every time she thought she had something figured, it turned out she was wrong. Plus, the man was a sphynx, never fully answering her questions about him. It didn't seem as though he was hiding anything, more like he simply didn't enjoy talking about himself.

That was typically a good quality to have, unless you were trying to get to know someone. Then it was downright frustrating. Shae closed her eyes against the thoughts swirling around, jockeying for attention. When she opened her eyes again Aiden was watching her.

"Everything alright?" he asked. "You're not getting a headache, are you?"

"No, I'm fine. I was just thinking," she said. Aiden looked as though he knew exactly what she meant and that unnerved her further. How was he so in tune with her?

"Can I take that for you?" he asked, reaching for her plate.

"Sure. I'm stuffed. I'm not used to eating this well every night. Thank you."

"You're welcome," Aiden said, clearing the dishes and packing up the leftovers.

Shae jumped up, "Please, let me do that. You've already done everything else."

"It's already done," Aiden said, that warm smile on his face. "Do you feel like taking a walk before dark?"

"That would be nice."

A sliver of moon rose as they walked, and the sky was particularly colorful that evening. Shae took a deep breath of fresh air as they walked. She felt Aiden watching her and looked over. He smiled and took her hand, twining his fingers with hers. He lifted her hand and pressed his lips against her skin.

Every thought stilled and evaporated. It was maddening. She couldn't think straight when he touched her. Her id took control, primitive and instinctual. There was no logic, no reason. Pure desire and a magnetic draw to this man were all that was left. How could she ever expect to make good choices where he was concerned if her brain left the building every time he was around?

"What are your parents like?" Shae asked as they passed the orange house at the end of the street. "You said they didn't let you watch TV. Are they anti-technology?"

"No," Aiden chuckled. "They're just disdainful of anything they find *lowbrow*. Television is only for philistines."

"What do they do?" Shae asked, glad he was finally opening up a bit.

"They're both teachers."

Shae waited, but he didn't elaborate. "What do they teach?" she finally asked.

"*Maman* teaches French, and my father teaches English and history. Or English history. He's quite the Anglophile."

"Did you ever think about teaching?" Shae asked. "With two teachers for parents, didn't they want you to go to college?"

Aiden gave her a questioning look. Shae thought maybe she'd made him uncomfortable. Maybe he didn't do very well in school, and it was a sore subject for him. She didn't want to bruise his ego by pointing out how much smarter she was than him.

"They did," Aiden answered slowly. "They're quite disappointed in me," he laughed. "They really wanted me to be Professor Love. But that wasn't the path that made me happy. I think we all need to follow our hearts, don't you?"

"To a point," Shae said. "You can't be silly about it. Following your heart is all well and good, but it won't put a roof over your head, or help you save for retirement. Doing whatever you want is fine for you, but what about the people around you?"

Aiden looked at her with wide eyes and she realized she had raised her voice. He'd struck a nerve and she knew it, but she couldn't stop the anger and hurt that swept through her.

"Sometimes you have to think about someone besides yourself!" she snapped. She pulled her hand away, crossing her arms over her chest and willing the tears back that pricked her eyes. She picked up the pace, walking fast toward home. She took several deep, calming breaths.

Aiden walked silently beside her, probably terrified. There was nothing she could do about that now, though. And she'd thought she was doing so well of late. She'd been missing River less, even feeling a warmth when Aiden called her *little firecracker*. But he'd hit on the one thing that could completely crush her.

"Aren't you coming in?" Shae asked when she stepped in her front door and Aiden hesitated.

"I don't have to," he said, a worried crease between his brows. "I'll just take a sleeping bag up to the deck."

"Don't be ridiculous," Shae said, grabbing his arm and pulling him inside. She'd never be able to move him if he didn't want her to, she realized as her hand closed around his huge arm. Her fingers looked small wrapped around the big muscle. She shook her head.

"Aiden," she sighed, unsure where to start. She closed the door behind him, feeling like she was imprisoning him against his will. He probably wanted to run away now. "Do you want to talk? Really talk, I mean?"

Aiden looked at her, his eyes still wide and unsure. He opened his mouth, then closed it, then finally spoke. "I do."

Shae looked at her hand on his arm, her fingers absently stroking the taught skin and bulging ridges. She choked on a groan and dropped her hand. She spun around so she couldn't see him. "If you want to go upstairs and fuck, we can do that, too," she blurted out. "I won't hold it against you."

Aiden was silent behind her. Then two warm hands gripped and stroked her arms. She closed her eyes and sighed at his touch.

"As tempting as that offer is, I've never wanted to 'fuck' you, Shae," Aiden said softly. Her whole body trembled. "Is that what you think? Is that all you want from *me*?"

Shae opened her eyes, shocked at the hurt she could hear in his voice. His hands tightened on her arms, and he spun her around and pulled her to him. She looked up and searched his face. His cobalt eyes drew her in, and she sank against him.

"I don't know what I want from you, Aiden," she heard herself say. It was the truth. She had no idea what to make of the extreme emotion he evoked in her.

"What the hell happened out there?" he asked.

"Do you really want to know?"

"Yes, I want to fucking know, Shae," he growled. "I want to know *you*! I don't know why, I don't know what it is about you, but you're all I can think about, ok? I've never felt this way about someone before. So yes, please tell me why you're angry with me!"

"I saw my brother die in front of me," Shae burst out.

"What?" Aiden whispered. His face dropped and he held her against his chest. "I'm sorry."

Shae laid her head against his chest, listening to his heartbeat. River used to hold her like this, too, when she had a bad dream or a bad date. She was so mad at him for leaving her. Shae pulled back and took Aiden's hand, guiding him up the stairs.

"I need to lie down," she said quietly. Aiden followed in silence. She wasn't sure if he would, but she was glad he did.

Upstairs she stripped down to her panties and slid between the sheets. Aiden stood still for a moment but followed suit soon enough. He laid down beside her and she rolled to face him.

"His name was River," Shae started. "I loved him more than I've ever loved anyone."

Aiden listened as she poured out the story of her adopted brother. He didn't say a word, his eyes locked on her face. His hand found hers and held it under the covers. It was warm and strong.

"River never brought his friends around me," Shae told him, her throat tightening as she got to the end of her explanation. "Especially the boys. He thought I was too young at fifteen to be hanging around twenty-year-olds. He was probably right. He hung with a wild crowd.

"The night he-" Shae swallowed hard, "-died, he told me he was in love. I didn't like her. She wasn't very nice to me. Not that she was mean, she just didn't acknowledge me. And I was jealous because he wouldn't let me come along when they hung out with their friends. River had less time for me when he started seeing her."

Shae paused, taking a deep breath. This was always the most difficult part for her to think about. Maybe if she hadn't been such a brat...

"I begged him not to leave me that night. He was going to ask her to marry him. It made me so angry. He'd always said he didn't believe in marriage. His parents were awful people who fought constantly from the day they were wed. I don't think he ever spoke to them again after he left the commune.

"I told him I'd never speak to him again if he chose her over me. We were in the middle of the Haight, in The City, on a Saturday night. It was the Fourth of July, and he was supposed to go with me to the show. The fireworks were starting. I still remember seeing the first ones over his head when he turned his back on me.

"There were people everywhere. I started throwing a screaming fit, trying to get his attention. He went to cross the street to go meet her and I couldn't stand it. I shrieked and he turned around, stumbling on the curb. A driver turned the corner and River fell in front of the car."

Shae couldn't go on. She buried herself against Aiden and trembled, silent tears falling from her eyes. Aiden held her, wrapping those strong arms around her, and she found the pain wasn't as bad as she expected.

"The last words he said to me were, '*We all have to follow our hearts, Shae*.'"

Aiden's grip on her tightened and her tears stopped. There was so much comfort in his arms. She almost forgot to be angry at River for leaving her, only remembering the happy times they'd spent together and the love she was lucky to have, even for so short a time.

"Oh, Shae, I'm so sorry," Aiden said quietly. "I say dumb things sometimes."

"And I act like a lunatic sometimes," Shae said into his chest. "I just thought you deserved an explanation for my behavior. It really doesn't have anything to do with you. You remind me of him. Your smile. And you're kind, like him. I think you would have been friends."

Aiden took a deep breath, his chest expanding and squeezing her tight. He sighed it out slowly. Shae let her lips brush his smooth skin and a surge of emotion washed through her. She tilted her head up and met Aiden's eyes. They were so beautiful, so dark in the dim starlight shining in through the bedroom windows.

Shae slid an arm up Aiden's chest, running her fingers through the short hair on the back of his head. He looked into her eyes and need arose in her, powerful and essential. She moved her lips to his, fitting them against him and finding everything she craved.

Aiden responded fervently, his kiss deep, his desire so keen she could taste it. Sliding her other arm free, she reached around his neck and pulled him to her. She needed him close. She needed him to hold her and not let go.

"I haven't watched a fireworks show since that night. Not until this year, with you," Shae whispered against his lips. "I feel safe with you, Aiden."

Aiden smiled, his eyes twinkling, "I don't remember watching much of that show."

Shae felt her whole being respond to him. The warmth in his smile drew her in, made her feel protected and cherished in a way she hadn't felt in a long time. He was being silly now, and it was exactly what she needed. The corners of her mouth turned up and she gazed up at him.

Talking with him, telling him everything had been so easy. She could never talk to her parents about that night without the dark shadow of guilt dragging on her. But telling Aiden had taken some of that away. She felt lighter, happier deep inside than she'd been since River left.

"I don't think I saw any of the show, actually," Shae whispered, "unless you count the explosions behind my closed eyes."

Aiden barked out a laugh and Shae found herself laughing, too. He gathered her close and kissed her cheek, then whispered in her ear, "Just thinking about you sends fireworks through me."

Shae gasped as he closed his mouth over the sensitive spot on her neck. His kisses were soft and hesitant, and her body responded with a burning desire. He still held her tight, but he didn't ask for more, and that small act, those little movements that showed her he would be happy just to hold her, set her on fire.

"Aiden?" she whispered.

"Yes?" he murmured against her skin.

"Will you make love to me?"

His only answer was a low noise that rolled through his chest, reverberating through her body. Her nipples tightened against him, and she ached for his touch. Aiden seemed to anticipate her, moving his kisses down her neck until his mouth was on her breast, warm and fervid.

Another groan from Aiden as he gently nipped her sensitive flesh sent her mind and body spinning. She was barely aware of her panties sliding down her legs, and only registered that Aiden had reached for a condom because the loss of his hands on her displeased her.

But then he was back, gathering her to him, looking into her eyes as he slowly sunk into her. Shae's breath caught, then rushed out as he parted and stretched her body with his own. She felt every hard inch of him pressing into her, until with a groan he filled her completely.

Shifting slightly, she angled her hips up, and squeezed. Aiden's whole body shook, and he choked on a moan. She felt him pulse inside of her and her core spasmed in response. Aiden pulled out an inch, rolling his hips as he thrust back in. Now Shae began to shake.

Every movement brought them closer together. Every little touch felt like an explosion. Shae was lost in the feeling. Her body climbed higher and higher, and her heart pounded in her chest. It felt as though it would leap out at any moment.

Without warning the dam burst. Every muscle in her body tensed and her lungs pulled in air, but it wasn't enough. Pleasure engulfed her and she cried out. Aiden gathered her closer, slamming into her, pulling her further into bliss. His own thunderous cry joined hers as he reached his peak, swelling and throbbing inside her, his body quaking around her.

Slowly Shae opened her eyes. Aiden rested on top of her, still breathing hard. She reached her arms further around him, holding him and burying her face against his collarbone. She let her lips play softly over the smooth skin there until Aiden shivered.

"Don't stop," he whispered. "Your lips are so soft."

Shae smiled and laid more gentle kisses along his shoulder and up his neck. When she got to his jaw he pulled up, one large hand moving to cup her face. His mouth moved to hers and he took her lips, moving against them until her breathing sped again.

Aiden stopped and stroked her cheek with his thumb. She opened her eyes again to see him watching her. In the dim light she could see the upward curve of his mouth and she smiled back.

"Thank you," she whispered.

Aiden made a sound, sucking in air like an inward sigh. His forehead dropped to Shae's shoulder, and he kissed the top of her breast. When he raised his head again his eyes flashed.

"I will make love with you anytime, little fire-. Oh, shit," Aiden cursed under his breath.

"It's okay," Shae said, meaning it. "I actually kind of like it when you call me that. Is that weird?"

"It's not weird. You've got such a beautiful soul, Shae," Aiden said quietly, leaning in for a kiss.

"I can't decide if you're a cowboy or a Hippie," Shae laughed gently.

"A cowboy?" Aiden asked, his eyebrow raised incredulously.

"It's the way you always say *howdy*," Shae said, imitating his voice.

Aiden laughed. "Ah. I thought it was the horse I keep in my backyard. I'll tell you a secret," he whispered. "I only say *howdy* when I'm nervous."

Shae thought back and giggled. "I think I like that I make you nervous," she said.

"Of course you do, Delilah," Aiden laughed back.

Shae tugged on a lock of his hair and leered at him. "I don't think your power is in your hair," she said, squeezing his cock inside of her.

"Holy fuck, woman," Aiden groaned.

"I need a shower," Shae said, shifting under him. Aiden let her up, following her into the bathroom. He discarded the condom as she stepped into the shower.

"After seeing your master bath it's been hard for me to use this one. I'm quite jealous," Shae said as she started the water.

"You're welcome to come over and shower anytime," Aiden's sultry voice came from the other side of the curtain.

"I might just take you up on that," Shae laughed. She was serious, though. Showering with Aiden would probably be an otherworldly experience, especially in that huge walk-in shower he'd constructed. She looked at the cramped plastic tub she was in and grimaced. No fun showering together in there. They'd more than likely kill themselves.

She heard Aiden brush his teeth and leave as she washed the sweat from her body. She washed her long hair, dreading how it would look in the morning if she went to bed with it wet. But she was exhausted and decided not to think about it now.

The sight that greeted her as she exited the bathroom put a big smile on her face. Aiden lay sprawled on his back, the blanket coming up just barely above his hips. One large arm was bent behind his head. His eyes were closed, and his chest rose and fell peacefully.

Shae stood in the doorway and took her time admiring him. He was all angles, hard and sharp, and a tingle tickled her belly as she looked. There was nothing hard in his eyes, though, when he opened them and met her gaze. A lazy smile spread across his face and the look he gave her was soft and warm. Shae pushed off the doorframe she'd been leaning against and sauntered over to him.

"Enjoying the view?" he asked with a chuckle. "I can close my eyes again if you like."

Shae slid in next to him and playfully shoved him. "You love it," she said.

"I do," he whispered, rolling over to take her in his arms.

Shae nestled in against him. She felt drained, emotionally and physically. She'd never opened up to someone like she had with Aiden tonight. Not her parents, not even Deja whom she'd been close to for over a decade. Of course, she'd talked to Deja about everything, and her best friend was sympathetic, but it was different with Aiden. While Shae knew Deja understood, Aiden seemed to be looking into her soul and reading her deepest feelings.

Was she romanticizing because the sex was so incredible? Sure, it felt like there was a connection. A wonderful, passionate, fulfilling connection. But was it real or was she kidding herself? How could she be falling for *Dr. Love* of all people? The more she thought about it, the more ludicrous it sounded. And yet she couldn't discount her feelings completely.

It didn't matter in the end. Shae was sure that she and Aiden were completely wrong for each other. She tried to convince herself that they had nothing in common. Once they really got to know each other they'd drift apart. Better not get too attached to this wonderful feeling, then, she thought as she began to drift off in Aiden's arms. She breathed in his scent and smiled as she fell asleep.

Chapter 13

Aiden had been walking on clouds all day. Last night was the best night of his life. Even replacing the siding on the exterior of his house, a job he normally loathed more than any other, had been enjoyable today.

He whistled while he worked, filling in the seams, painting on the primer, and only laughing when he found another spot of dry rot he'd missed. His phone rang in his pocket, and he pulled it out.

"Gabe!" he whooped. "How is every little thing?"

"It's really great," Gabe said, sounding like he meant it. "Did you already talk to Tabby?"

"No, should I have?" Aiden asked as he continued his work.

"No, you just sounded so excited, I thought maybe she'd told you already."

"Told me what?" Aiden asked, his mind not fully focused on the conversation, or else he would already have guessed the reason for this call.

"We're pregnant!" Gabe shouted.

"We?" Aiden laughed. "As in, you and me?"

"Asshole," Gabe laughed. "You could at least act happy for me."

Aiden laughed. "I am happy for you. I figured it out a long time ago, though. I'm glad you finally know. Congratulations!"

Gabe laughed again. "How the hell did you know? Is there something I should know about you and Tabby? You two were always way too close."

"Please," Aiden chuckled. "The big boobs? The mood swings? It was probably obvious to everyone but the two of you."

"Right," Gabe laughed. "I finally got her to go see a doctor and that's almost exactly what he said. Shit, I hope we're better at figuring out what's going on with our kid," Gabe said, sounding terrified.

"So, when's the happy event?" Aiden asked.

"February second," Gabe said.

"Groundhog Day!" Aiden laughed. "His emergence will foretell whether we shall have an early spring or six more weeks of winter."

"Very funny," Gabe said, not amused.

"So, all my poetry has paid off for you. Guess you won't require the services of Dr. Love any longer," Aiden said.

"Actually, I do. That's why I'm calling you. I'm fucking dying, man!" Gabe cried. "Tabby wants more and more. She's still moody, and if I don't whisper sweet nothings to her every night and then satisfy her, it's not pretty. Can you give me some more stuff to use tonight?"

Aiden laughed. "Sure, no problem. How do you like this?" Aiden started to speak, but Gabe cut him off.

"Hold on a sec, I'm going to record this. Ok, I'm ready."

"What is a kiss? A pledge properly sealed, a promise seasoned to taste, a vow stamped with the immediacy of a lip, a rosy circle drawn around the verb 'to love.' A kiss is a message too intimate for the ear, infinity captured in the bee's brief visit to a flower, secular communication with an aftertaste of heaven, the pulse rising from the heart to utter its name on a lover's lip: 'Forever.'"

"Is that it?" Gabe asked.

"Trust me," Aiden said, "she'll love it. Just whisper it near her ear giving her soft kisses between the sentences while you brush her hair aside and run your fingers down her neck."

"Alright. Hey, is it weird that we do this?" Gabe asked.

"Probably," Aiden laughed. "But it worked for Cyrano. Well, actually it worked for his friend Christian, but in this case you're Christian, so it's all good."

"What the hell are you talking about?" Gabe asked, exasperatedly.

"You know, Cyrano de Bergerac? The play where the guy falls in love with his beautiful cousin, but she's not interested in him because he's unattractive, so he convinces Christian to woo her, but Cyrano writes the poetry she falls in love with."

"I hate it when you talk about theater," Gabe said. "Almost as much as when you tell me about art gallery openings."

Aiden laughed. "I know. But you're happy to use my knowledge for your own ends."

"Anything that gets me some peace," Gabe sighed.

"You're a good husband," Aiden said. "And you'll be a great dad, too."

"Yeah, I can't help it. I just love my woman too damn much."

Aiden laughed, and a warm feeling spread through him. He and Gabe talked shop for a bit, then Gabe was called away to check something on the job site. Aiden's mind was immediately on Shae again, the warm feeling filling his chest as he painted.

He decided to quit early to get dinner ready for everyone. As he made his way to the shower, he realized he hadn't thought about a single thing other than Shae all day. His mind was usually filled with project ideas, things he'd read, gaming strategies to use at the next Mensa meet, or when it was really working overtime, practicing mathematical proofs in his head.

It was blissful to get a break from the constant racket in his mind. Still, he had another project to complete, and he should be working the kinks out. But he felt a goofy grin spread across his face as he thought about the hilarious joke Shae told him that morning instead.

His phone rang again, and he answered it before he even looked at the screen, his head still in the clouds.

"*Bonjour mon fils, comment vas-tu?*" his mother asked.

"*Maman!*" he said, his head snapping up and his mind clearing. "Just fine, and you?" he continued in French.

"Your father and I are both well. We are looking forward to seeing you Saturday after missing our usual dinner this week," his mother said, a guilt-inducing tone in her voice.

"Yes, I am as well," Aiden said brightly. He *was* looking forward to seeing his family, he realized, even if it was at a faculty function.

"You sound happy," his mother commented, a smile in her voice. "Any special reason?"

"It's just a beautiful day," Aiden said. "And I'm ahead of schedule on my project."

"Oh, I'm so glad to hear that. I know everyone is going to want to know all about your work with Architects for Humanity. Tell me, what were you doing this time?" she asked eagerly.

Aiden sighed internally. Of course, she meant his volunteer work. She'd never be so excited about the work he did with his hands. "I meant the house I'm refurbishing. It's turning out to be my best yet," he said, excited. "You and Father are invited to dinner when it's done. Shouldn't be more than a few more weeks now."

"Oh, yes, of course," his mother said, less enthusiastically. "We'd love to. But tell me about your real work."

"This is my real work," he snapped before he could control himself. He felt his anger flaring and took a deep breath in through his nose.

"Aiden, really. I know all the girls must love the big muscles and macho job, but it's a waste of your intellect. Still," she clucked her tongue, "at least we'll have something relevant to tell everyone on Saturday. You do have a project, don't you?"

"Yes, Maman, I do. And I'll be happy to parade it out in front of your friends for you. Just once I'd like you to support my interests, though," Aiden sighed, tired of this argument.

"Which interests are those?" his mother said sarcastically. "Tom-catting around or manual labor?" she said, as if manual labor were the less desirable of the two.

"Mom," he said in English.

"I'm sorry, honey, I didn't mean that," she apologized.

"Yes, you did. But it's alright. We can just agree to disagree."

"Fine," his mother said.

"Was there something you wanted to talk about?" Aiden asked.

"Yes! I almost forgot. Will you be bringing a date? I'll need to know by tomorrow how many seats to have at the table. And what meal she'd like. I believe they're serving chicken piccata or roast beef."

Aiden tensed as he realized Shae had never answered him about Saturday night. He'd tried to bring it up a few times, but she always managed to change the subject. "I'll text you tonight," he said. "I have to make sure her calendar is clear. And if so, she'll be having whatever the vegetarian option is with me."

"Oh, Aiden!" his mother squealed. "Is this a real date? Not a job date?"

"Yes," he said almost shyly. He'd never spoken to his mother about a woman before. He'd never been with a woman he wanted to talk about.

"Well, I just can't wait!" his mother said, lapsing into English, her Ohio accent coming out in full force. "I'll let you go now. I love you. See you Saturday!"

"Love you too, *Maman*," Aiden said.

He took a long shower after that conversation. He was unnerved by his mother's interest in his dating life recently. He couldn't be too upset over that, though, considering how happy he was about it. He scrubbed hard at the paint on his arms as he thought more about her other comments concerning his job.

He was fed up with everyone's focus on him using his big brain. His family, his colleagues, the Mensa people. Yes, he liked to engage at the Mingle nights and flex his mental muscles, but then Hestia popped into his head, and he shuddered. She had been so fixated on his IQ.

What was wrong with enjoying working with your hands? Aiden wished that just once he'd meet someone who was interested in him for who he was. He thought he had a lot to offer outside of his big brain, or big biceps. But it seemed women were only interested in one of those two things. But that wasn't true. They also liked it if you had a fancy job.

By the time his shower was over, Aiden had worked himself into a metaphorical lather. He banged pots as he fixed dinner until he cooled down. His mother could rile him up like no one else. He stopped for a moment, closing his eyes and clearing his head.

A bubbling sound from the stove made him jump and he just barely saved the sauce for the potatoes. He threw them together and put them in the oven to finish while he chopped up a salad. He relaxed a little, realizing that Shae would be back soon with Vern and Veronica. Last time Veronica had read his palm and told him some interesting things. He hoped she'd do it again. He was fascinated by her insights. He doubted it was truly a psychic ability, more likely she was just good at reading people, but he had fun with it either way.

He heard a car door close and went to look out his front window. He saw Shae and her parents go inside. She looked gorgeous again today. She was always dressed so well, in an old-fashioned, conservative way that managed to emphasize every round curve of her body. Aiden swallowed hard. He was hungry for her already.

The oven timer went off and he began packing everything up. He took his time, wanting to give Shae a few minutes to settle in with her parents. The hot casserole dish was a bit tricky, but he managed to wrestle everything into cloth sacks. He hauled it all over, but when he got to the front door, he wasn't sure what to do. Shae had told him to come and go as he pleased over the last few days, but now, with her parents there, it felt different.

Aiden decided knocking was the best option, but his hands were too full. He pressed his elbow against the doorbell and waited. In a moment the door opened, and Shae's beautiful eyes looked into his.

"I told you, you don't have to ring the bell," she started. "Oh! Let me help you with all that!" she exclaimed when she noticed all the packages.

"It's ok, I've got it," Aiden said, jostling the bags. "Just open the door wide."

Shae stepped aside and Aiden made his way into the kitchen where he was greeted with huge hugs from Vern and Veronica after he deposited the mountain of food.

"You brought enough to feed an army!" Veronica exclaimed as she wrapped her arms around him. "It's so kind of you to go to all this trouble. We hardly eat anything; I don't know how we'll make a dent in this feast!"

"I know, Shae told me not to make a lot for you. This is all for her," Aiden said, pulling back and smirking at Shae. She returned his smile and her parents laughed.

"In that case you should have made more," Vern chuckled. Shae rolled her eyes at him.

"Come on, what is this, gang up on the hostess night? What can I get you to drink?" Shae asked Aiden.

"Anything is fine," he said, glancing at the glasses on the table. "What are you drinking?"

"I brought a batch of kombucha!" Veronica said. "It's the best scoby I've ever made. Just look at that!" Veronica held up the gallon-size glass jar and swirled it around to show Aiden the slimy, mucus-looking blob at the bottom of the amber liquid. His stomach revolted.

"Wow," he said, trying to sound impressed. He glanced at Shae and saw she had her hand over her mouth, trying not to laugh. He gave her an imploring look, but she just shook her head. He was on his own.

"Let me get you some," Veronica said as she poured out a glass. "There's a little apple cider vinegar in there, too. Your gut will thank you."

Aiden tried his best not to wince when she handed him the glass, watching him with wide, expectant eyes as he raised it to his lips. He tried not to breathe through his nose as the acidic liquid flowed down his throat. It didn't help much and he almost gagged.

"Mmm," he managed as his eyes began to water. "That's great."

"You hate it!" Veronica exclaimed, then burst out laughing. Soon the three of them were laughing wildly as Aiden stood there baffled. "It's alright, dear. Shae hates it, too. I won't make you drink any more."

Veronica swiped the glass from his hand before he could react. His instinct was to object and finish the revolting drink with as much of a smile on his face as he could manage. It would only be polite. He was relieved when Veronica downed the rest of his glass in one gulp before taking up her own.

"Alright, slow down, Mom," Shae said. "You'll get tipsy."

"It's not that strong," Veronica objected, but she let Shae take her glass and place it on the table.

"Oh please," Shae scolded, "I know how you roll, Mom."

"For what it's worth, Veronica, that's the best kombucha I've ever had," Aiden said.

"You're such a sweet man," Veronica said, taking his face in her hand and squeezing. "Look at that handsome face, too, Shae. No wonder you're so hot for him."

Aiden blanched and froze as Veronica gave his cheeks another squeeze. He looked at Shae, assuming she would be as mortified as he was, but she only gave him an almost lascivious smile. Suddenly the floor was the most interesting thing in the world, and he was unable to look anywhere else.

"Mom, you've embarrassed him," Shae said. "Please you two, just sit down and Aiden and I will get dinner on the table."

"I don't know what there is to be embarrassed about," Veronica went on. "From what you've told me he should be proud of his skill as a lover, not embarrassed."

Aiden wished the floor would open and swallow him up. He wasn't prudish by any means, but discussing his sex life with someone's parents, especially Shae's, was too much, even for him. He shuffled his feet and reached for a bag to begin setting food on the table.

"Don't worry about them," Vern said when Aiden stepped next to him to set the casserole dish out. "They have to talk about everything. If they start talking about your aura being too dark, then you can worry."

Aiden dared a quick look at Vern and saw he was smiling. He hadn't even known whether Shae had divulged that they were seeing each other, and now it seemed she'd said a lot more than that. Vern gave him a pat on the arm and Aiden relaxed.

"I hope you like scalloped potatoes," Aiden said as he opened the food.

"You *know* it's my favorite," Veronica said, beaming at him.

"Yes, I do," Aiden laughed. "Shae tells *me* secrets, too."

Veronica laughed. "I'm sure she does. Maybe you can get her to loosen up a bit."

Aiden stared at Veronica for a split second. He couldn't imagine a family any *looser* than this one.

"Ugh, Mom," Shae objected. "You're really on a roll tonight, you know that?"

"What?" Veronica asked. "It's just nice to see you with someone kind and generous like Aiden. Not like those uptight, corporate types you always go for. You'll be good for her," she said to Aiden.

He couldn't help but blush. "Thank you, Veronica," Aiden said, genuinely touched. "I'm lucky Shae even looked twice at me."

"And modest, too," Veronica laughed. "I'd bet most women look more than twice at you. Probably some men, too."

"Alright, enough flirting, Mom," Shae laughed.

Throughout dinner Vern and Veronica shared the most entertaining stories Aiden had ever heard about their colorful lives in communes and various vehicles. Aiden had lived in one house his entire life until he moved to the dorms in college. Part of him longed for the freedom of living in a van, able to go wherever and whenever you wanted. Maybe that was why he was never able to settle in one place for long.

"And that was how we ended up here, building the cabin. Suddenly there was a huge demand for designer weed," Vern said. "And I thought, if there's one thing I know about, it's how to grow some good buds-"

"Dad," Shae scolded.

"Excuse me," Vern said in a hoity-toity manner. "I mean *cannabis*." Everyone laughed except Shae.

"Aiden doesn't need to hear about you being a drug dealer," Shae said.

"Marijuana is not a drug any more than alcohol or cigarettes or caffeine," Vern argued. "I only sell to dispensaries, not kids on the street. Wouldn't you agree, Aiden?"

"I, uh," Aiden began, not sure what to say.

"Dad," Shae said harshly.

"We call her Saint Shae, you know," Vern said, smiling slyly at Aiden. "She'd never touch the stuff."

"I didn't want to kill all my brain cells," Shae said defensively.

"You've never smoked?" Aiden asked. He was surprised after the stories he'd heard tonight. There was certainly no lack of substances for her to have tried had she wanted to.

"No," Shae said, almost smugly. "I knew how to read when I was four years old. I graduated at the top of my high school and graduate school classes. And my Stanford–Binet Intelligence Scale score is 131. That puts me in the top four percent for IQ," she said, explaining to Aiden.

"You had your IQ tested?" Aiden asked, a knot in his stomach. He didn't enjoy the way she'd said any of that.

"Yes. It was always my dream to be a member of Mensa. I missed it by one percentage point, though," Shae said glumly.

"You see what I mean?" Veronica asked. "Sometimes you just need to let it go, Shaky."

"Mensa's great and all," Aiden said, "but don't you think other things are more important than some bullshit test?"

"Here, here!" Veronica said, taking another gulp of kombucha. "We've been telling her that her whole life. She's always been so obsessed with meeting these mediocre standards imposed by people whose opinions really shouldn't make any difference to her."

Shae stood abruptly from the table, grabbing her mother's glass from the table before Veronica could pour herself another. Shae's mouth was set in a grim line, and she refused to meet Aiden's eye.

"Alright, enough, Mom. Now you really are getting drunk," Shae said, clearing dishes to the sink. "I think it's getting late. We should get you both home." Shae clattered a dish loudly in the sink and Aiden jumped.

"I am not getting drunk," Veronica protested. "You're wound more tightly tonight than usual. I have my oils and crystals in my bag, lie on the couch and I'll help you release some of this negative energy."

"I don't need you to wave crystals over me right now," Shae said sharply.

"You do," Veronica answered, "you're just too stubborn to admit it. I can't see what this block is inside you, but whatever it is, you're imposing it on yourself. Listen to the universe, Shae, it's trying to guide you. River is even trying to help."

"Enough!" Shae yelled, dropping a large serving spoon into the sink with a bang. It was the most Aiden had ever heard her raise her voice. When she turned it looked as though she might cry. "Don't start talking to River right now, please."

"I'm not," Veronica said. "He's been coming to me in my dreams lately. He's worried about you. And that's all I'm going to say about it." Veronica put her hands up in the air defensively as Shae glared at her again.

Vern stood and wrapped his arms around Shae. She tensed visibly but didn't pull away. Aiden was frozen in his seat. His family meals were never this emotional, and he had no idea how to handle it.

"It's ok, Shaky-Bakey," Vern said quietly. "We just want you to be happy. You sure you don't want Mom to adjust your energy field?"

Aiden saw Shae roll her eyes, but then she smiled a little. "No," she said. "My field is just fine."

Aiden relaxed and took a deep breath. It seemed Vern's quiet words had a soothing effect on Shae. He really felt like he blew it, though. He couldn't tell if she was angry with him for calling IQ tests bullshit, or at her mother for everything else. Before he could think much more about it, Veronica was up out of her chair and grabbing his hand, dragging him into the living room.

"I need to talk to you," she whispered quietly as she dragged him out the front door.

Aiden glanced over his shoulder, but Shae and Vern didn't appear to be following. He let Veronica lead him, curious what she wanted, but he really wished to be back inside with Shae. He didn't like the tension he'd felt between them.

"I lied," Veronica said after she'd closed the front door. "I do know what's blocking Shae. She's going to make herself sick one of these days if she doesn't go easier on herself. You need to help her, Aiden."

"I'm happy to do anything I can, but I'm hardly qualified to-" Aiden began.

"Twaddle," Veronica said, making Aiden chuckle. "You're exactly the man for the job. Shae just hasn't accepted that yet, but she will."

"I'm afraid I don't follow you," Aiden said, confused.

"She thinks she knows what she wants, but she's wrong and only making herself unhappy chasing empty notions. You have to show her what's really important."

"What is it she thinks she wants?" Aiden asked, completely lost as to what Veronica was asking of him.

"You know, someone driven, uptight, snobby. Corporate. And intelligent above all. Based on society's measure. For some reason she judges success on a very narrow scale. She'll only be a success when she is recognized by people who like to give out trophies. I try to tell her the point of life is to enjoy the journey, not win the prize, but she won't listen to me.

"She would have listened to River. He left at the worst possible time in her life. Right as she was becoming a woman. She isn't the same kind of woman I am, and she dismisses my advice because she thinks I'm flighty. But you know, all I have to do is look at her and I know I've done well in life. She's a good person who contributes so much to the world. Her and River. He was such a sad child when Shae brought him home to us. But the more love we poured into him, the more he gave back. For the short time he was here he made the world a better place," Veronica ended wistfully.

"Shae loved him very much," Aiden said quietly. He didn't know what else to say. Everything Veronica said resonated with him. Some of it made him happy, but some of it bothered him.

"Yes, she does," Veronica said. "And if she would only listen to him now! He sent you to her, you know."

"What do you mean?" Aiden asked dubiously.

"He sent you. He told me about it, in my dreams, you know."

Aiden's face must have betrayed him because Veronica laughed, patting his arm.

"Ok, you're skeptical. It doesn't matter. River told me he was there when you saw the house," she said, motioning next door. "He pushed you to buy it."

This was a lot crazier than the palm reading. Veronica was talking to dead people, and he was supposed to believe they were controlling his actions? Yet he couldn't deny the feeling that came over him the first time he'd seen the house. It was as if he had to buy it. Something had driven him to it. He scoffed, shaking his head. Yes, his truck had driven him to it, nothing supernatural. But then Veronica asked him a question and his conviction was shaken.

"Had you ever called anyone *little firecracker* before?"

Aiden froze, his mind reeling, trying to find an instance in the past where he'd used that term. He couldn't think of a single one. He'd never even thought the two words together as far as he could remember before meeting Shae. And yet it had rolled off his tongue naturally, without a second thought.

"No," he said finally.

"Well," Veronica said quietly, patting his arm again.

Aiden stood there, his logical mind trying to reason with the part of him that wanted to believe what Veronica was telling him. He liked the idea that people could still look out for you after they'd passed. And he really liked the idea that River approved of him. In a lot of ways River was still the most important person in Shae's life. Aiden was reminded of how much he loved and admired his grandfather, and how so many of his choices had been guided by the man even after he was gone.

"Papa wants me to tell you tough tomatoes," Veronica said.

"What?" Aiden gulped, almost falling over.

"That's what I said, but he assured me he wanted me to say tough tomatoes."

Aiden fell into a squat, his legs going weak. He ran a hand over his face as the front door opened, spilling light out onto the walkway. Shae and Vern stepped out, both smiling, but Aiden was too overwhelmed to respond to them. How had Veronica known anything about his grandfather, especially the thing he used to say anytime Aiden came to him with a silly problem? It had become a private joke between the two of them, something he hadn't thought about, much less mentioned to anyone in years.

"Aiden, are you alright?" Shae said, kneeling beside him, her gentle hands flitting over his shoulder, his arm.

"I'm fine," he said, coming back to himself. He stood, pulling her up with him. "You'll stain your slacks if you kneel on the grass."

"Mom, what did you do?" Shae said, turning accusing eyes on Veronica.

"Nothing!" Veronica said innocently. "If anything, it was the strange message his grandfather sent."

"Oh, mother," Shae groaned. She turned to Aiden and took his hand. "Don't let her scare you. She's harmless, I promise."

Aiden looked into Shae's eyes and for a moment forgot everything. She looked at him softly and her concern sent warmth spreading through his chest.

"It's fine," he said with a smile. And it was. Whether he'd received an actual message from beyond the grave or not, he was filled now with happy memories of his childhood and the special bond between him and his grandfather. He looked over at Veronica and she smiled lovingly at him, too.

"I hadn't thought of my grandfather in a long time, and it overwhelmed me, that's all," he told Shae. "I used to spend summers at his ranch in Ohio and we were very close. He passed away about seven years ago."

"I'm sorry," Shae said quietly.

"You have such a big heart," Veronica said, snatching his hand from Shae and wrapping it in both of hers. "I've never seen someone so open, with so much pink in their aura; since River, that is. You have a very similar aura. Come on, you'll sit with me in the back and tell me all about Ohio." She pulled him toward Shae's car.

Aiden hesitated, "I was going to stay and clean up-"

"No, no," Veronica said. "Shae will enjoy the company on the way back. You can clean up later. You'll be back before ten, and you young people have plenty of energy. That's not late for you."

Aiden glanced at Shae, and she shrugged, smiling again as if she were as powerless against the force of Veronica as he was. He let her lead him into the tiny backseat and folded himself in. He was curious now to see what else she would tell him.

"So, what exactly is a pink aura?" Aiden asked as they pulled out.

"Pink indicates romance, love, generosity, and faithfulness. In your case, your color is leaning toward magenta, which means you are also independent, funny, and big-hearted. Now, there is a lot of yellow, and a blue bordering on turquoise as well-"

"Mom, come on," Shae said from the driver's seat.

"Fine," Veronica said. "I won't even bother to mention how much gold I see in your aura lately, Shae. I'd rather hear about Ohio, anyway."

Aiden found that once he began talking about the ranch he couldn't stop. Memories came flooding back, and he was amazed when he realized how much of his grandfather's wisdom he'd taken to heart. As he talked a thought hit him that had never occurred to him before, and it knocked the wind out of him.

His grandfather was the one who sparked his interest in architecture. There was always some problem to be solved on the ranch, or something that needed to be built or repaired. When he was eight years old Papa had handed him a toolbox and some nails and sent him out to the scrap wood pile with instructions to build a chicken coop for the second flock of chickens Nana wanted to raise.

That was it. No instructions, no supervision. Aiden had worked his tail off building that coop. When it was built, he painted it Nana's favorite color, lavender. It was lopsided, too small, and difficult to move, but Nana had used it for decades until it finally rotted. The chickens didn't seem to mind.

Papa had passed away the day before Aiden found out about the city building project that changed the course of his career. He remembered being distraught. His grandfather was in good health and his death was unexpected. *Maman* had called him and told him over the phone. Pneumonia they said, from the flu. It happened quickly. He wished his mother had told him in person. He had no one to turn to in his empty office. No friendly shoulder to cry on.

He saw now how much it had impacted his reaction to the news the next day that his pet project, his baby, was being ruined beyond recognition. He also knew how much happier he was now, working with his hands, on tangible projects of his choosing that helped people. He thanked his grandfather for opening that path to him.

All this ran through his mind as he told the story of the chicken coop. He didn't voice what he had just discovered about himself, wanting to think more about it later.

"I'm sorry," Aiden said as they pulled into a dark driveway. "I've been monopolizing the conversation."

"We loved every second of it," Veronica assured him with a pat on the hand. "You had quite the childhood."

Aiden chuckled at her statement. His childhood was a complete bore compared to Shae's, but he'd loved it. "It was pretty great, I'll admit."

Aiden stood and stretched his legs as everyone climbed out, but he remained by the car, saying his goodbyes outside and giving Shae a few minutes alone with her parents. He felt a bit guilty about taking up her evening with them, and for the added tension his presence caused. But he had enjoyed his time with them even more than their last dinner.

Was it possible to feel like you fit perfectly with another family? Surely, he wasn't betraying his mother and father by feeling so at home with Vern and Veronica, was he? He loved his mother deeply, but sometimes he wished she could be as open and accepting of him, as appreciative of his aspirations as Veronica was.

"What are you thinking out here in the dark?" Shae's voice interrupted his thoughts.

"Lots of things," he answered honestly. "Would you like me to drive?"

"No, I'm ok," she said, stepping close to him.

His body immediately stiffened as he leaned against the car, reacting to the heat and the scent of her so close. He hadn't touched her all night, pushing his desire for her to the background until they could be alone. It had been a monumental endeavor, and now here they were, in the dark, and he couldn't hold back any longer.

He reached for her without thought, wrapping his arms around her slender waist, pulling her into his embrace until she was pressed firmly against him. She responded with a smile and a sigh, and lightning flashed through him.

"You still like me?" Shae whispered, gazing at him.

"Of course, I do."

"I thought my mom might have scared you away. But you're not easily spooked, are you?" she said with a grin.

"Nope. If anything, I like you more." Aiden tilted his head toward hers and her eyes fluttered shut. Her soft lips parted as he tenderly kissed her. He felt her body melt in his arms, and he pulled back. Shae opened her eyes and gazed up at him. He wanted to hold her like this forever.

"We should go," Shae said breathlessly, but she didn't move.

"We should," Aiden echoed. He straightened, placing his hands on her waist and moving her away from him a few torturous inches. He opened the passenger door and stepped in. Shae looked confused for a moment, then took her seat behind the wheel.

Aiden needed answers, so many answers, to questions he was afraid to ask. One answer he needed now. It seemed a simple question, so why did trepidation grip his heart as he opened his mouth to speak the words?

Chapter 14

S hae reluctantly sat behind the wheel, her mind and body conflicted. On the one side, she could stay in Aiden's arms for all eternity. It felt so damn good there. On the other side, she was mad at him. Clearly, he didn't value the same things she did. He scoffed at her academic achievements, belittling her IQ score, of which she was immensely proud. He seemed more interested in her mother's inane ramblings about auras and chakras.

That just wasn't what Shae wanted. She needed someone who took life seriously. Someone who wanted to do more than swing a hammer, drink beer, and screw. Although the screwing was very nice... Damn, and there was her dilemma. She loved the screwing, but at some point they would have to talk to each other, and then what? Aiden would be bored by her talk about statistical analysis and carbon nanotubes, and she would be bored by watching ESPN.

"Have you decided about Saturday night?" Aiden asked beside her in the darkened car. They hadn't gotten back to the main highway yet where the streetlights started. She couldn't make out the expression on his face in the dim light.

"Saturday night, right," she said, stalling for time. She didn't want to have this conversation. Still, maybe it was easier this way when they didn't have to look at each other.

"I need to let them know tonight to reserve your seat. It's a sit-down dinner. There will be an open bar, though, if that makes it sound any less banal," Aiden laughed.

Shae's ears perked up at his use of the word banal. A fancy word for Mr. Muscles to use. "Tell me about it again?"

"It's the annual faculty dinner. My mother is insisting on parading me in front of her friends, so fair warning, you'd be subjected to their scrutiny as well. She asked if I'd like to bring a date, and I thought of you."

Again, her thoughts struggled against each other. But she shouldn't lead him on. She couldn't go on a date and meet his parents and all their friends as if she were his girlfriend. Not when she was so unsure about him.

"I can't, Aiden," she heard herself say. She pressed her lips together before she could change her mind. Her body pulled toward him, begging her to give in, to let go and see where this could lead. He was the funniest, nicest man she'd met in a long time, after all.

"Ah," he said quietly. "Perhaps another time, then."

Shae could sense his disappointment and it bit at her. She realized she felt let down, too. A bigger part of her than she'd realized wanted to go.

"It's just too soon," she went on. Might as well lay it all out on the table. "I think we should keep it casual right now, don't you? Friends with benefits if that's alright."

Aiden didn't say anything, and Shae felt like she couldn't breathe. What was he thinking right now? Had she offended him? Hurt him? Was he fine with what she was offering? Most men would be ecstatic with her offer. Was he?

"I mean, we don't have a lot in common when you think about it," Shae went on, filling the uncomfortable silence. "You'd get bored with me if we dated. I'd always want to go to art shows, or theater, or just stay home and do the Sunday crossword. I'm sure you'd rather go to a bar or a sporting event." Shae glanced over briefly as she finished and caught the grim expression on Aiden's face.

"Or a sports bar?" Aiden said bitterly. Damn, she had offended him.

"Maybe?" she said timidly.

"Whatever you want, Shae," he said shortly.

"No, not whatever I want, Aiden," she said, getting annoyed now. "It's whatever we want together. We both have to agree."

"Tell me this, then," Aiden said, turning and looking directly at her. "Would you ever enjoy going to a baseball game or a football game, or whatever thing involving throwing a ball people like to watch, with me? Would it matter at all to you that I was there, or is your enjoyment on a date solely dependent on the venue?"

Shae was taken aback. She didn't have a response. She truly didn't know her own mind at this moment. She opened her mouth, a few sounds coming out, but closed it again. "I, uh,".

"Because it wouldn't matter to me," Aiden said, turning back to face front. "I like being around you, Shae. I like you, but Veronica is right. You need to loosen up."

Now she found her voice. "Don't tell me what I need to do. I'm not going to be your subservient little house frau, and that's part of the problem here. You and I want different things. I don't want to wash your socks and clean your house while you drink a six-pack in front of the T.V. every night."

Shae clapped a hand over her mouth, gripping the steering wheel with the other, and wished she could have bitten back those words. Having him side with her mother was too much. She was sick of hearing she needed to loosen up. She'd been hearing it her whole life, and she'd overreacted.

"No one's asking you to," Aiden said coldly. "I was merely asking you out on a date, not to enter into an indentured servant contract. Now that I fully comprehend your opinion of me, I can see why you would refuse. But for your information, yes, I do enjoy beer once in a while. But I do not watch sports of any kind. In fact, I can't remember the last time I even watched television at all. I apologize for suggesting you loosen up. That was rude."

Again, he had her speechless. He apologized with ease, admitting his fault while maintaining his integrity. It might have been the sexiest thing a man had ever said to her. He didn't put up any false pretense of masculinity, and he didn't watch sports? What American male, especially one that looked like him, didn't watch sports? She was even more confused now.

"You didn't answer my question," Aiden said quietly beside her.

"I'm sorry," Shae said, her voice quavering. She felt all wrong. What was she doing wrong? "What was the question again?"

"Never mind," Aiden said and pulled out his phone, holding the screen at an angle so she couldn't see what he was doing. He typed for a few seconds and then replaced it in his pocket.

"You know," Aiden said after a moment, "I was so happy this morning when I heard about Gabe and Tabby's news."

"Who?" Shae asked, bewildered.

"You don't know Tabitha Martinez?" Aiden asked, sounding surprised.

"No, doesn't sound familiar."

"Huh," Aiden said.

They rode in silence the rest of the way. When Shae parked in the driveway, Aiden stepped out and walked to the door. Shae had no idea what he was thinking. Clearly, he was coming inside. Was he staying the night again? Should she say something? She should say something, but she had no idea what.

She unlocked the door and Aiden marched straight into the kitchen where he began to wash dishes. Shae stood behind him, in the middle of the room, watching him wrap food in foil and pack his bags. She wished he would turn around. She wished he would hold her in his arms again.

She reached out her hand to touch him, but the set of his shoulders stopped her. There were only a few feet between them, but it felt like a mile. The pain it caused her was almost unbearable. Need for him permeated her being, and she gulped back a lump that was forming in her throat. She moved next to Aiden and began loading the dishwasher.

He didn't move away. He was so close she could feel the heat of his skin. She watched him out of the side of her eye, but he didn't look at her. Finished with his task, he turned and gathered his bags.

"I'll call you tomorrow," he said quietly, moving toward the living room.

"I'll be out late," Shae said, closing the dishwasher. She didn't want him to go. "I have a thing." Why couldn't she ask him to stay?

Aiden looked at her and nodded once, turning to go again. She followed him, the ache in her chest growing. He opened the front door and stepped out, turning, and finally meeting her eye. He looked at her with longing, his dark eyes almost black in the dim porchlight.

Shae imagined throwing her arms around him, kissing him until he came back inside and took her upstairs. She wanted to feel him, to be close to him again so badly she could almost taste it. But she couldn't do it. Something stopped her. She almost growled in frustration. Why couldn't he be happy with what she was offering? Why was he making it into more than it should be? Didn't he see it would never work for them beyond the physical?

Aiden looked into her eyes a moment longer. He seemed to be waiting for something, but Shae was frozen. Everything inside was mixed up and no words came to her.

"Well, goodnight," Aiden said, then strode quickly across the lawn and disappeared into his house.

Shae closed the door behind her, startling when she felt a tear run down her cheek. "Stupid," she murmured, wiping it away.

Her house felt cold and dark. Only the kitchen light was on. She went in to turn it off and looked around. Neat and clean. He'd made dinner *and* cleaned again. Guilt stabbed at her. He was too nice. But there wasn't such a thing as too nice. Just too nice for her. Maybe she didn't deserve him.

Shae turned the lights out and climbed the stairs. She realized the last two times she'd gone up these stairs Aiden had carried her. He could be carrying her now if she wasn't such an idiot. She could feel those strong arms wrapped around her, the large hands spread across her, supporting her effortlessly. The thought made her annoyingly happy. Why did he have to be so damn amazing?

She went through her evening routine in a daze. When she climbed into her bed the sheets were too cold. It was July, it shouldn't feel cold, but it did. She got up and looked out the window. Aiden's light was on in his bedroom, but the blinds were closed. She laid down again and stretched out in the big, empty space. She remembered how much she hated sleeping alone. It had been so nice to have a large, warm man beside her the last few nights.

As she drifted off, she gripped the pillow, and Aiden's scent filled her head. In her dreams she saw herself in a white satin dress. She had flowers in her hair and River was there, smiling like he always did when he had a surprise for her. She smiled back, excited to see him, and unable to wait another second for him to give her the gift. He kissed her cheek and his smile turned impish.

"Loosen up, little firecracker," he said. "I meant what I told you. We all have to follow our hearts." Then he began to slide away.

"Wait!" Shae cried, trying to yell, but her voice wouldn't work. "Stay, River! Wait!"

Her phone began to buzz its morning alarm and Shae bolted upright in bed. "River!" she sobbed. What a way to start the day.

She slammed her hand across the phone screen, silencing the noise. She felt as though she hadn't slept at all. "Thanks, big brother!" she shouted at the ceiling. "You're suck a fucking asshole. Couldn't resist the urge to taunt me, even from beyond the grave!"

Shae could almost hear River's laughter. Her shoulders slumped and she got ready for work.

"ADVANCED," SHAE SAID, helping Jacob sound out the word. "The knights advanced upon the ancient castle."

"The air was thick with mo... mo..." Jacob read, becoming stuck again.

"Moisture," Shae helped.

"Moisture," Jacob read. "The fog seemed to hem them in from all sides."

"Ms. Mitchell, what does 'hem them in' mean?"

"It means it surrounded them," she explained. "I think it would be terrifying if you were expecting a fire-breathing dragon to leap out at you from the fog at any moment. Raaarrr!" Shae growled, and clawed the air in front of Jacob. He jumped and laughed.

"I like reading with you," the little boy said. "You're funny."

"I like reading with you," Shae said, giving him a hug. "And you're getting so good at it. I'm proud of you."

Jacob smiled and went back to the story. Shae loved watching him bloom. She'd been volunteering to teach children to read at the group home for ten years now. It was the most satisfying thing in her life. Soon Jacob wouldn't need her, and she'd be assigned to a new child. There were always so many. She hoped Jacob would find a loving family soon. He was such a good kid.

Shae had loved reading since she could remember. River was her first student. His parents hadn't read to him or bothered to put him in any kind of school. He loved listening to Shae read, especially fantasy stories. She must have read The Hobbit to him at least one hundred times. Then she'd taught him. He picked things up quickly. He was smarter than anyone Shae had ever met.

"Time for bed, little man," Deja said, stepping over just as Jacob finished the chapter.

"Aw, man!" Jacob complained.

"Don't give me any lip, you," Deja teased him. "It's a school night."

"I know," Jacob groaned, hanging his head.

"Thank you for reading to me," Shae said, unfolding herself from the beanbag chair they'd both been curled in. Her body complained. She couldn't sit in 'bean' furniture anymore. She was too old.

"You're welcome, Ms. Mitchell," Jacob said.

"I'll see you next Thursday, alright? Be good in school," Shae said, hugging him.

"Ok. Bye!" he said, running off toward the bedroom area.

Deja made a huffing, groaning sound, stretching her arm above her head. "I am beat. And hungry."

"Me, too. I didn't sleep very well last night," Shae told her.

Deja got a wicked look in her eye and hustled Shae out the door so fast she barely had time to say goodbye to Mr. Elkers the house manager. As soon as the door had closed behind them, Deja spun around in front of her, blocking her path.

"You are going to tell me all about it," Deja stated. "Has *Dr. Love* been keeping you up all night?"

"You can lose the drool," Shae said, irritated. "He didn't even spend the night last night."

"Then who did?" Deja asked, grinning.

"No one." Deja knew her too well, Shae thought as Deja's smile became a confused frown.

"Come on, this requires pie," Deja said, dragging Shae to the car. She drove to the diner where they'd had dinner every Thursday night since Freshman year. And it always included pie.

"Banana cream, please," Shae told the waitress after she'd finished her grilled veggie panini.

"Blackberry," Deja said. "Thank you." The waitress left and Deja narrowed her eyes at Shae. "You only eat banana cream when it's really bad. What happened? He knock you up?"

Shae burst out laughing. "God no. You're terrible." Shae stopped laughing and looked at Deja. "It's worse."

"What could be worse?" Deja asked.

"I miss him," Shae said miserably.

"Oh, girl," Deja said quietly. "You fell in love with him?"

"What? No!" Shae said incredulously. "Let's just say the rumors about his abilities are true."

Deja made a sound of disbelief through her lips. "But you said you missed *him*, not his disco stick. I'm sorry. I thought you would be immune to anything like this. Just don't hire him again, for goodness' sake."

"It's not like that," Shae said. She hadn't divulged what was going on with Aiden, being so overwhelmed with it all herself. "I never hired him."

"What?" Deja asked, her eyes wide.

"Yeah, funny story, actually. I showed up at the bar and my new neighbor was sitting there."

Deja choked on her pie, spitting a few crumbs onto her plate. She took a long drink of her water, then spoke, "Aiden?"

"The same. Turns out he has a secret identity. Anyway, we ended up spending the last week together, and now..." Shae trailed off.

"Now you really like him. So, what's the problem? Is he out on a date, is that why your face is hanging so low?"

Shae sat up straighter. "I have no idea," she said, eyes wide. "I didn't even consider that he might be working."

"It *is* his job," Deja pointed out.

"We never discussed it. I mean, I broke up with Liam before I went on the first date. I didn't want to feel like I was 'cheating', even though we never made any commitments to each other. Seems like Liam didn't care that much anyway. I haven't heard from him since."

"Fuck Liam," Deja said sourly. "I never liked him. He's a prig. No wonder you fell for the first real man who came your way."

"Liam is not a prig. He's a good man. He does lots of pro bono work for the underprivileged." Shae was surprised she was defending Liam. She didn't think she felt that strongly about him. Maybe she needed to go backpacking deep into the redwoods and sort out her feelings. The large slice of pie she'd just inhaled wasn't helping.

"So, what are you going to do about it?" Deja asked.

"I don't know. He wanted to call me today, and I sort of blew him off. Now I wish I hadn't," Shae moped.

"So, you know where he lives. Go over there and jump him," Deja laughed. "Just knock first. In case he's on the job."

"Very funny," Shae said. Deja's comment stung. The thought of Aiden with another woman sent a burning pain so sharp through her chest she almost sobbed.

"You don't look so good," Deja said, her brows pulling together.

"I think I ate too much pie," Shae fibbed. She knew it wasn't the pie causing the acid in her stomach.

"Liar," Deja said quietly.

"I shouldn't want him," Shae said miserably. "It could never work."

"He probably has commitment issues. Don't take it personally," Deja comforted her, patting her hand.

"You don't understand. He wants me to meet his parents."

A look of understanding crossed Deja's face and she leaned back, judgement flashing in her eyes. "I get it. He's not good enough for you."

Shae cringed away from the accusatory tone in Deja's voice. "We just don't enjoy the same things or have anything in common."

"You know," Deja said, "I have never said this to you because I love you and think you're a wonderful person, but you need to step down. This is just like that time you wouldn't even give my cousin Steven a chance because he didn't have enough college degrees for you. There are more important things, Shae. You pass up all the nice ones chasing after status."

"First of all, Steven is like ten years younger than me," Shae defended herself. "And second, what exactly do you think I'd have in common with a male escort?"

"I don't know, but from everything you've said about Aiden over the last several weeks, I'd say it would be worth finding out."

Shae stared at the table, fidgeting with the edge of her napkin. She and Deja didn't speak when they paid the check, or as Deja drove Shae back to her car.

"You know I'm right," Deja said when they arrived, as Shae stepped out.

"You always are," Shae said, meaning it. "I'll see you tomorrow."

Shae unlocked her car and stepped in. She rested her arms on top of the steering wheel, laying her forehead against them. Sighing, she closed her eyes. Deja honked loudly, making her jump. She waved Deja away and was relieved when she drove off. Shae started her car and drove slowly home.

She was so lost in thought that she was parked in her driveway and getting out before she realized there was another car there. As she pulled herself out of the fog, she realized whose car it was. Before she could react, however, Liam was standing in front of her, his mouth already moving with words that Shae had to struggle to understand.

"Finally," Liam said, stepping too close to her. "I've been waiting here for three hours. I want to talk to you."

Shae fell back a step, widening the distance between them, but Liam only moved closer to her, until she bumped the car behind her. Then his arms were coming around her and he held her tightly.

"Liam, please, come inside," she said, her voice shaking with surprise. He released her and followed her to the door, taking her hand as soon as they were inside.

Leading her to the couch, he pulled her down and forced her to face him. "That wasn't very nice of you, you know," he said. "My whole week has been a mess and my most important case is falling way behind. How could you just dump me and then refuse to take my calls?"

Shae was shocked. Liam looked at her with hurt in his eyes. "I didn't think it mattered to you," she said quietly.

Liam's expression turned to surprise. "How could you think that?"

"I don't know," Shae said, a bit put out. "You never call, I barely see you, and when I do it's a quick shag and you're out the door. You don't take me out, we don't do anything together. We never discussed it, so I assumed I was just convenient for you. It became inconvenient for me recently and I felt that letting you know was the polite thing to do."

Liam dropped her hand and leaned back, blowing out a breath through pursed lips and moved as if to push his fingers through his perfectly combed hair. He seemed to think better of it and dropped his hand.

"Shae, I came back a day early because I couldn't go another minute without you," Liam said earnestly. "You know how important my career is, and I told you I'd be busy for a while, but please know that I thought we were heading somewhere serious."

Liam looked into her eyes, searching. Shae sucked in a breath, her heart racing. She should be happy at his revelations, but all she felt was anxiety. "Liam," she stuttered.

"Don't run away, Shae," Liam said, sensing her hesitation. "Tell me what you need from me."

"I need you to be around," Shae said, thinking only of how lonely she'd been over the past few months; how ignored she'd felt.

Liam sighed. "I will," Liam said. "But I can only do so much. I thought you understood how demanding it is for me right now, trying to make partner. I need a strong woman like you behind me. Sometimes that means being patient. When I make partner, and we're married, things will be easier."

"Married?" Shae gasped. She could feel her face pale.

"Yes, Shae, that's what I'm trying to tell you, but I'm having a surprisingly difficult time for someone in the business of words," Liam struggled. Then his demeanor changed, and a question entered his eyes. "Wait, what did you mean it's been inconvenient for you lately? Is there someone else?"

Liam almost choked on the last word and Shae's chest squeezed. "Yes," she admitted.

"Is it serious?" Liam asked quietly.

"Yes," Shae said automatically. Then, quickly, shaking her head, "No."

"Well, which is it?" Liam asked impatiently.

"No," she decided.

"I see," Liam said, staring at the far wall. Then his eyes shot back to hers, flashing. "Who is it?"

"It's irrelevant," Shae said.

"Of course," Liam agreed. "Please, Shae, can we put this all behind us and agree to be exclusive? You should know, there's never been anyone else for me."

Liam moved closer to her, one arm sliding around her waist to pull her into him. He was so close now, she could feel his breath, smell his cologne. The scent used to entice her. Now it smelled too strong. She pulled back before he could kiss her.

"I'm not sure, Liam. You're a good man," she said gently, sensing his ego was beginning to bruise. "I don't know if I can be that patient. You know how I am."

"Yes, I do," Liam almost growled. She'd never heard him sound so animalistic. "I'll try harder. I'll make time." He pulled her close again.

"Please, Liam," Shae said, wriggling out of his arms.

He released her and straightened his tie. "I want to take you out," he said firmly. "Tomorrow night. I'll clear my schedule and we can spend the night in The City. There's a photography exhibit at the DeYoung I've been wanting to see."

"Yes," Shae said. "The Art of Architecture. I wanted to see that, too."

"Excellent," Liam said, looking hopeful.

"I need to get some sleep, and I'm sure you're tired as well," Shae said, standing and motioning toward the door. Liam's face fell a little.

"Of course. The firm has tickets to an exclusive evening showing tomorrow. Shall I pick you up at seven? I won't have time for dinner before, unfortunately, but there will be passed hors d'oeuvres. They're usually good."

"Seven? I don't know," Shae said, shuffling Liam out the door. She couldn't focus on what he was saying.

"Yes, there are several people I'd like to introduce you to," Liam said as she almost shoved him out.

"I have to think," Shae mumbled.

"Goodnight!" he said as she rebuffed his attempt at a kiss and almost closed the door in his face.

Her mind reeled. Shae was not the kind of woman who liked juggling men. She had closed the door on Liam in her mind and in her heart the minute she'd decided to go out with Dr. Love. But tonight, he'd practically proposed.

Logically he was a perfect match for her, handsome, driven, intelligent. And satisfying in bed. Shae wondered if she'd ever really be satisfied with anyone but Aiden again. She thought of him now and her skin tingled. Desire swept through her, and Deja's advice came back to her.

Shae was out the front door before she could think. She didn't even slip her shoes on; something she realized when her feet hit the sharp bark pieces as she walked across the space to Aiden's door.

With every step she felt lighter, and her smile widened. She wanted his arms around her, his warmth, his love. He had so much love, and he wanted to give it to her. It was more than she deserved. She'd been so closed off to him. Not anymore.

It didn't matter what his job was, as long as they loved each other. And she did love Aiden. "I'm in love with you, Aiden," she whispered, practicing it to herself as she timidly rang the doorbell.

She waited, but there was no answer. His truck was in the driveway, so he should be home. She tried again, moving to the side of the house to see if she could peek in the front window. It was dark, but she heard a muffled voice. She stepped around the side of the house and realized Aiden was on the rooftop terrace speaking to someone.

Shae wondered, with a twinge of jealousy, who he could have up there with him. She couldn't hear another voice and she resolved not to listen in any case. She wasn't going to spy on him. But she couldn't help hearing what he said as she walked back to her yard.

"I crave your mouth, your voice, your hair. Silent and starving, I prowl through the streets.

Bread does not nourish me, dawn disrupts me. I hunt for the liquid measure of your steps.

"I hunger for your sleek laugh and want to eat the sunbeam flaring in your lovely body. I pace around hungry in the twilight, hunting for you, for your hot heart, like a puma in the desert barren."

Aiden laughed low and long, and Shae ran. He'd been quoting Pablo Neruda's famous love sonnet. Pretty accurately if Shae remembered her Freshman English lessons. She hid inside her house as his laughter trailed off. Whoever he had up there must be melting into a puddle now. Shae's heart had raced at the way Aiden's velvet voice wrapped around the alluring language until she realized he wasn't saying it to her.

She wished he were. As she leaned against the door a sharp burning spread from her chest, dropping into her stomach and lodging in her throat. The air felt thick, and her eyes filled with hot liquid.

She couldn't do this anymore today. Sleep. She needed sleep. She ran up the stairs, tearing clothes off as she went, slipping into bed and sleep before the knowledge that Aiden had already moved on lodged too deeply in her heart.

Chapter 15

It was only the third time in her life Shae had called in sick to work, and the only time it had been a lie. She knew she wasn't physically ill, but her chest ached, and she couldn't face the world today.

Aiden spent the day working in his front yard. Shae didn't have a good view of him from inside, but she could hear him out there. He'd finished painting the house. It looked gorgeous. Now he was tearing out the awful crabgrass lawn and planting bushes. Shae wished he would call.

He didn't. He must know she was home since her car was parked in the driveway. But he didn't drop by, didn't text, didn't seem to acknowledge her at all. He must truly have moved on. The thought made the ache throb anew.

Exactly when she'd fallen in love, she couldn't say. And it didn't matter now, anyway. She'd missed her chance. If she'd ever had one. He liked her, that much was obvious. But it couldn't have been love on his side, and that knowledge cut her to the core.

Shae resolved to move on as well. By early evening she'd managed to stop feeling sorry for herself and conceal her puffy, red eyes. She chose a flattering A-line dress and pulled her hair up into an elegant bun. At seven o'clock on the dot her doorbell chimed.

"You look gorgeous," Liam breathed, his eyes widening as he took her in. He leaned in and she let him kiss her cheek.

"Thank you," Shae said demurely. She closed and locked her door, turning to follow Liam down the driveway. Her eyes strayed to Aiden's yard of their own accord and her heart almost stopped.

Aiden stood there leaning on a shovel. His tight t-shirt was smeared with dirt and his large arms glistened with perspiration. Her eyes met his and he lifted one gloved hand in a friendly wave. Shae's breath caught and she looked away as panic gripped her.

"Howdy," she heard Aiden say, along with his approaching footsteps.

"Hello," Liam responded.

"How are you, Shae? Going out?" Aiden asked when she didn't respond.

She had no choice but to meet his eyes now. She searched his expression for something, anything akin to the pain she was feeling, but he gave nothing away.

"Yes," she finally said in response to his question, but she couldn't bring herself to say another word.

"Hi, I'm Aiden," she heard as she dropped her eyes to the ground again. Aiden removed a glove, extending a large hand to Liam. The two men shook briefly.

"Liam Kline, pleased to meet you," Liam said in an overly polite tone.

"The Mercedes must be yours," Aiden said. "Nice car. I was surprised to see it back in the driveway last night. I thought Shae must have gotten rid of it a few weeks ago."

Shae raised her eyes and Aiden's gaze pierced right through her. She didn't miss the accusing tone and cold set of his lips. She cringed back.

"Yes, well, I've been away," Liam said, his hackles up now. "But I'm back."

"I can see that," Aiden said simply. Shae couldn't meet his eyes again.

"There are those who can extrapolate from incomplete data," Liam said, reading Aiden's shirt. Shae glanced up to see Aiden smiling. She looked to Liam and his eyes were hard.

"It's a joke," Aiden said. "You see,-"

"I understand the joke," Liam said shortly. "I just don't find it that amusing."

"You must be the one with the big IQ Shae was telling me about," Aiden said.

Shae's eyebrows raised in question. She had never said anything about Liam or his IQ to Aiden.

"Yes, well, that's a bit of a sore point for her," Liam chuckled. "I tell her four points really isn't that much of a difference, but she's a bit stuck on it, you know."

"Yes, I do," Aiden said quietly. "Well, have a lovely evening." Aiden turned, walking back and picking up his shovel, his back to them as he worked.

"Come along," Liam said, his hand lightly pressing her elbow. He guided her to the passenger door, depositing her inside.

Shae fumed. How dare Liam talk about her as if she weren't standing right there! And he taunted her to boot! Liam slammed his door shut and pulled out of the driveway rather quickly. Shae looked at his face and he didn't look happy.

"That's him, then?" Liam growled. For a moment Shae didn't realize what he was asking.

"What do you-" she began.

"Don't condescend to me, Shae. Never mind. I can see the attraction. It's my own fault, really. I know you are an excessively physical woman and I left you alone for weeks with that neanderthal in such close proximity. It's to be expected, really. At least I know now that I don't have any real competition."

Shae sat with his comments for a few agonizingly quiet minutes. What did he mean, 'excessively physical', and where did he get off calling Aiden a neanderthal? "He's a nice person," Shae said quietly, feeling a strong desire to defend Aiden, but realizing Liam wouldn't care to hear it.

"I'm sure," he said. "Let's not discuss the landscaper any further." Liam reached down to the radio and turned on the classical music station.

Shae hated that station. As much as she longed to belong to the part of society that appreciated art and culture and academic achievement, she'd never been able to enjoy classical music. She preferred the bouncing rhythms and horns of jazz.

"Would you like to go to Tulsa with me next month?" Liam asked after a long stretch of silence.

"On a work trip?" Shae asked.

"Yes."

"You've never offered to take me along before," she said, encouraged. Maybe Liam really meant it when he said he wanted to spend more time together.

"Tulsa isn't the most exotic destination. I didn't think you would care to take time off work to travel to the mundane places I must go. Still, if you think you'd enjoy it, I'd like to have you with me."

"I'll think about it," Shae said. She could guess why he'd suddenly rather have her with him than at home unsupervised.

They both talked about work as they drove and rather than intellectually stimulating, Shae found it boring and mundane. Liam couldn't tell her any of the truly interesting details about his cases, and he didn't seem to find her shop talk engaging, either.

Shae ran out of topics as they sailed over the Golden Gate Bridge. The sun was setting behind a wall of fog that rolled across the bridge. Sailboats glowed below, string lights twinkling from their masts. It would have been beautiful and romantic, Shae thought, if she were here with the right person.

Liam pulled into one of the claustrophobic parking spaces in the museum's underground garage. Shae stepped out and they made their way to the elevator and directly to the museum's lobby. Shae breathed deeply, enjoying the smell of the place. Art had a smell, and she loved it.

"Kline," an older gentleman in a suit called out. Liam led her over, shaking hands with the man. People milled about, drinking cocktails and sampling hors d'oeuvres, and Shae realized she was quite hungry. She tried to catch a server's eye, stepping away as one passed several feet away, but Liam's hand on her arm made her turn back.

"Allow me to introduce Shae Mitchell," Liam said to the other man.

Shae suffered through introductions to several people, catching the word partner here and there. She understood that she was to treat those people to extra attention. At last she was able to procure a crab puff, moaning in delight as the light, creamy bite hit her tongue.

"Shae," Liam hissed in her ear.

"What?" she said, dabbing her mouth with the napkin.

"Must you moan in public?" he said in an exasperated whisper.

"Sorry."

She managed to grab a mini spring roll with some delicious, spicy sauce as Liam hustled her into the gallery. She hadn't even gotten a drink. And now she wanted one. The food was only out in the lobby, but they were passing champagne in here. Shae lifted a flute as the tray passed by and sipped. It was sweet and good.

"Don't get tipsy, please," Liam mumbled. "I might need you later."

Shae rolled her eyes before she could stop herself. No wonder she and Liam had limited their rendezvous to the bedroom. He was an absolute bore outside of it. Liam didn't seem to notice her impertinence, moving on to talk to yet another old man in a suit.

Shae began to peruse the exhibit, which was actually quite extraordinary.

"I apologize," Liam said, appearing at her side. "I have to take a phone call. I'll be in the lobby if you need me. Shouldn't be too long."

Shae nodded, downing the rest of the champagne as he walked away, swapping it for a fresh glass as a tray passed by. She began to enjoy the photographs even more.

"This one is my favorite, though I may be biased," an elegant older woman commented to Shae as she admired a large photograph of an art deco style building.

Shae realized she'd been staring at the picture for at least ten minutes. "I love it," Shae said. "The building in this picture, it's, well, *c'est magnifique.*"

The woman responded with a string of perfect French, causing Shae to smile broadly. She hadn't been able to stretch her lingual muscles in quite a while.

"It's my son's work," the woman was saying in French.

"*Oui?*" Shae responded. "Angela is a very strange name for a son," Shae said, reading the photographer's name on the plate below the frame.

"No, no, no. He was the architect on the building, not the photographer," the woman laughed.

"His work is exquisite," Shae said. "I can't seem to take my eyes away. I'm glad this is one of the larger photos. The detail is beautiful, and I've never seen a building with these particular angles. Forgive me, I don't know the technical terms, but I can see why Angela chose to shoot this."

"I'm glad to hear you say that. I'm not completely biased, then."

"No, no," Shae assured her. "It's truly genius."

"My son *is* a genius, top 0.5% IQ, but I suppose it doesn't necessarily follow that he would produce genius level work. In this case, though, I will agree with you," the woman laughed.

Shae was momentarily put off by the woman casually mentioning her son's genius status. It was like she couldn't get away from that topic tonight. But the woman took her hand then and led her to another photograph. This one of a blocky, almost Seussian building.

"Tell me what you think of this one," the woman said.

"It's awful!" Shae blurted before she could think. Maybe she should slow down on the champagne. "I'm sorry, this one can't be your son's as well?"

"Hah! It is!" the woman laughed. "But don't worry. He hates it. It's the one that broke him. Not much of his original design is left here, so don't judge his talent by this."

Shae and the woman walked through the rest of the exhibit arm in arm as she told Shae all about her son. By the end of the evening Shae knew the story of his entire career. It was so much for someone who must only be in his thirties at most, judging by his mother's smooth skin.

Shae found that she'd told the woman about herself as well, surprised at how easy it was to get along with her. Their conversation flowed, and Shae enjoyed being able to speak without being understood by those around them, as they appeared to be the only French speakers in the room. It gave her a sort of freedom to speak her mind without being afraid of offending anyone with her strong opinions.

"I agree with you again," the woman said. "You and I are very much alike. Wait!" the woman suddenly said, stopping Shae with a hand on her arm. "We haven't even exchanged names!"

Both women began to laugh a little too loudly, turning heads in their direction. They shushed each other and giggled more quietly. "Shae Mitchell," she said, holding out her hand.

"*Madame la Professeure* Rosalind Moore," she said, grasping Shae's hand. "It is a pleasure to know you. At the risk of being too bold, my dear, I wish my son would find someone like you to settle down with. Are you single?"

Shae blushed deeply, her face flaming. "No," Shae said quickly. Mme Moore's son sounded like a dream come true to Shae, but she could barely deal with the two men currently wreaking havoc in her life.

"Oh, that's too bad," Mme Moore said. "Not married, though?" she asked, eyeing Shae's hand.

"No, most decidedly not," Shae said, an unpleasant feeling coming over her as she remembered Liam's almost proposal.

"Gay?" Mme Moore asked.

"No," Shae said, intending to explain further when Liam returned to her side.

"I'm so sorry," he said. "I promise I'm yours the rest of the evening."

"Liam, this is *Madame la Professeure Moore*," Shae said. "We've been touring the exhibit together."

"A pleasure, *Madame*," Liam tried, his accent lacking.

"Ah! And this is my other half," Mme Moore said as a gentleman with a full beard and a tweed suit approached. "James, meet my new friends."

Mme Moore introduced Shae and Liam as her husband smiled kindly at them. There was something familiar about his smile. And his eyes, Shae thought.

"Professor James Love," he said just as Shae had the thought. Suddenly she knew exactly where she'd seen those deep blue eyes before.

"Do you teach English and History, by any chance?" Shae ventured.

"I do," Professor Love confirmed.

"And you must teach French," Shae said to Mme Moore.

"Why yes, although I don't get to teach as much as I like anymore since taking over department head," she answered. "But how did you guess? Did you attend Cal?"

Shae nearly fell over. Aiden had told her his parents were teachers, not professors at the most prestigious university on the West Coast. And department head? Wait! Aiden was the genius son she'd been talking about all evening who volunteered to design villages for devastated communities and had amassed a list of accolades a mile long over his short career?

Shae felt faint. Her head spun and she placed a palm against her forehead. She stumbled back half a step and Liam gripped her arms.

"Are you alright, Shae?" he asked.

"Yes, I think so," she stammered. "I'm suddenly not feeling very well, though. I would like to go home."

"Oh, I do hope you're alright," Mme Moore said. "I would love to stay in touch, if you wouldn't mind. I've just enjoyed our conversation tonight so much."

"I'd like that, too," Shae said weakly. "I'm on all the social media. My middle name is Indigo. I'm easy to find." Shae felt faint again, stepping into Liam for support.

"I really should get her home," he said. "Goodnight."

"Goodnight, and take care," Mme Moore said as Liam guided her out.

"Shae, are you alright?" he asked when they got to the lobby.

"I think so. I'm just hungry, and the champagne. I'm sorry, could you please take me home?"

"Yes, of course. I talked to everyone I needed to meet with tonight already. I'll just cancel the hotel room," Liam said, pulling his phone out as she gripped his arm for support.

Relief flooded through her as she realized she was going home and not to a hotel with Liam. She couldn't imagine spending another night with him, and she was surprised she'd ever thought he was right for her. He was absolutely wrong, and everyone had seen it but her.

Liam finished swiping at his phone as they got to the car. She fell into the seat and closed her eyes, leaning her head back. In a moment they were moving, and Shae kept her eyes closed, hoping Liam wouldn't speak to her until they were closer to home.

"Did you enjoy tonight?" Liam asked. No such luck, Shae thought. Reluctantly she opened her eyes.

"The exhibit was incredible," Shae said. "Did you get to see much of it?"

"Yes, I made one round. I enjoy black and white photography," Liam answered.

Shae wondered when he'd had time to look at anything. He'd been talking to people the entire evening, in person or on the phone. She hadn't seen him stop in front of a single piece long enough to really see it.

"How are you feeling?" Liam asked. "I'm happy to stay the night with you. Although there is a lot of work I could do if you're not feeling up to it. I'll have to work all weekend as it is, with this little diversion tonight."

"Why do you want to be with me?" Shae asked.

"What do you mean?" Liam asked. "I would think that would be obvious. You're intelligent, beautiful, and I think we're a good match." He slid a hand over her knee, and she twisted uncomfortably.

"How are we good together?"

"Well, sexually, obviously," he said, a self-satisfied smirk on his face. "And people like you. You'll be a good wife."

Shae closed her eyes, squeezing them against the tears that wanted to come. Her words from the other night came back to her, when she'd accused Aiden of wanting a good little wife. He'd been appalled. Now Liam told her that was exactly what he wanted, someone to look pretty in front of the partners and suck his cock whenever he deigned to come home.

As they got closer to town, Shae opened her eyes and steeled herself. "Don't spend the night, Liam," she said firmly. "I can't see you anymore. This isn't what I want. It isn't what I *need*. I'm sorry it's taken me so long to figure that out."

Liam turned to her, his mouth hanging open for a second before he turned his eyes back to the road. She saw them narrow and fill with anger. He didn't say a thing.

As they pulled into the cul-de-sac, Shae wondered if Liam was ever going to speak to her again. He slammed the car into park and turned to her.

"I think you're making a mistake," Liam said coldly.

"It's not a mistake," Shae said. "If you really knew me, you would know that. I haven't been honest with you, or myself. I truly hope you'll find someone who wants everything you have to offer, Liam. It's just not me."

Liam looked away; his eyes fixed straight ahead now. Shae wondered fleetingly what he would think of her monthly moon rituals. She opened her door and had one foot on the ground before she turned back. "I'm sorry," she said again.

She left quickly, sensing that there was nothing more to be said or done. Liam was disappointed, she was sure, but in all of his declarations he had never once said he loved her. She knew he didn't, and it was more of a relief than anything.

Shae ran up the stairs, pulling pins out of her hair and shedding the tight-fitting dress. She opened a drawer and pulled out the long, colorful dress she'd bought with her mother at the festival. It seemed like such a long time ago, but it had only been a few months. How much things changed in that time, Shae thought.

She took everything off, pulling the dress over her head and feeling free for the first time in days. She ran back down the stairs, only hesitating a moment at the front door. Aiden might not be home, or he might have company. He might never want to speak to her again, but she was going to take the chance. She didn't think it was true, anyway. She heard the hurt in his voice when he'd spoken to her and Liam. She only regretted that she hadn't run into his arms then, even if he had been covered with dirt at the time.

Aiden's truck was there, but the house was dark. It was almost midnight. He was probably sleeping. With a deep breath, Shae rang the bell anyway. She waited, then pounded on the door. In a moment there was rustling, a dim light came on inside, and the door opened.

Aiden stood there in his underwear, his hair tousled and his eyes sleepy. She *had* woken him. Her heart raced as she took him in. She knew his skin would be warm and soft and she longed to touch him.

"Shae?" he said, registering her standing there. "What's wrong?"

"Nothing's wrong. Can I come in, please?"

"It's midnight," he said, hesitating in the doorway.

"Please, it's important," she said as calmly as she could. Her body hummed and her voice barely obeyed her.

Aiden moved back, opening the door wider to allow her to pass. When she stepped inside, her eyes widened in surprise. He'd finished everything, and the room was now full of beautiful furniture. It was a style she would have picked out if she could have afforded it. She'd had the same living room set since college.

Aiden motioned for her to sit on the couch, and she complied. He sat down on the opposite end, as far from her as possible, leaning back and yawning, his arms stretched over the arm and back of the couch. He looked like an underwear model, Shae thought. It wasn't fair how incredibly gorgeous he was.

"You look different," he commented, waving a finger at her. "Date over already?"

Shae couldn't tell what he was thinking from the tone of his voice. She didn't know whether she wanted him to be upset or not. It was easier if he wasn't angry with her, but that could mean he didn't care, and she didn't want that, either.

"There was no date," Shae started, wanting to clear the air. "Not really. Liam showed up out of the blue last night. I sent him away tonight. I've been so wrong about everything, Aiden."

Aiden sat up, his eyes locking on hers. "You have?" he asked.

"Yes," she said, but then found she didn't know where to start. She was suddenly terrified that Aiden would reject her. Pain shot through her with the thought and her mind went blank. She bit her lip, tears falling from her eyes as she looked at her lap.

"Shae," Aiden said softy, and he moved to her, his hand on her arm. His touch was warm, just as she knew it would be, and pleasure rippled through her.

She took a deep breath and looked up. His dark eyes were fixed on hers and she felt the connection to him that she'd always known was there but had denied for all these months. Yearning broke free from somewhere deep inside and poured out of her. She needed Aiden in a way she'd never needed anyone before. Throwing her arms around his neck, she placed her lips against his.

A spark of fire ignited inside of her, the flame spreading from her chest, into her stomach, and down her legs. Aiden's arms came around her, pulling her into him, his heat adding to the fire that moved to lick her toes and fingertips. But then his hands slid down to her waist, and he pushed her away from him.

"Shae," he said in a strangled whisper.

"You won't believe what happened tonight," she said, trying to hide the pain that his pushing her away caused.

"You mean on your not-date," Aiden said, anger tingeing his words.

"It wasn't a date," Shae insisted.

"Just one last hurrah?" Aiden said bitterly. "Why are you here, Shae? Friends with benefits doesn't extend to midnight booty calls."

"I'm here to tell you I was wrong about that. It was a stupid thing to say. I'm stupid," Shae blurted out. She'd never called herself stupid before but, in this case, she thought it was warranted. It felt strange but liberating. She didn't have to pretend in front of Aiden. She felt like she could tell him anything.

Aiden looked surprised, then like he might laugh. But he didn't say anything.

"I see I'm not going to get any disagreements from you," Shae teased. One corner of Aiden's mouth twitched up. "I met someone at the DeYoung tonight."

Aiden's mouth turned down again. "So, you went on one of those get dressed-up, go to the art gallery, not-dates. I suppose you had a wonderful time, since it wasn't a sports bar."

Shae sighed. "Stop, or I'll kiss you again," she said. She expected he might laugh, or at least smirk, but he did neither. Instead, he looked at her with an intense heat that burned to her core.

She wanted his kiss, his touch so badly her body ached. She could tell he wanted it, too. But he didn't move, his eyes piercing into her, and his mouth set in a firm line.

"I was looking at this piece, something about it drew me in," Shae said, pushing the ache away. "I must have been there for ten minutes when a woman approached me, and we started talking. We spent the next hour chatting, and by the end of the night she'd practically told me everything about her son. She was so proud of him. I have to admit, it was all very interesting. I told her my life story, as well. So, yes, I was having a very good time."

Shae's breath caught in her throat as she met Aiden's eyes again. He watched her impassively, but his nearness was doing things to her, and she had to drop her eyes before she could go on.

"I think we're friends now," Shae said quietly.

"This is all very interesting," Aiden said, "but when you said friends with benefits, I didn't think you meant coming over at midnight for girl talk."

"I told you that was stupid," Shae growled playfully. But she'd had enough of him bringing that up. "I don't want that Aiden. I want you. I'm trying to say I'm falling in love with you."

Shae launched herself onto him, straddling his lap and sinking down until her core was pressed against him. Her mouth was on his before he could say a word. This time he didn't push her away.

Aiden responded with hungry kisses, his mouth devouring hers as if it were the very air he needed to breathe. Shae could barely get a breath in herself as he tightened his arms around her and swelled, hard and hot between her thighs.

"You're not wearing anything under this dress, are you?" Aiden purred against her neck as he nipped at her skin. She felt his tongue on her earlobe and he bit down. "I can feel you."

"Ohh!" Shae cried out as a rough palm skated up her thigh under her skirt, gripping her hip. Aiden held her tightly and pressed against her. She kissed him again, trembling with anticipation.

"Oh, you're hotter than fire," Aiden groaned, moving under her. She swiveled her hips, moving up and down the length of him and he moaned again.

"Do you want me?" Shae asked breathlessly. "I mean, not just for the benefits," she said, pulling back to look into his eyes.

"Shae, I've wanted you since the moment I saw you," Aiden said, but then his expression soured. "You were with him that night, too."

"Please!" Shae said, exasperated. "Can we not talk about Liam anymore! I told you it was over before I even went out with you the first time. You have nothing to be jealous about."

"His car was in your driveway all evening, and then you left with him. What am I supposed to think, Shae? And I can't think at all with you in my lap," Aiden sighed.

"Stop thinking, then," Shae said, pressing her lips to his. But his kiss was half-hearted now.

"Why did you come over now? And why were you telling me about the gallery?" Aiden asked. "What happened to Liam if you spent the whole night with your new friend?"

"Stop thinking about Liam!" Shae said with a huff. "I came here as soon as I could because, like I said, I realized I was being stupid. Liam made me realize how backward I've been, so really, you should be thanking him."

"Yes, I'll be sure to do that," Aiden said sarcastically. Shae placed her hands lightly on either side of his face until he looked into her eyes. She smiled and kissed him softly.

"I'm sorry it took me so long," she said quietly. "I can be stubborn and single-minded."

Aiden blew air out through his lips in a scoffing sound. Shae dropped her hands to his chest, intending to give him a reprimanding tap. Instead, she became momentarily distracted by the rounded muscles under her palms. She stroked him once, her eyes roving over him.

Aiden's hand came down on hers, snapping her back to attention. She raised her eyes to see him looking at her with an impish grin. He was so cocky she just wanted to kiss that smug smile right off his face.

Instead, she tried to climb off his lap. The immediate look of panic in his eyes made her giggle. He held her in place, and she grinned down in triumph.

"I thought my being on your lap was too distracting," she teased.

"It is, but I like having you here nonetheless." He looked up at her, shyly she thought. "Are you really falling in love with me?" he asked.

"I really am," Shae said softly, leaning in for a kiss. "But you still haven't told me how you feel," Shae said, doubt creeping into her. "There are a lot of things you haven't told me."

"What do you mean?" Aiden asked, his fingers in her hair as he dragged her lips back to his.

"Why didn't you tell me about your work? It's beautiful," Shae breathed, shivering as his other hand slid down her back.

"What work?" Aiden whispered against her collarbone.

"Two of the photos in the exhibit tonight were of your buildings," Shae gasped. "Your mother told me all about them."

Aiden stopped, his hands dropping from her body. "My mother?!" he said harshly.

"Yes. My new friend. I didn't know until we'd talked for a couple of hours. When your father introduced himself, I made the connection. You look so much like him," Shae said, still surprised at how strong the resemblance was.

Aiden seemed to blanche, but it could have been a trick of the pale light coming from the little table lamp. Shae couldn't be sure, and his expression had changed to something completely unreadable.

"So," Aiden said slowly, "you came straight over here after meeting my mother and learning all the wonderful things about me?"

His words were cold, and Shae was unsure of how to respond. "Yes, I suppose so, but Aiden-"

"So, she must have mentioned my Pritzker, my Aga Khan, and my Progressive Architecture awards," Aiden said.

"Yes, but-"

"And of course, she told you I was the youngest professor ever to be offered tenure in a UC," he said accusingly.

"She did, but-"

"And how could my dear mother ever have a conversation about me without mentioning her crowning glory, her golden child, her greatest accomplishment, the son with the genius IQ, Mensa member extraordinaire? And when she was done with all that, she told you how I've fallen woefully from grace, giving it all up to swing a hammer in obscurity."

With every sentence Aiden's voice became louder, his tone more defensive. He lifted Shae off his lap, setting her gently on the couch beside him. He stood and paced, his back to her, his hand in his hair.

"She didn't say anything about swinging a hammer," Shae said quietly. "She told me about your volunteer work."

"Oh, well, you missed out on the whole epic saga, then," Aiden said, his back still turned.

"Are you angry?" Shae asked, bewildered by his reaction.

"I'm not angry, Shae," he said, turning to face her. She almost gasped when she saw the pain in his eyes. "Just disappointed."

"I don't understand, Aiden," Shae said, standing and walking to his side. He turned away from her again.

Aiden's voice was quiet as he spoke, and he kept his eyes averted. "I thought you finally saw me, Shae. I thought you were finally giving me a chance, giving us a chance. I thought you felt as much for me as I feel for you. But I see I was wrong."

Shae reached out her hand and placed it on his shoulder. "You're not wrong," she said fervently. "I meant what I said. I got past the fact that you're a construction worker and the whole escort thing. I fell for you anyway."

"I don't want you to have to look past it, Shae," he said, looking her in the eye now. "That's who I am. If you can't see that, if you only want me because of my degrees and titles, then I can't be a part of this."

"Aiden," Shae cried. "I'm doing this all wrong." She wrung her hands, trying to find the right words.

"Please go," Aiden said quietly.

"Go?" Shae croaked, her voice small and fragile.

"Go home," he said as if he were exhausted.

"I don't want to go home, Aiden," Shae said more firmly. "Why are you being this way?"

"My mother has praised me my entire life, Shae," he said, sounding angry again. "From my first memories she was always telling me how much better I was than the other children; how much smarter I was, how much more talented. Every achievement I made was her achievement, too."

"But isn't that what a mother is supposed to do?" Shae asked, trying to soothe whatever was causing him to turn away from her again. "Your mother is such a lovely person. And she loves you very much. That much was obvious from the way she talks about you. I wish my mother would be as proud of me."

"You have no idea what you're talking about," Aiden said darkly. "Your parents support your dreams, even if they don't agree with them. My mother never misses a chance to tell me how much I'm wasting my life since I've veered from the path she set me on."

"Hah!" Shae scoffed. "My parents have never once praised me for my accomplishments! You heard them at dinner: *Shae needs to loosen up, Shae's academic achievements are used as a way to mock the establishment.* I had nothing, Aiden! Nothing! The only person who ever supported my dreams was River, and even he left me in the end!"

She saw Aiden soften, a little widening of his eyes, but then the hardness was back. "You have everything, Shae! Your parents are incredible, and they love you to no end!"

"So do yours!" she retorted.

They stood silently for a moment, glaring daggers at each other. Shae couldn't figure out where everything went wrong. She only knew she was hurting worse than she'd ever hurt before. Aiden didn't understand. Maybe he didn't care about what was important to her after all.

"Fine, I'll go," Shae said through the tears that were starting. "I don't know why I ever believed you. You're good at your other job, too, *Dr. Love*. Oh my god, that's your real name! *Dr. Love* is a world-class seducer. You made me fall for you, Aiden. You! Before I even knew anything your mother told me.

"I came over last night," Shae continued through the tears that now fell freely down her face. "I heard you reciting love poetry to whomever you had on the roof. I wished so badly that you could have been saying those words to me! And even after I heard that- stupid, stupid girl that I am- I came back tonight. Hoping that it was only a job; that I was the one you really wanted..." A sob broke from her chest, and she turned and ran out the door.

Aiden didn't say a word. He didn't try to stop her. She wished she didn't want him to. She wished that the scene of him chasing after her, begging her forgiveness and taking her in his arms, wouldn't play in her head over and over again as she ran home and hid under the covers.

The extra pillow in her bed smelled like Aiden and the scent may as well have been a knife through her heart. She pulled it to her chest, inhaling deeply, letting herself believe for half a second that he was there, next to her, in love with her.

But that wasn't real life. Real life kicked you in the teeth and when you tried to stand back up, it cut you off at the knees. For the second time in her life, she felt as though she might die from a broken heart. She punched the pillow, then pinched herself.

Aiden wasn't dead. He hadn't left her so completely, so irrevocably as River had. She was being melodramatic. Since when did she need a man to validate her existence? She would find joy in all the things she had before Aiden James Love had walked into her life.

That was what she told herself as she fell asleep. When she woke in the morning, she saw it for the lie it was. She could never go back to the way things were again.

Chapter 16

Laughter drifted in through the open window, permeating Aiden's dreams and pulling him into consciousness. With a growl he rolled out of bed, stumbling over to the window and slamming it shut.

"Why are those kids out so damn early?!" he shouted to the empty room. He fell back on the bed, stabbing at his phone until it displayed the time.

Ten o'clock! He knew he'd slept in but hadn't thought it could possibly be after seven. Shae had really messed with his head.

Sleep had not come again for Aiden until the sky began to lighten with the coming dawn. He'd cried. It had surprised him. He couldn't remember the last time he'd cried. Then it came to him. It was in his office after his mother had told him about Papa's death.

Aiden decided crying alone was terrible and he wasn't going to do it anymore. He walked into his shower and turned the hot water up. He wasn't crying if he couldn't feel the tears.

After showering he put on a pair of shorts and made his way downstairs. Halfway down he smelled the coffee. He groaned. It was going to be burnt and awful. He'd set it for five a.m.

In the kitchen he turned off the pot and poured the coffee down the drain. He didn't want it today. He didn't have the energy to work, though he had a list to get done. The house was almost ready to go on the market, and after last night that couldn't happen fast enough.

Living next door to Shae would be pure torture. He wanted her. He wanted her so badly it felt like every cell in his body was being pulled toward her. But she'd lied to him.

She may not have thought of it as a lie, but it was just the same. How else did you explain the fact that she left with Liam, but came running back to him the minute she heard he was the better deal? And all that stuff about falling in love with him, well, that was the lie. She was even fooling herself.

And he couldn't even trust his own mind on this matter. From the moment he'd first set eyes on her, he was drawn to her. He remembered exactly what she'd looked like that night as she flew into Liam's arms. The image of her long, chestnut hair flowing over the rounded tops of her breasts in that lacy blue bra was burned into his memory. He'd been jealous that night; wishing, no, *hoping*, that she would come to him like she did to that jerk in the suit.

Since that night he'd been bordering on obsessed with her, but she seemed to actively avoid him. She never wanted him. He had been blind to her disdain because of his overpowering attraction to her. But now his eyes were fully opened.

Aiden closed all the windows and blinds. He didn't want to take the chance of seeing her. He had to leave at five for the faculty dinner. He only had to hide out for a few hours. He set his laptop on the coffee table and spent the next several hours watching old television.

By late afternoon he felt like a zombie. Methodically he tied his bowtie and twisted his cufflinks into place. He wasn't a big fan of French cuffs; he found them too fussy. But he did enjoy playing with the little cufflinks. They were like game pieces, and he liked the fiddly bits in board games.

His throat closed up and he dropped his hands to the dresser. He pressed his palms flat against the surface as he tried not to cry again. He remembered Shae showing him her game room, and how impressed and excited he'd been to challenge her to a match. She was almost the perfect woman.

Almost.

Anger burned through him. He shouldn't love her, not this strongly and deeply. He thought her heart was pure and kind, the love she was capable of shining through every time she spoke about her brother. But her heart was cold and calculating, after all. She loved numbers, and he just happened to have some of her favorite ones. You couldn't build a relationship on such superficial nonsense. She didn't love him for who he really was.

He'd tried to show her. He'd tried to give her his true self, the important things, the things that mattered. Hadn't he? Doubt crept into his mind. He *had* held some things back. At the time he thought it was to protect himself, to be sure she wouldn't be lured in by his awards or anything else his mother might have trotted out.

Had he been *too* guarded? It struck him now that he had absolutely no qualms telling people about his escort gig, something many people found shameful. But wasn't his work as an architect just as much a part of who he was? The irony of the fact that he went to great pains to hide that part of his life was not lost on him.

He hadn't hidden it from Shae, though. She simply hadn't asked the right questions. He'd shown her his office and she made assumptions. That should have sent him running had he thought about it. She was incredibly intelligent. When he'd shown her his workspace, had she not been completely blinded by her own prejudices, she would have seen who he was.

Yes, he had given her every opportunity to see him, and she'd still needed more. She'd needed something she could brag about, just like his mother. And now he had to go spend an entire evening pretending to be the man they both wanted. He gritted his teeth as he walked out the door.

He opened the truck door and hung his tuxedo jacket on the hook behind the seat so it wouldn't wrinkle on the drive. If he was lucky the drive would take an hour. If there was traffic it could be longer. He pulled at the French cuffs, adjusting them before sliding behind the wheel. He put on a podcast to distract his mind. He'd rather not think tonight.

"*Coucou mon fils chéri!*" his mother greeted him as she spotted him making his way to their table.

"*Bonjour, Maman,*" Aiden responded, kissing her cheek. She beamed up at him and he felt himself smile back, despite his annoyance.

"How have you been, son?" his father said, standing and embracing him. Aiden froze for a moment, unused to the physical gesture. It wasn't that the man never hugged him, it just wasn't his typical greeting.

"I've been well," Aiden answered. His attention was diverted to the six other people at the table as he said his hellos to the familiar faces. It seemed he'd been seated with four married couples. Typically, he was at the singles table at these events. A pain shot through him, particularly when he saw the unoccupied seat next to him. However, he was soon relieved when he realized there would be no pressure to flirt or be flirted with.

He poured himself a glass of wine and lifted it to his lips, preparing dialogues in his head for each person he was likely to speak with tonight. But before he could get too comfortable, his mother's face lit up with a grin, and she tapped his arm.

"Here she comes now," she said, looking over Aiden's shoulder.

Aiden set the glass down and turned in his seat. He immediately turned back, shooting daggers at his mother.

"Well, stand up!" she whispered to him.

Aiden stood, turning again to face the last person he wanted to see tonight. He pasted a false smile on his face. "Hestia, what a surprise to see you here," he said, kissing her cheek as she reached the table.

"Hello, Aiden," she said in her chipper voice.

"A surprise?" *Maman* asked, perplexed.

"Oh, yes," Hestia jumped in. "It's true, Aiden didn't know I was going to come tonight."

"Ah," *Maman* said. "That must be why he texted me and told me you weren't going to make it. Well, I'm so very glad you did after all. And I made sure to special order the vegetarian meals for both of you."

Aiden was lost. What in the world was Hestia doing sitting next to him? And why did his mother seem to know more about it than he did?

"Vegetarian?" Hestia asked.

"Oh!" *Maman* said, looking sheepish. "Aiden said you would prefer that. Aiden, are you trying to convert another person? He thinks everyone should go vegetarian."

"It's better for the planet," he said, irritated by her mocking tone. "And I wasn't talking about Hes-"

"Oh, of course," Hestia jumped in. "He's so adorable, always thinking about those things."

"Hestia," he said quietly to her, "can I speak with you, please?"

"Not now, honey, the salad is here," Hestia answered brightly. Servers surrounded their table and salads were set in front of them. Hestia began chatting with the woman on her other side and Aiden turned to his mother.

"*Maman, qu'est-ce qui se passe ici?*" he demanded.

"We shouldn't speak French at the table," his mother said to his surprise. "No one else here is fluent. And aren't you happy that Hestia was able to make it tonight? You've been seeing each other for a while now. Things must be getting somewhat serious."

Aiden sat back in surprise. "Why would you think that?" he asked.

"You sounded so happy when you told me about her the other day," his mother said joyfully. "It was wonderful to hear you talk about having a real relationship. I just don't understand why you haven't introduced us! Of course, we've known Hestia for years, but you could have brought her to dinner."

"You've known her for years?" Aiden had no idea where to start with this.

"Yes, through her father. Fred, not Edgar. He's an adjunct in the history department. They're right over there," his mother said, waving. Aiden looked up and two men met his eye, giving them a wave back. He couldn't be sure, but their expressions, though smiling, appeared somewhat less than friendly.

"We'll all go over and catch up after dinner," *Maman* went on.

Aiden was unable to tear Hestia away from the table all through dinner. She seemed to either be deep in fascinating conversation or enjoying her food too much to be interrupted. She flirted with him shamelessly, at one point sliding her hand up his thigh under the table. He quickly removed it, excusing himself to the restroom.

"Come to the dessert bar with me, Hestia," he said as the dinner plates were cleared.

"I don't need a dessert, thank you," she said demurely, trying to turn away from him again.

"Wouldn't you like a coffee?" he asked, standing and taking her hand. But his escape was blocked by Fred and Edgar who now stood behind him.

"Fred, how nice to see you," Maman said as the men approached. "And how have you been, Edgar?"

"*Bon soir*, Rosalind," Fred said, kissing her hand. Edgar leaned in for a kiss on her cheek. They said their hellos around the table and Hestia stood by Aiden's side.

"Dads, this is Aiden Love," she finally said.

"Pleasure," they mumbled, shaking hands.

Aiden couldn't take this any longer. "Hestia and I were just about to get some fresh air. If you will all please excuse us," he said abruptly, taking her hand and dragging her outside before she could object again.

She was so small, he felt like he was towing a reluctant child. Outside he kept walking until they were at a far enough distance from the building that he was sure they wouldn't be interrupted. He dropped her hand and crossed his arms in front of his chest, staring down at her expectantly.

"Isn't it a lovely night?" Hestia asked, nervously looking at the sky.

"I have no idea," Aiden said. "Can you please explain to me why my mother believes you and I are dating? Why are you here, Hestia?"

"I work in the H.R. department," Hestia said. "I'm on the party planning committee. I come every year."

Aiden's gaze didn't waiver, pinning her in place until she answered the rest of his question.

"I didn't tell her that, if that's what you think. I told her we'd gone out once. She assumed the rest and I didn't correct her, that's all," Hestia said defensively. Then her face softened, and she smiled up at him. "We could go out on a date," she said, running a hand up his arm.

Aiden dropped his arms, stepping back from her touch. She looked momentarily discomfited, but then her face set with determination.

"I had fun with you. And it seemed like you enjoyed yourself," she said with a hint of bitterness. "I think we should do it again.

Tonight's a lovely night. There's champagne, dancing..." She moved closer, running her small hands up his chest. Her arms barely reached around his neck as she tilted her chin to him in clear invitation.

"Hestia," he sighed, taking her hands, and placing them at her sides.

"If you won't go on a real date with me," she said, "then I want to hire you again. Right now. You're here alone."

Aiden winced as a sharp pain hit him in the chest. He was alone, so alone. "I must decline," he said softly.

Hestia's face fell and her lip trembled. "Why?" she asked, her voice squeaking.

"I am no longer pursuing that line of employment. In fact, I haven't been for some time now. Please, don't take it personally," he said gently.

"How can I not take it personally, Aiden?" Hestia said angrily.

"I have to apologize," Aiden said, feeling guilty. "I never meant to lead you on. I thought we were both just blowing off some steam that night. I mean, you practically threw me out."

Hestia looked guilty now, her eyes darting to the side. "I did, you're right. And you don't owe me an apology. I thought I was just 'blowing off steam', as you put it, too. I saw your mother the next day and mentioned that we'd met at the Mensa meeting, and she started gushing about you. The more she talked, the more I realized I liked you, and then I heard you weren't taking jobs and I hoped it was because of me..."

"What do you like about me, Hestia?" Aiden asked.

Hestia laughed incredulously. "What's not to like? You're smart, and handsome, and successful. Not to mention great in bed."

"Is that all you're looking for?" Aiden asked. "Is that all every woman is looking for?"

"What else is there?" Hestia asked.

"Everything," Aiden mumbled.

"I can't speak for all women," Hestia said contemplatively, "but you always hear things like sense of humor and sensitivity. I think people are just pretending when they say they're looking for those qualities. I don't personally want a man acting goofy all the time, or too emotional."

Aiden's mind was tangled with thoughts. He couldn't follow any of the threads. As soon as he'd grab onto one thought, another would cross his mind, diverting him down a different path. He'd never felt so mixed up in his life.

"Aiden?" Hestia prodded.

He pulled himself out of his head. "I don't think I'm the kind of man you're looking for, then," he said.

Hestia looked surprised. "No?"

"Terrible jokes are sort of my calling card, especially puns," Aiden laughed.

"Oh," Hestia said. "I loathe puns."

"You don't think they're very punny?" he smirked. Hestia frowned at him.

"Maybe you're right," Hestia conceded.

"Are we good here?" Aiden asked.

"Yes," Hestia sighed. "Quite disappointing, though. Your mother didn't mention anything about your sense of humor."

No, she wouldn't have, Aiden thought. "Shall we rejoin the party?" Aiden asked. "*Maman* will be quite put out if I don't make the rounds with her."

"Sure," Hestia said.

Aiden escorted her inside where she joined her parents and some others and was immediately deep in conversation. Aiden realized she almost never stopped talking, her high, squeaky voice carrying across the room. He thought of the comfortable silences he shared with Shae. And when she did speak, her voice was calm and soothing to him.

He stopped and checked himself. He shouldn't be thinking of her. He made his way over to say hello to some friends. It wasn't long before his mother found him, a group of friends surrounding her.

"Here is my son," she announced. Aiden fought the urge to roll his eyes.

"And here is my beautiful mother," he said, hugging her.

"Aw," she said. "You see! Didn't I tell you how sweet he is? Aiden, I've just been telling them about your work. I thought you might have some pictures on your phone? Everyone is curious to see. I told them Dad and I haven't seen it yet, so I couldn't tell them much about it."

"I don't have any pictures of the Haiti project," Aiden began.

"Oh, no, no," his mother said. "I mean your house. We all can't wait to see this one. The others were all so beautiful."

For a moment Aiden's jaw dropped. He quickly closed his mouth and pulled his phone from his pocket. He'd taken pictures for the real estate listing. He pulled them up and passed his phone around.

"And he does this all himself," his mother said, the usual proud tone in her voice.

"*Maman*," he whispered as the others poured over his photos, "I thought you weren't interested in my projects."

"Oh, don't act so surprised," she laughed. "I'm interested in everything you do. I had a most eye-opening conversation last night, though, and it started me thinking. I don't give you enough credit."

Aiden laughed so loudly heads turned in his direction. "I don't think that's ever been true," he said more quietly.

"Well, you're probably right about that," she laughed. "At any rate, I realized that I've been too focused on what I want for you, and not enough on what you want for yourself. So, from now on I want to know all about your work. Well, not the *other* work, feel free to keep that to yourself."

Aiden laughed again. He grabbed his mother in a hug, startling her. "That means a lot to me," he said quietly.

"Oh, well, you mean a lot to me," she said.

"And just so you know, I am no longer providing those *other* services," Aiden said. It was strange to be talking about this with his mother. They'd never been so open about it.

"Oh thank goodness," his mother said, stringing the words together in one long exhale. "Hestia has captured your heart, then?"

"No, not Hestia," he said. "She and I only went out the one time. We've realized we're not right for each other."

"But there's someone?" his mother asked with surprise.

"There was. I don't know if it's going to work out," he said, the pain stabbing through his chest anew.

"Oh, I'm sorry, honey. Well, I met the loveliest woman last night, and like I said, some things she said really made me stop and look inside myself, you know? I think you would like her. Maybe I'll introduce you. She was with a date, but I don't think she'll be with him for long. There was nothing between them, I could tell."

His mother stopped talking to take a sip of her drink. Aiden was on the edge of his seat. He started to ask her to continue but was interrupted when his phone was handed back to him. People were suddenly full of questions, which he politely answered for what seemed an interminably long time.

"*Maman*, what did you tell Sh-, I mean, the woman you met last night? What did you talk about exactly? This is important," he said when he was finally able to get his mother alone.

"Well, I talked about you, mostly, of course. She was admiring a picture of the Algoro building for a very long time. I noticed and couldn't resist telling her it was yours. She said something in French and the two of us just couldn't stop after that. Come to think of it, she talked a lot more than I did, really. I didn't get to tell her all the wonderful things about you. I never even told her your name!"

"She said the building was a work of genius, or something to that effect, and I told her you were a genius, and about all your awards. She was duly impressed, but then she started to tell me about a friend she'd met recently, and how he'd made her realize that we all have to follow our hearts, and maybe my son, meaning you, was just following his heart. The way she explained it, I just, I don't know. It struck me."

Aiden nearly fell to his knees. Shae hadn't been lying; to him or to herself. She'd tried to explain it to him, but he hadn't listened. He'd been the judgmental one, not her. The sharp pain in his chest became an agonizing ache to be with her. It would have been pure joy if he was sure she would welcome him back with open arms.

There was absolutely no guarantee that she would. She'd heard him reciting a particularly sensual poem to someone on his roof, and he hadn't denied or explained it. Would she believe him when he told her he was talking to his friend, Gabe, an even bigger and burlier construction worker than himself? Would she laugh or would she toss him out on his obviously deceitful ear?

"Aiden, are you alright?" his mother asked.

Shaking his head, he focused his eyes. He had to go. "*Je suis désolé, mais je dois y aller*," he said. "Please say my goodbyes, *Maman*!"

Aiden ran all the way to the parking lot. He tore his bowtie off as he ran, stuffing it in the pocket of his tux and then stripping the jacket off as well. He threw it on the front seat and tore out of the parking lot. Every stop sign caused him to curse until he was finally off campus.

He had an hour on the road. He spent the time going over everything Shae had ever said to him. She laughed at his jokes; really laughed. She inhaled his cooking. She got turned on when he did the dishes.

She saw his heart. She'd said it. She'd told him he reminded her of River because of his heart. How could he have been so blind? She was telling him she loved him in so many words. She probably just didn't realize it herself. But he should have.

They had both let their prejudices and chipped shoulders get in the way of something that would make them boundlessly happy. He couldn't believe he'd been so stupid for someone who was supposed to be smart.

He owed *Maman* an apology, too. He saw her through Shae's eyes, and realized how much his mother loved him. She may have been more vocal about it than he would have liked, but her support had allowed him to get where he was today. And now he was in Shae's driveway.

His heart sank when he saw her car wasn't there. He jumped out and pounded on the door anyway. He laughed as he remembered the first time he'd pounded on this door and how she'd dragged him inside. It had been like a fantasy coming true. She was so beautiful that day; all hot and flushed from standing over the boiling jam pots. The memory had him sweating.

He pounded again, but the house remained dark and silent. He pulled out his phone and called her. "Pick up, pick up, pick up," he chanted quietly. Straight to voicemail.

"Damn!" he yelled as her soft voice directed him to leave a message. "Shae, please call me as soon as you get this. We need to talk. I really screwed up. Please call me."

He ended the call and typed out a text. He couldn't sit still and wait. He needed to act. He thought about places she might go. The only place he could think of was her parents' house. He wasn't sure he could remember the way there. And it was late. They went to bed early. But if she was there, they might still be up.

He was in his truck driving West on the highway before he could think. He knew the general area, but Shae had been driving last time and he hadn't paid close attention from the back seat. Plus, it was dark and things weren't generally marked out in the county. He didn't even remember a street sign.

He took the exit he remembered and then just hoped. He kept his eyes wide, scanning the darkness for something familiar. He took a few roads that ended up being wrong before he found one that looked vaguely familiar. Yes! He'd definitely seen this road before.

He drove on, beginning to worry after a few minutes that he'd gone too far. But luck seemed to be on his side as he spotted an oak tree that had toppled over at some point and grown sideways along the ground instead of up. He'd remarked upon it before.

A few more minutes and he'd located the dark driveway. He pulled in cautiously at first, hoping this was it and he wasn't going to be attacked by guard dogs. People didn't like you rolling up on their property in the middle of the night on the farms out here.

The house looked dark, but as Aiden killed his engine a light came on inside. He stepped out and walked boldly up to the door. He was going to do this despite his heart wanting to leap from his chest. Before he got to the door, Veronica stepped out, a big smile on her face. His shoulders dropped in relief.

"I thought we'd be hearing from you tonight," she said, stepping up to give him one of her hugs. "What took you so long? We were just about to go to bed."

"I'm sorry it's so late," Aiden said over her shoulder as she continued to squeeze him. "Is Shae here?"

"She was here, but she's gone now. She was very upset, Aiden," Veronica said almost accusingly. "I've never seen her aura so black."

Aiden wanted to cry again. "I'm sorry again," he said. "I never wanted to hurt her. I'm trying to make it right. Where can I find her?"

"I know," Veronica said soothingly. "Don't worry. It'll all work out. I already saw it on your palm." Veronica winked at him and dragged him toward the door.

"I just want to go tell her I'm sorry," Aiden said, resisting her attempts to move him.

"You're not going to find her tonight," Veronica said. "Come inside and have some tea and tell us what happened. Shae wouldn't reveal anything, but she couldn't hide her feelings from me. You broke her heart, young man."

Aiden went weak at her revelation and let her drag him inside. Vern already had the kettle on and was setting three cups on the table. He looked up as Aiden was dragged in.

"Well, there you are!" he said. "Mint or chamomile?"

"It is very kind of you to offer, but neither, thank you. I would really just like to talk to Shae," Aiden said, struggling to steady his voice.

"She's gone up to Armstrong Woods on a spiritual retreat," Veronica said. "She came over this afternoon to borrow some camping gear. She's deep in the woods by now. So why don't you sit down and have some tea." She patted a chair and Aiden sat, resigning himself to the tea.

"Mint, please," he said to Vern. "Do you know which campground?"

"She said she was going to take the East Ridge Trail. That one goes about nine miles straight up the mountain. Near Bullfrog Pond," Vern said. "She won't be on the trail, though, or in a campground. She went out to find herself. She'll be as far from people as possible, especially since she's camping with black Matilda."

"What?" Veronica yelled, jumping up from the table.

Aiden jumped at her sudden movement and the startled expression on her face. Until this moment he had been sure

Veronica's mood never moved above mellow. "Who is Black Matilda?" he asked.

"You gave our daughter peyote and sent her out into the forest?! How could you, Vern!" Veronica was shouting. "She has no idea what she's doing!"

"She asked and I thought it was about time she had an awakening," Vern said defensively. "I only gave her a little. She's probably in her tent laughing right now."

"What if she's walking off a cliff, instead! You never go on your first trip alone, you know that!" Veronica said, wringing her hands.

"Tell me exactly where she went," Aiden said, standing from the table. "I've been there plenty of times. I'll find her."

"Oh," Veronica moaned. Her distress was making Aiden extremely worried. He felt like he was going to jump out of his skin.

"I'll show you," Vern said quietly. He looked a little crestfallen and Aiden began to worry even more.

Vern had some old trail maps and one ancient headlamp that he thrust into Aiden's hands. He showed him on the map the most likely destinations to spiritually find oneself. Aiden folded the map and headed for the front door.

"Wait!" Veronica said. "Give us your hands."

She and Vern each took one of Aiden's hands and Veronica closed her eyes. She began mumbling something, her eyebrows drawn together, causing a deep crease in her forehead. When she opened her eyes, she looked peaceful.

"It'll be alright," she said decisively. "River is watching over her. But please go, Aiden. There's only so much he can do for her."

"I'm gone," Aiden said, jumping for the door.

"River will help you," Veronica called out as he opened the door. He nodded once and closed the door behind himself.

Aiden wasn't sure he believed in ghosts guiding you from beyond the grave, but one thing he was sure of was that River would be watching over Shae if there were any way he could. He hoped that would extend to helping him find her.

He headed for the redwood forest. Thirty minutes to get there. Thirty minutes of torture while he worried about her. He told himself she was fine. She was smart enough to take care of herself, even if she was under the influence of psychotropic drugs.

The woods were dark as he pulled in, the park closed up for the night. As he drove through the towering redwoods, one lonely light on the ranger's station was the only artificial illumination. But there were stars galore. It was an unusually clear night, the marine layer that typically settled along the coast conspicuously absent.

As his truck climbed the hill toward Bullfrog Pond, Aiden was acutely aware of the futility of this mission. Trying to find someone in the dark in eight hundred acres of forest was ludicrous. He didn't even know how to begin. But he knew he had to be with her, and he couldn't wait until she decided to come out of the woods.

Yet finding her was almost as frightening a thought as not. Best case scenario she was having a good trip on the peyote and wouldn't mind him being there, seeing her through it. Worst case... No, he wouldn't even let his mind go there. He clenched his jaw, more determined to find her than before.

The parking lot at Bullfrog Pond had exactly one car in it, a little hybrid that had relief spiraling through him as soon as he spotted it. He at least had a jumping off point now. He parked next to her car and strapped the headlamp on.

Cold air hit him when he stepped out of the truck. It was freezing. He reached back in and grabbed his tuxedo jacket, laughing at the absurdity of it all. Nothing like a midnight hike in a tuxedo. Maybe he would start doing this more often.

He walked the perimeter of the parking lot, locating the trailheads and the campground. As quietly as he could, he walked through the campsites. All empty. Vern had said she wouldn't be in the campground, but frustration still rolled off him in waves. Why couldn't she have gone for a spa weekend like a normal woman?

He smiled as he answered his own question. Because Shae wasn't a normal woman- far from it. She was the most extraordinary woman he'd ever met, and of course she would be up on a mountaintop going on a spiritual journey. For as much as she eschewed her alternative upbringing, deep down she embraced it.

Aiden loved that about her. He loved her stodgy, button-down, throwback to the fifties facade that barely concealed the wild woman beneath. He'd been attracted to her cutie-pie look, but he'd fallen in love with her untamed and impassioned soul.

He chose a trail; the one Vern had said went deepest into the woods. Going slowly, he swung his head from side to side to see if she'd gone off trail. Unlikely, as that could be damaging to the forest, and he was reasonably certain Shae would be mindful of that. But he looked anyway, unsure what her state of mind was when she got here.

Veronica said he'd broken her heart. The pain he'd been feeling, as wretched as it was, had been brought on by himself alone. He'd chosen to walk away from her. Shae had come to him, offered her heart to him, and he'd told her to go. He imagined her saying the same to him now, and his chest felt like it would split apart and tear him in two.

A rustling sound caught his attention and he stopped in the middle of the trail. Holding his breath, he listened, hoping he wasn't about to run into any large wildlife. Another rustling, but it didn't sound like underbrush. It sounded like nylon fabric, followed by a low muttering. Aiden removed his headlamp so he wouldn't blind whoever was coming around the bend ahead.

His heart nearly stopped and then skipped with joy when he saw her. Shae was marching down the trail, a large bundle held awkwardly in her arms. She was grousing quietly to herself. Aiden couldn't see her expression, but he guessed it would be adorably annoyed from the sounds she was making, and the picture in his head made him grin like a fool.

She froze when she finally saw him standing there. He was so happy to see her that he ran toward her, covering the twenty yards between them in a few seconds. Shae dropped her bundle and when he reached her, he realized his mistake. She stepped back into a slight crouch and the knife in her hand glinted in the beam of his headlamp.

"Shae!"

Chapter 17

This camping trip had been a bad idea from the start, Shae thought as she pulled off her wet thermal and pulled her only dry shirt from her backpack. She changed quickly in the wet tent, the thin walls barely keeping her warmer than the outside. At least the wind wasn't biting into her.

She exited the tent and collapsed it. She didn't bother rolling it up or putting it away. It was soaked and she'd have to set it out on her deck to dry when she got home anyway. She bundled it into her arms and started back down the trail to her car.

She'd hiked all day. Her body was exhausted, and she would be sore tomorrow, but it was doing nothing to dull the pain she was feeling in her heart. She'd hoped to be sleeping by now, or at least having an out of body experience. She'd like to be out of this body, this life, for at least a little while. But nothing was going right lately, and this failed attempt to look deeper into herself was no exception.

At first the fresh air and dark forest floor had been a nice change of scenery, diverting her mind from the constant need she felt to be near Aiden. She'd fallen into a relaxing pace, concentrating on the rhythm of her footfalls on the spongy ground. By early evening she'd reached her destination: the furthest, most remote rustic campground in this forest. She hadn't seen another hiker for hours, and that was the way she wanted it.

She set up camp and stretched out on the ground to eat a granola bar that her mother had shoved into her hand as she left the house.

She watched the sky turn from brilliant blue to pink, then scarlet. It was beautiful.

"Aaaaaa!" Shae screamed, jumping up. Large, black ants were crawling all over her, and a few began to bite. She jumped up and down, brushing them off and smacking the stinging spots. She went to escape into the tent, only to find they had invaded there, as well.

In the fading light she saw there were ant hills everywhere in the clearing. She looked about for a better spot for her tent, but the little buggers were everywhere. Finally, she decided to move down the mountain to a peaceful spot she'd seen a few miles down the trail. She'd liked the look of it on her way up but had opted to go further into the forest.

Climbing back down was faster than going up the hill, and she reached the site not long after sunset. It was darker there, being further under the canopy of the trees, and even with her headlamp she had a hard time locating a flat spot and setting up again.

At last, everything was in place, and she crawled into the tent, hoping no ants had managed to get inside her sleeping bag which she hadn't had a chance to unroll at the first site. It was getting cold, and she snuggled into the smooth, soft bag.

Shae took out her water bottle and the peyote her father had given her. She laughed to herself as she remembered the look on his face today when she'd asked him. Surprise at first, then almost wistful. Or proud, maybe? He'd waited so long for her to 'expand her mind'. She made sure her mother was nowhere in earshot at the time, knowing she would object.

Shae thought she could handle it, though. She'd been confident that she wanted to see what all the fuss was about. Anything to stop the pain. She never wanted to go through this again. Maybe, if she could find her deepest self, she would be able to recognize the next time something good came along.

Not that she expected something this good to ever come her way again. She counted herself lucky to have known such strong, pure love twice in her life, even if she had to lose it both times. It gave her hope that there were good people in the world, and maybe she would learn more about herself from this experience.

But now she couldn't do it. She looked at the powdered cactus her father had given her. She was supposed to mix it with her water and drink it. As she held the water, though, she chickened out. All sorts of things started going through her mind. She could be allergic, or it could interact with whatever was in her mother's weird granola bar. She could trip over a root as she wandered around in a daze and bump her head and die alone in the forest.

Shae began to regret coming out here. She put the baggie back in her backpack and laid down. She couldn't do it, and now the tears came again. She didn't know what she was going to do with herself. It hurt too much.

The tears soaked the sleeping bag under her head, and she fell asleep in a puddle. She woke sometime later, her whole body feeling uncomfortably wet. She wondered how much she'd cried. She slowly came back to consciousness and realized that her left side was soaked.

Shae sat up and pushed the sleeping bag off. A puddle of water was seeping through the bottom of the tent and had wet right through her sleeping bag. She cursed and untangled her feet from the bag. She felt so stupid for not bringing a tarp.

She felt even worse when she got out of the tent and the cold air froze her wet left arm. She lifted up the corner of the tent and discovered she'd placed it directly on top of some sort of natural spring. Her weight had pressed down into the damp earth and her sleeping bag had absorbed all the damp. Just great.

"I give up! Is that what you want to hear, universe?" she said to the sky, throwing her hands down at her sides with a loud slap. Why did the heavens have it out for her this week?

There was nothing to do now but go home. Clearly, she wasn't getting anything out of this experience. Ice cream and television seemed like a better salve for her soul at this moment. Grumbling she wadded up the tent and headed down the trail.

She'd been half walking, half stumbling in the dark for an hour when a hulking figure appeared before her on the trail. Shae froze, her body going straight into fight or flight mode.

There was no way she was going to outrun anyone on the dark trail when she could barely walk without falling. She dropped the tent and flipped the pocketknife open that she'd been carrying in case an animal came at her. She wasn't expecting the animal to be a person.

The would-be-murderer ran at her, and she held her knife out, prepared to fight for her life. When he got close, though, her mind refused to believe what her eyes were seeing, and she almost dropped the knife.

"Shae!" he yelled, stopping in front of her.

"Aiden?!" she cried, bewildered. Had she taken the peyote, then? Was this a hallucination? If it was, she thought drugs were the best thing she'd ever tried in her life. Her lucid mind would never have conjured Aiden in a tuxedo running down the forest path.

"Shae, it's me," he said, turning the light so she could see his face. "I'm sorry I scared you."

"Aiden!" she said again, still frozen in place.

He smiled and put his hands out to the sides in a submissive gesture. "I know I probably deserve it, but could you possibly consider not stabbing me? I did go to an awful lot of trouble to find you out here."

"Oh," Shae said, feeling the knife in her hand. She straightened and flipped the knife closed, placing it in her pocket. "God, you look good," she sighed, sure that this was some sort of vision.

Aiden chuckled. "You look incredible."

Shae looked down at herself, the beam from her headlamp reminding her that not only was she rumpled and dirty, but she was wearing ridiculous headgear. Now she knew she must be dreaming. Only in her fantasies could this be happening.

"Shae," Aiden said quietly. "I'm so sorry."

She looked up, meeting his eyes, but her light blinded him, and he squinted, his hand coming up to block the beam. Shae reached up and took it off her head, pointing it to the ground. "I'm glad you're the one guiding me," she said.

Aiden's soft laughter filled her with longing. He was so close, he seemed so solid, like she could reach out and touch him. How real were the visions, she wondered. Could you actually feel things that weren't there? She took a step forward.

"Are you ok?" Aiden asked. "Are you having any hallucinations?"

"Only you," she answered, reaching her hand out to stroke his lapel. It was soft and smooth, and solid. "You feel so real."

"I am real," Aiden said, his hand coming down on top of hers. He pressed her fingers to his heart, and the heat of his hand spread up her arm. He was always so warm.

Shae looked up again, her face close enough to see his eyes, even in the dark. What she saw there made her heart race. He looked at her with the same longing she felt deep in her soul. It was the way she wished he would have looked at her last night. If this was a dream, she didn't care. It was wonderful.

"Will you come back to the car with me, Shae?" Aiden asked gently. "There's so much I want to tell you."

Shae nodded and Aiden's hand slipped off of hers. He moved away, bending to pick up the tent she'd dropped on the ground.

"What did you do to this thing?" he asked as he gathered the bundle.

Shae shook her head. This was too real. "You're really here," she said, still not believing it.

"Yes, don't worry. I'll stay with you until the effects diminish. It'll be ok," he said tenderly.

"I haven't taken any drugs, you idiot!" Shae said, exasperated. "Is that why you're here? How did you know, anyway?"

Aiden stopped fumbling with the tent. After a beat he began to laugh softly. "That's not why I'm here, though you don't know how relieved I am to find you lucid and in one piece."

"Then what in the world are you doing here? Dressed like that!" Shae was beyond vexed with him.

"Call me and an idiot again," he said earnestly.

"What?!" Shae exclaimed.

"I need to hear it," Aiden said. "I need to hear it from you every day for a very long time. Well, maybe every other day after the first few months."

Shae threw her hands to her sides, giving up on his riddles. The man never said what he meant. She always had to infer his meaning and she hadn't done a very good job at it thus far. She wished she hadn't told him she was sober. If she had the excuse of not being in her right mind she could walk over there and kiss him right now.

Shae dropped her headlamp to the ground at the same time she let her backpack slide off her shoulders. She marched over to Aiden and knocked the tent out of his hands, kicking it to the side. She stepped into him until her breasts brushed the front of his tux. Her breath hitched as she looked up into his surprised face.

"Idiot," she whispered.

His eyes softened and he shifted closer to her. She saw his arm move, but then he stopped just short of touching her. Her gut twisted and she stilled the whimper of frustration that rose up her throat.

"Forgive me, Shae," he said with pain in his voice.

It was all she needed to hear. Shae closed the last few inches of space between their lips, her mouth meeting his in the sweetest kiss of her life. She felt Aiden's face tense, then his arms were around her. He hauled her up against his chest, lifting her feet off the ground. Her arms were trapped against Aiden's chest, and she couldn't move, but it didn't matter.

Aiden kissed her ardently, long and hard, until she was gasping for breath. At last, he pulled back, resting his forehead against hers and breathing hard. Shae opened her eyes to see a crease between his brows, his eyes shut hard. His chest trembled.

"You're crying," she said softly, wriggling one arm free to stroke his cheek as she laid another soft kiss against his lips. Aiden opened his eyes.

"Don't tell anyone," he smiled. "I hear women don't like it."

"That's ridiculous," Shae said. "Do you care what women think?" she asked, insecurity creeping back in.

"Only one," he whispered. "Only you. I love you, Shae. I've loved you since the Fourth of July, maybe even before. I'm sorry it has taken me so long to tell you. I *am* an idiot."

Shae stopped him with a finger to his lips. "We've both been idiots. Let's not talk about it anymore."

With a low rumble he kissed her again, holding her so tightly she couldn't breathe. But who needed air when you were being kissed like this? He let her body slide down until her feet touched the ground, then one warm palm cupped her backside, pulling her against his rigid erection.

Shae wanted to fall to the ground with him. She wanted Aiden to take her right now on the trail. But he stilled and looked at her quizzically.

"Why are you soaking wet?" he asked.

"Because of you," she said with as straight a face as she could manage.

Aiden looked at her a moment then erupted in laughter. "I think that might be a medical condition. Your pants are soaked through," he teased.

"I set my tent up in a puddle, if you must know," Shae said, abashed. "This whole camping experience has been one big catastrophe. First there were ants, then I was too chicken to take the peyote, then there was the puddle, then-"

Aiden kissed her again, his lips coaxing her to open to him, his tongue dancing over hers until she began to see fireworks behind her eyes. His hand moved to tangle in her hair, the other skating up her side, skimming her breast before drawing her against him again.

"We could stay here tonight," he whispered, his breath ragged. "I'll set up the tent in a campsite, no puddle." He gripped her hair, tugging gently to give him access to her neck. His lips roved slowly down her neck and her body burned.

"There's a perfectly good tree right there," she whispered. She wrapped one leg around his waist, then the other, linking her ankles behind his waist.

"Uunnhh," he groaned, as if he were in pain. "No condom."

"I don't care!" Shae moaned back. She needed Aiden badly, more than she needed her next breath.

"Yes, you do," he said, pulling back and tapping her on the nose. "No moon, either."

"I'm sorry I ever told you about that," she pouted.

"Too late now," he said with a smile. "I'll set up the tent and we'll see if we can't work around this little roadblock."

Shae released her legs from around his waist and stood in his arms with her lower lip jutting out. "I don't want to stay in this nasty forest anymore. I'm covered with dirt and ant bites and now you're refusing to make love to me."

"I would never refuse you, my beautiful little firecracker," he whispered. His lips found hers again and his kiss was tender and sweet. "How about a shower?"

Shae's body lurched in his arms. "Yes, please," she begged.

"Shall I carry you down the mountain?" Aiden asked, rocking her playfully.

"I can walk. I made it up, didn't I?" she said, grinning up at him.

"But I don't want to let you go," he said, smiling back.

"Oh, I hadn't thought of that," Shae said, disappointed. "We'll do it fast. Like ripping off a bandage."

"Ok, you go first," Aiden said, his arms still firmly around her.

"You have to let go," Shae pointed out.

"I told you I don't want to," he said impishly.

"Do you always get what you want?" she asked.

"Most of the time," he admitted.

Shae placed her hands flat on his chest and summoned all her willpower. She pushed out of his arms and walked over to retrieve her backpack. She bent over slowly, being sure to give Aiden the best possible view. His pained groan behind her made her giggle.

"You little minx," he growled as he bundled up the tent.

Aiden offered her his hand and they made their way back down the trail. Shae smiled as she imagined the picture they made with their headlamps, the wadded-up tent, and Aiden's tuxedo. God, he looked good in that tuxedo.

They reached the parking lot and Aiden tossed the tent into the bed of his truck. He reached for her backpack, sliding it off and tossing it in, too. Then he grabbed her, his hands tight around her waist. He pulled her into an embrace, pinning her to the side of the truck, his mouth hot and urgent on hers.

"I really don't want to let you go," he growled. "We could come back tomorrow to get your car."

"Professor Love, I don't want to leave your bedroom tomorrow," Shae said firmly.

A deep rumbling came from Aiden's chest, and he gripped her tenaciously. "I'll drive you to work on Monday, then. Please, get in the truck," he begged.

Shae complied, her mind and body singing. She wished the truck had a bench seat so she could slide closer to Aiden. Being this near, but not quite near enough, was torture.

Aiden took his jacket off and hung it behind the seat. He slid behind the wheel and closed the door. One large hand gripped the steering wheel, while the other reached over to cup her face. He leaned in for a kiss, smiling and cradling her cheek in his hand.

As he pulled out, Shae couldn't take her eyes off him. His white shirt was unbuttoned at the throat, enough of his skin exposed to make her picture undoing the rest of the buttons. Her eyes moved down his arms and fixed on the mother-of-pearl cufflinks at his wrists. Oh boy.

Aiden glanced over and noticed her staring. "These belonged to my grandfather. Do you like them?" he asked.

"Papa," Shae said absentmindedly.

"Yes," Aiden said with surprise.

"Oh, Mom told me all about him," Shae explained. "At least, what she thinks she knows about him," she said quickly, realizing she sounded a bit loony.

"It's so strange," Aiden said.

"My mother? Yes, she is that," Shae admitted.

"Well yes, and I mean that in the best way, believe me, but no, not her," Aiden said. "When I was getting dressed tonight, I opened my drawer and there they were, just right in front. I keep these cufflinks in a special box. They were the ones Papa wore on his wedding day. I wasn't going to wear them tonight. I've been saving them for a special occasion. But there they were, like they just got up and jumped out of the box."

Shae watched his lips. They curved into a smile as he spoke. He was so sexy, she thought, just the shape of his mouth gave her wicked thoughts.

"Don't you think that's strange?" Aiden asked, turning toward her.

"Oh yes, very," she said quickly. He smiled a warm smile at her.

"Did I tell you how in love with you I am?" he asked, still grinning.

"Not how *much*, no," she teased.

He turned his eyes back to the road, shaking his head and blushing shyly. God, every time she thought he couldn't get any more adorable...

"More than I should probably admit to," he said quietly. "It's alright if you don't feel the same way. I haven't exactly earned it."

Shae jumped in her seat as if she'd been stabbed. He watched the road, his expression uncertain, his brows drawn together slightly. She realized with some guilt that she hadn't returned his affections in so many words. Her heart opened to him even further. She reached over and placed her hand on top of his where it rested on his thigh.

"I love you, too," she said. Her voice was quiet, her heart still a bit tender from the emotions of the last few days.

Aiden's cloudy expression cleared, and he smiled shyly again. Shae wondered how a man with the experience he had could still be shy. Then she realized that being in love was something much different than being in lust. Hadn't she always compartmentalized the two herself? Her own smile turned shy when she realized that they were both in love for the first time.

"Aiden, would you drop me off at my house and give me a few minutes?" she asked as they turned down their street. "I'd like to get cleaned up."

"Don't you want to *get cleaned up* at my place? Bigger shower," he said, raising his eyebrows and winking at her. Shae laughed.

"Raincheck?" she asked.

"Of course," he said, parking in her driveway. "I'll walk you to your door."

"No need," she said, placing her hand on his arm to stop him as he started to get out. "I'll be over soon, I promise."

Shae leaned over and kissed him on his handsome cheek. She gave him a little smile and hopped out, almost skipping to her door.

"Hit the garage button!" Aiden called after her. "I'll lay this wet tent out for you."

Shae's heart jumped in her chest as she unlocked the door, and she couldn't stop the enormous grin that spread across her face. She kicked off her boots and ran upstairs, straight to the shower. She scrubbed the dust off as quickly as she could, relieved when she found the ant bites weren't as ugly and red as she worried they might be.

As much as she wanted to christen Aiden's new shower with him, she was still too self-conscious to do it when she was actually covered with grime. Besides, she had something she wanted to wear tonight; something she'd been thinking about since he'd made the comment about her resemblance to Bettie Page and his secret crush on the woman.

She ran the blow dryer over her hair, just enough to keep it from being dripping wet. It would have to do. She was too eager to fuss with hair and makeup tonight. It was already after midnight and Shae didn't know how tired Aiden was. She should be exhausted, but adrenaline coursed through her system.

She threw her favorite wiggle dress over the red satin bra and bloomers set and grabbed her black T-strap, peep-toe heels. She hoped Aiden hadn't undressed yet. She was dying to see him in that tux one more time. And to watch him take those cufflinks off.

Her phone buzzed loudly from her pants pocket on the floor, alerting her of a text message. She grabbed it and saw that Aiden had texted her several times. She eagerly opened the texts and her heart swelled as she read. He'd just sent the last one, telling her to text her parents that she was ok.

"Silly, sweet boy," she said as she turned the phone off. Her parents didn't have cell phones, and they'd be sound asleep by now. She could call them sometime after dawn. She didn't plan to be asleep before then.

Chapter 18

Heels in hand, Shae ran down the stairs and out the front door. She slipped her shoes on as she ran, skidding to a stop at Aiden's door. Should she knock? No, she decided, that seemed silly. She tried the handle, and the door was unlocked. She opened it and peeked her head in. It was quiet and dark. The only light came from a dozen tea lights that led up the stairs.

Shae closed and locked the door behind her. She tilted her head, hand over her mouth. The little candles were so pretty. She followed them up the stairs and saw that they continued up the spiral staircase to the roof.

"Oh, Aiden," she sighed.

Aiden stood on the rooftop deck with his back to her, his hands in his pockets, giving her a very nice view of his firm backside. He turned when he heard her take the last two steps. He'd put his jacket and tie back on and she nearly swooned when his dark eyes met hers, flashing in the candlelight.

"Oh my," Aiden said, his already deep voice lowering a full octave.

Shae loved what she was doing to him, as much as she savored what he was doing to her. She walked slowly toward him, running her palms down her hips. Mostly to draw his attention to her body, but also because her palms had begun to sweat.

She was nervous. Her heart fluttered uncontrollably, and her mouth went dry. After everything she and Aiden had talked about, everything they'd declared to each other, she was still scared. She'd never been so invested in another person, not since River.

And now she knew the real reason it had taken her so long to admit her feelings to herself. She couldn't stand the thought of ever loving someone that deeply and losing them again. But it wasn't something she had control over. Aiden had lodged himself deep in her heart and there was no going back now.

"Aiden, I..." she began, but words failed her. She didn't know where to begin, how to explain everything she'd just come to understand.

But he seemed to know already. He looked into her eyes, and everything felt right, whole. He reached for her, taking her in his arms, his hand gentle on her cheek. With a small smile he leaned in slowly, his full lips brushing hers in the softest caress.

Leaning against him, Shae brought her arms around his neck, her fingers weaving through his hair. His soft kisses continued, and Shae melted into his embrace.

"Tell me I never have to let you go," he whispered as he moved his lips down her throat.

"Never let me go," she sighed, laying her head on his shoulder. She closed her eyes and breathed him in, the light scent of his cologne spinning her head.

Aiden shifted and grasped her right hand, lifting it in his. His other arm came around her waist and he started to sing. He moved her slowly, laying his cheek against hers as his velvet voice slipped over her.

The very thought of you makes my heart sing
Like an April breeze on the wings of spring
And you appear in all your splendor
My one and only love
The shadows fall and spread their mystic charms
In the hush of night while you're in my arms

I feel your lips, so warm and tender
My one and only love
The touch of your hand is like heaven
A heaven that I've never known
The blush on your cheek whenever I speak
Tells me that you are my own
You fill my eager heart with such desire
Every kiss you give sets my soul on fire
I give myself in sweet surrender
My one and only love
My one and only love

Aiden spun her in slow circles a few moments more. Her body was not her own. She felt as though she would float out of it at any moment and drift to Heaven. But she was already there.

"The stars are so beautiful tonight," Aiden whispered. "Do you like to look at the stars, Shae?"

"I do," she sighed, shivering when Aiden's lips closed over her earlobe. "I know all the constellations."

"Really?" he said, lifting his head. "Will you show me?"

"I will if you'll put your cheek back against mine," Shae said, looking up into his eyes.

"Come over here," he said, leading her to the double lounger. He laid down, pulling her down with him. He wrapped his arms around her, drawing her against his warm body and placing his cheek up against hers.

Shae smiled. It was perfect. "The stars are incredible up here," she said in wonder. "I didn't know there was a view this good so close to town."

"It thrills me that you like it," Aiden said softly.

Shae raised a hand and pointed to the heavens. She began pointing out constellations, her finger gliding across the dark sky.

"Here is Aries," she said. Aiden snuggled closer to her. "Pisces, Perseus, Cassiopeia, Cepheus, Camelopardalis, Andromeda."

With every constellation Aiden moved against her. Just a stroke down her arm, a nuzzle against her neck, but each little touch stoked the fire that had been burning in her since the first time Aiden had spoken to her. The day he'd come over while she was making jam, and left her so hot and bothered she'd had to-

"Oh," she breathed as his palm skated over her breast. "And there is Ursa Minor," she said, trailing off on a moan. Aiden's large hand closed over her breast, gently kneading.

"I thought that was the Little Dipper," Aiden whispered.

"It is," Shae sighed, turning her head away from the sky, seeking Aiden's lips. "Don't pretend you didn't know that."

"I didn't, truly," Aiden said, kissing her softly. "I never paid much attention to astronomy. It's not one of my interests. And, as we've already established, I'm an idiot."

Shae giggled against his lips, and he pulled her under him, pinning her down with a kiss that seared straight through her until she was sure the cushion below her would catch fire. His fingers twined with hers and he moved her arms above her head as his mouth moved down her neck to the center of her throat.

"It's astrology, not astronomy," she breathed, moaning as his lips made their way to the valley between her breasts.

"I'm fairly certain it's astronomy," came his muffled reply.

"Not the way I learned it. Oh!" Shae cried out as Aiden's hand slid down the length of her, sliding her dress off one shoulder so quickly she hardly had time to react.

His teeth were nipping at her shoulder now, his hands squeezing and caressing and tickling. Every touch was pure ecstasy. Her lungs expanded, but she couldn't seem to get enough air to keep up with her wild heart.

"What are you wearing?" Aiden moaned. Shae smiled, elated.

"Something just for you," she managed to say between panting breaths.

"I didn't think it would get better than this dress," Aiden said, his own breathing hard.

"As good as Bettie Page?" Shae asked demurely.

"Bettie who?" Aiden mumbled.

Shae pushed against his chest, and he sat up. She pulled at the edge of his bowtie, and it came undone. She untied it and began to open the buttons that had been driving her crazy the entire drive home. Reaching down to his waist, she unbuttoned the tuxedo jacket as well.

"Did you put this back on just so I could enjoy taking it off?" Shae asked. "Because I love it," she said, spreading his shirt open and kissing his neck up to his sharp jaw. "Now take it off."

"With pleasure," Aiden responded. He stood and Shae followed. She stood in front of him and pulled her dress over her head. Aiden choked.

"You like?" she asked. She turned and crawled onto the lounger on her knees, then laid herself out to watch him. For a moment she worried Aiden might faint. He froze, his eyes locked on her. "Well, your turn," she prodded.

He snapped back to attention and slid his jacket off, laying it over the back of a chair. Shae swallowed hard as he reached for the cufflinks. She couldn't stop herself from sitting up and leaning toward him, her eyes hungry.

Click, click, and they were off. In another second his shirt was gone, too, along with the undershirt that had been driving her mad, concealing the golden expanse of his chest from her. Unconsciously, Shae ran a hand over her body, eager for Aiden's touch. Dying to touch him.

Aiden tore the rest of his clothing off, his eyes burning as they ran up and down her body. "You're like a dream," he said, coming softly to her. "I don't want to wake up."

He moved over her slowly now, every touch a gentle caress, like the lick of a flame that left a burning trail wherever his skin touched hers. Soon she was consumed by the fire that raged through her, and the only relief was more of his touch.

He hovered over her now, the curves of his chest and arms hard under her fingertips. She explored and mapped his skin, like silk stretched over warm sand, hard but giving at her touch. Aiden moved his lips over her neck, her shoulders, taking her waist in his hands and lifting her to caress down her ribs with his tongue. She arched into him as he moved to the soft mound below her belly button.

Shae kicked her heels off, desperate to be rid of the last bits of clothing covering her body. Aiden followed her cue, his fingers gently slipping under the waistband of her lingerie and drawing it down as he kissed along her hip. His movements were tender, reverent, and her heart burned as deeply for him as her skin.

"Kiss me, Aiden," Shae whispered, her hands smoothing over his shoulders. He complied, and in a moment his body was on hers, pressing her down into the soft surface.

Aiden looked down into her eyes, running his fingers over her cheek. His eyes were soft and he smiled tenderly as he took her lips. How could it be that the touch of his lips on hers conveyed so much more than any other touch, any words could ever say? In this kiss was a sweet surrender, by him and to him, a promise to each other.

Aiden's arms slipped around her, releasing the clasp on her bra. His kiss continued as he moved it down her arms, his fingertips grazing her skin and making her shiver. Finally, there was nothing between them, and Aiden settled against her with a contented groan.

"I love you, Aiden," Shae whispered, stroking his jaw as she found his eyes. "I love your silly jokes, and your amazing cooking," she said. Aiden pinched her side, tickling her and she laughed. "And I love your kind heart."

Aiden gathered her in his arms and buried his face in her neck. He inhaled deeply, his nose nuzzling against her. "I love you so much, Shae," he said softly.

Raising up, he looked into her eyes. His fingers gently grasped her thigh, and she felt him, hard and ready. He pushed the broad head of his cock into her and her mouth opened in a gasp. Slowly he pressed, sliding into her inch by deliriously sensuous inch, until her mind and body were filled with him.

They moved together, eyes never straying, her right hand twined with this left. With every stroke she cried out, soft and muted, the exultant pleasure moving her close to tears. They moved faster and Aiden's lips brushed hers, ardent and fervid, another promise, this one more passionate. A promise not only to love her, but to want her, to need her as much as she needed him.

"I love you, Shae," he whispered again. "God, I love you."

Her body and mind quaked with pleasure. The raging fire condensed to a single point, then burst forth in an explosion of raptus. Her eyes closed as every nerve came to life. She could feel Aiden, his body at once surrounding and filling her, completing her. His voice close to her, deep and rolling, cried out as he surged inside her, bringing her to a peak she never could have dreamed of before.

Aiden's breathing was hard, his chest heaving against her, every breath he took a moaning sigh. His body shook, small tremors that seemed to race between them, making her limbs quiver. Shae opened her eyes to a black sky full of brightly glowing stars. She felt as though she'd never truly seen them before.

Aiden's lips pressed tenderly against her neck as he rested his head next to hers. His warm breath ghosted across her skin, sending a thrill through her unlike any feeling she'd known before. More visceral than physical, an emotion manifested in feeling, indescribable and empyrean.

"Aiden," she said, stroking his soft hair.

"Hmm?" he mumbled, his hand languidly traversing up and down her left side.

"It's never been like this before," she stated simply. So much was meant in those words, and she hoped he would understand, hoped he felt the same.

"Never," he stated firmly, lifting up so he could see her face. "I don't say this very often, or ever, but I don't understand it. From the moment I set eyes on you I've been changing, evolving. I'm better because of you. I don't know how to explain it."

"You don't have to," Shae said, closing her eyes. "Just kiss me."

AIDEN WOKE TO A SOFT nuzzling against his neck. In his dream he was a child again, and his favorite dog on Papa's ranch was waking him to come play with her, as she often did. "Stop it, Lily," he mumbled. "I'm still sleepy."

"Who is Lily?" a soft voice drifted into his dream. He was pulled back to consciousness as warm desire spread through him. That voice...

He opened his eyes to a soft, gray sky. The fog had finally rolled in sometime before dawn and settled around them, muffling the sounds of the world. He burrowed deeper under the heavy comforter, pulling Shae closer to him. "Mmm," he sighed in contentment.

"Is she the one you had up here the other night?" Shae asked, her tone wounded.

"What?" Aiden asked in confusion.

"It doesn't matter," Shae said, shaking her head slightly. "Sorry I woke you. I can't resist your neck." She ran a finger along his jaw and down his neck.

"No, wait," he said, turning to her. "Lily was Papa's dog. She used to nuzzle me just like that. Try not to be too jealous," he laughed.

Shae smiled, but she still looked a little sad. "I'll try," she said, as if it would be a great effort.

"What's the matter, sweetheart?" he asked, concerned now.

Shae groaned in frustration. "I promised myself I wasn't going to be like this. You know I love you and support everything you do, right?" she asked.

"Of course, I do," Aiden said, taking her in his arms.

"I'm just having a difficult time with your work," she said guiltily. "I'll get over it, I will, I promise. Just give me some time to get used to the idea."

"Shae, what are you talking about?" he said exasperatedly. "I'm almost done with the house. If it bothers you that much I won't buy another one. I told you last night I'd do anything for you. I'll even go back to teaching if that would make you happy."

To his relief she smiled a genuine smile. "Not the house building," she said, "the other work. The work you were doing up here Thursday night. Although, if you did go back to teaching, I would be sitting in the front row of every lecture, studiously taking notes in my little pleated skirt."

"Jesus," Aiden said, taking her lips and kissing her deeply. He almost wanted to go back to teaching now. "Wait, I wasn't doing any work up here Thursday night. I was up here drinking beer and drowning my sorrows alone."

"But I heard you," Shae said, her voice hurt again. "You were reciting Pablo Neruda. Very well, in my opinion. But it's ok!" she said quickly.

"Shae," Aiden soothed, finally figuring out what she was saying. He tried not to laugh before he explained. "I was on the phone," he said, unable to hide his smirk.

He stretched an arm across her, reaching for his phone on the little table by their makeshift bed. He had to reach far enough that his body pressed down against Shae's. He couldn't resist tasting her sweet lips again as she lay there under him. She was so distracting.

Clearing his throat, he laid back, pulling up a picture on his phone. "This is the friend I was talking to, Gabe," he said, handing her the phone.

Shae's eyes widened for a moment, but she quickly schooled her expression. "Oh, I didn't realize you were..." she said.

Aiden couldn't hold back his laughter any longer. He erupted in a full-throated howling fit. She was so adorably wonderful, so accepting. But as funny and cute as it was, he was also angered by part of what she'd said.

"Gabe is my best friend," Aiden said when his laughter finally subsided. He wiped a tear from the corner of his eye. "And as adorable as I find your openness to a romantic relationship between him and me, that's not the situation. Not that he isn't a good-looking man. I was helping him with his wife. She likes poetry, he doesn't know any. Thus..."

Aiden could see Shae's relief written all over her face. He smiled and stroked her hair. "That's nice of you," she said.

"But you have made me angry," Aiden chastised, putting on a disapproving face. "And I'm going to need an apology."

Shae's face fell and she drew her eyebrows together. "I'm-"

"Ah-ah-ah," Aiden said, a finger to her lips. "If you know my heart, Shae, and I believe you truly do, then you know that since the first time I laid eyes on you, there has been no other woman, no other person in existence that could hold a candle to you. I never have, and

I never will love someone, down into the depths of my soul, the way I love you."

"I do know, Aiden," she said quietly. "That's what I'm trying to tell you. I know you love me, and that's why it's ok that you keep working."

Aiden felt his heart squeeze painfully in his chest. "Shae, I haven't worked a day since the first time you acknowledged my existence. Well, except the date that turned out to be with you. I don't know why I decided to respond to your text that night. Something just told me I should."

Shae giggled. "I only texted *Dr. Love* that night because I was too afraid to admit my crush on you. Secretly I wished it was you that I was meeting that day."

"Really?" Aiden said in disbelief, his heart overjoyed.

"Yes," Shae said, a naughty smile on her lips. "I was already masturbating to your face several times a day. I couldn't take it anymore. Deja said *Dr. Love* could help me. Seems to have done the trick. I'm cured!"

Aiden leaned over and nibbled her neck, tickling her in the side. "Stop being so incredibly cute and distracting! How am I supposed to stay mad at you?"

"Why are you mad at me?" Shae asked playfully.

"Because the thought of you with another man makes me so angry, I get physically ill. I don't want to date other people, for work or otherwise, and I don't want you to be ok with it!" he said vehemently.

"I'm sorry," Shae said sincerely, then laughed. "And here I was thinking I was being such a stick in the mud for wanting you to drop your escort job. You have to realize that the way I was raised, the relationships I saw, was not conventional. My parents were the anomaly in our circle. Free love and all that. I wanted to be ok with whatever your heart needed."

"Oh, my lovely," Aiden sighed, holding her tight. "My heart needs *you*, all of you, *only* you. It has driven me mad all these months, seeing you with another man, not being able to have you, or to even get you to speak to me. I will never be ok with sharing you, and if that makes me a barbarian, so be it."

"You know I'll love you no matter what you do, though, right?" she asked, sounding unsure.

"I do," he said softly. "I know. But you've given me quite a tempting reason to go back into teaching." He chuckled and kissed her lips.

Shae shifted under him, wrapping her legs around his waist. His blood surged, his body readying to make love to her. But a second later, he found himself on his back, a warm, soft Shae straddling him and pinning his arms above his head with her slender hands.

"Someday you will have to teach me how you do that," he whispered as she worked her way down his chest, her hot, wet lips closing over his left pec.

"I would be happy to teach you, Professor Love," she replied, and the way she said his name made his heart fly.

Suddenly she shot up, startling him with her quick movements. She moved much too quickly this early in the morning. Her heavy breasts swayed, and he leaned up, taking a nipple gently between his teeth.

"You can't see my yard anymore!" she said, staring at the wall he'd put up.

"You can," he said, trying to draw her back down, "if you go over and look around the side. I didn't want to ruin the entire aesthetic, but now at least, if you're in your yard people will have to make a real effort to see you. Now come back down here."

Aiden gathered her to his chest, and she smiled, her beautiful hazel eyes gray and blue in the foggy morning light. "Why did you do it?" she asked.

"I didn't want anyone else to look at you. After that night when Gabe and I saw you performing the moon ritual..." He stopped, gulping as he realized what he'd just said.

"It's ok," she laughed. "I'm sure it wasn't that good a show."

Aiden growled. "I almost tore Gabe's head off. You were the most beautiful thing I'd ever seen. Say, there's a full moon in a couple weeks, do I get front row seats this time?" he laughed.

"Whatever you want, lover," she said, kissing him ardently.

"Whatever *we* want, sweetheart."

Chapter 19

A iden watched Shae as she helped Tabby hold another tiny blue baby outfit up to her rounded belly. Tabitha sat in a chair surrounded by piles of eco-friendly wrapping paper and organic cotton infant items. Shae's glowing smile seemed to light up the room as she cooed over the clothing.

"We are two damn lucky son of a guns," Gabe said, watching the festivities beside him. He tapped the neck of his beer bottle to Aiden's.

"I couldn't agree more," Aiden said, finishing off his drink. "You want another?"

"No, I'm good. Tabby gets jealous if she smells alcohol on me. I swear the woman is going on a bender next month as soon as that kid gets evicted. I'll probably join her. This sneaking one beer at a time is nonsense."

"You know she's planning to breastfeed," Aiden pointed out. Gabe's face fell.

"What does that mean?" he asked warily.

"No drinking," Aiden said, stifling a laugh at Gabe's stricken expression.

"Yeah, well, we'll see who's laughing after a few more months, buddy. Doesn't Shae mind you drinking without her?" Gabe asked.

"No, she doesn't. She's pretty amazing that way," Aiden said, his eyes locked on her face.

"Oh, god, here we go again," Gabe said with mock sarcasm. "I changed my mind, I'm having another." Gabe headed for the kitchen.

Aiden knew everyone was sick of him mooning. But he couldn't help it, and he really didn't care. Every day he fell deeper in love with her, especially now, when her little baby bump had popped out, and her skin glowed like some ethereal being.

"She really is beautiful," his mother said, echoing his thoughts. "She makes pregnancy look good."

"I couldn't agree more," Aiden said, wrapping an arm around his mother's shoulders.

"I have to tell you, Veronica is such a hoot! She just read my palm. Apparently, your father and I have some big romantic thing coming up. I can't wait!" she laughed.

Aiden found himself taken aback yet again by this change in his mother. Not only had she and Shae become the best of friends seemingly overnight, but she and Veronica got along as if they were sisters. Rather than eschewing the spiritual lifestyle the Mitchells espoused, his mother had embraced it, finding her inner Hippie. She even began drinking kombucha, to Aiden's horror.

"So, did you two find out? Are you going to tell us all or keep us on pins and needles?" his mother asked.

"We know," Aiden said. "Shae wants to tell everyone after the presents. You won't have to wait much longer."

"Well, I already know, too," she said mysteriously.

"What? How?" Aiden asked, thinking Shae must have told her without informing him.

"Veronica told me. She's been communicating with the baby's spirit already, apparently."

Maman said this as if it were an everyday, normal occurrence. As if people often communicated with infants in the womb.

"She said she can't wait for you to finally meet River in person," she went on.

Aiden rolled his eyes, but he smiled. If it made Shae's mother happy to believe their baby was her reincarnated son, he didn't see the harm. He knew that either way, everyone already loved this baby beyond measure.

Shae came back into the room with a huge chocolate cake. Aiden ran over to help her, swooping in to clear a space on the table and lifting it from her hands.

"Thank you, my big, strong man," she teased him.

"Hey, it looked heavy. You're in a delicate condition," he said, rubbing her little belly.

Shae leaned in until her lips almost brushed his. "Remind me to show you how delicate I'm not, later," she whispered. His pulse quickened and his cock filled. And she knew what she was doing to him, too.

"You're in so much trouble later," he growled. He turned and ran to the kitchen to grab the plates and forks before anyone could notice his state. When he returned, he set them on the table and Shae slid her arm around his, gripping his bicep and squeezing. She looked up at him and his heart melted for her.

"Ready?" she asked.

"Sure. But you should know, your mother already told everyone," he laughed. Shae returned his smile, adding an eyeroll of her own.

"Everyone!" Shae said. "Aiden and I wanted to say how excited we are that our very good friends are going to welcome their little boy into the world in only a few weeks now. Congratulations to Tabitha and Gabe!"

A round of applause and raised glasses followed, and Aiden took Shae's hand, kissing her fingers. He raised his voice as the cheering died down, "And we would also like you all to know that in three months, we will be welcoming our own little boy!"

The cheering erupted again, and Gabe came over and slapped Aiden's hand. "Our boys are going to be like brothers," Gabe said.

"You know it," Aiden agreed. "I finished the gate between our yards yesterday. Did you see it?"

"I haven't been out yet, with everything going on inside. Thanks," Gabe said.

"Hey, not a problem. I can't imagine having better neighbors. I don't think Shae would have sold her house to anyone else." Aiden said.

"Well, be careful what you wish for," Gabe laughed. "I'm expecting a lot of help with the renovations since your place turned out so nice."

"Can't wait," Aiden said. It would be a lot of fun working on Shae's house, though it wasn't her house anymore. Still, he would always think of it that way, no matter who lived there.

Aiden turned to Shae, taking her hand. She looked at him questioningly but didn't resist as he led her to the den. He pulled her inside and closed the door, pressing her back against the wall with his body.

"I love you," he said, his hands sliding up her full skirt.

"I love you," Shae moaned.

"When are you going to make an honest man out of me and marry me, Shae Indigo Marley Mitchell?" he asked, lips sliding down her neck.

"You know I want a summer wedding," she breathed. "You're so impatient for a piece of paper."

"It's not the paper. I want you," he growled.

"But there's a party out there."

"You started this with your flirting," Aiden laughed as she began to breathe harder. He lifted her and pressed between her legs.

"But there's cake," she squeaked, clinging to him.

"I remember a time when you let the cake wait until after," Aiden teased her.

"I'm pregnant now," she teased back. Aiden kissed her and sighed. He tried, he really did. But keeping his hands off her was too difficult.

"Never stand between you and your chocolate cake," he laughed.

"Damn straight," she said. "And *you* are my favorite kind."

The End

Also by J.C. Fairbanks

Love and Desire
Two Days In Florida
A Kiss in Carolina
Love and Desire in Paradise
Daphne, Woman of Law

Love by the Golden Gate
Love Next Door

Standalone
Eternal Flame

Watch for more at https://www.facebook.com/jcfairbanksromance.

About the Author

I love to write about love. True love, passion, and romance are the best things about life. I fall in love with all of my characters in every story, and I hope you will, too. In my real life I am living my happily ever after every day with the love of my life and our four little ones. But let me tell you the story of how I started writing. One night I had a dream. It was incredible and I couldn't stop thinking about it for weeks. This dream was not your usual dream. It was so real that it felt like it had actually happened. In it I met Julia, Camile, Anika, Leo, David, and the whole family. I now knew these people and I was dying to find out what happened to them after I was yanked from my slumber by the alarm clock. It was nearly impossible to get out of bed that morning and even harder to stop thinking about them. My first novel, Two Days In Florida, was born. But I still had to know more. The stories just keep getting steamier and more romantic. I can't wait to see what happens next!

Read more at https://www.facebook.com/jcfairbanksromance.